The Swords
of December

ROBERT YORK

The Swords
of December

Charles Scribner's Sons
New York

Copyright © 1978 Robert York

Library of Congress Cataloging in Publication data

York, Robert.
    The Swords of December.

    1.   Thomas à Becket, Saint, Abp. of Canterbury,
1118?–1170–Fiction.   2.   Henry II, King of England,
1133–1189–Fiction.   I.   Title.
PZ4.Y636Sw   [PR6075.067]   823'.9'14   78–24026
ISBN 684-16142-7

1 3 5 7 9 11 13 15 17 19   O/C   20 18 16 14 12 10 8 6 4 2

Printed in the United States of America

Prologue

I fled once from my duty, rather than face your
swords; this time I stay. You will find me here.

Thomas of London, December 1170

'Even as my lord, Thomas, lay dead upon the steps, his sacred blood darkening the stone, and while the whole cathedral was in a tumult, many ordinary people wishing to touch him and the monks trying to prevent them, Henry of Auxerre came to me and said that men-at-arms were pillaging my lord's quarters, searching for gold and silver and jewelled chalices.

'Now Thomas had kept no gold and certainly no jewels in his rooms, and thus I did not believe what Henry told me. Suddenly, as if Thomas still lived, I heard him speak as he had spoken to me that very morning in the privacy of his chamber: "Guard well your day-books, my friend; they may bear witness for all time, long after we are dust." And I remember how, long ago, he had said of these same books that at all times they must be locked in the strongest of secret hiding-places, because they were the only witness, myself apart, of what he truly thought and did.

'Then I knew without hesitation or doubt, by some instinct or prompting of Thomas's departed spirit, that it was not gold or jewels that the intruders sought, but those very manuscripts.

'I turned and ran past Thomas's body, pushing through monks and townspeople into the cloister, retracing the steps by which, not half an hour before, he had reached the cathedral. I was aware that one followed me, and thought him to be that same Henry of Auxerre. I could hear sounds of shouting and the breaking of wood from my lord's quarters. I ran past the steps leading thither to a small room of which only I kept the key; here, among vestments, the books were hidden behind a cunningly contrived panel seeming to be part of the wall. I seized them and turned, to find that by some blessing of Providence he who had followed me was not Henry but that Edward, lay brother of Northampton, who had chosen to share Thomas's hardships and exile.

'This good man cannot have known what the books contained, but me he knew very well, and he could read the panic on my face.

He said, "This way, my lord, there are horses in the orchard." As we ran past the Archbishop's hall someone within saw me and shouted my name, and a man leapt down the steps to bar my way. He did not see Edward behind him with drawn sword. I pray that he died at once, for it was an ugly wound. We ourselves made haste to the orchard where there were indeed tethered horses, whose I do not know, and thus we rode from Canterbury upon that terrible night, none following, to the house of a trusted friend some nine miles distant. I blessed Edward for saving my life, and bade him ride swiftly northwards, taking advantage of darkness, to Lincoln where his sister lives with her husband; they will hide him as once they hid four other fugitives.

'Now it is the first hour, and still I sit by the dying fire in this small chamber, staring at the three volumes of parchment which are a certain promise of my own death.

'Soon I will draw the taper close and make a record of the fearful day which has passed, for did not Thomas say to me but eighteen hours ago, "Write simply and clearly of what you see today; I doubt if any other will do so." Well, he is dead, and so I must bear this great weight of truth alone; and I see, as he assuredly saw, that it is not merely an account of the day that I must write, but of all the days leading up to it. If I do not, the world will come to believe the flood of gibberish, false evidence, convenient omissions, outright lies, with which the Christians will all too soon surround his death and demean his life; for they intend to have him as a saint, which is irony indeed!

'Yet my books contain much which none save my Brethren may read, so I must take them and tear from them all the sacred things, and make of the rest that "witness for all time" which Thomas desired, and which his sacred memory demands of me.

'How will I find the time and the place in which to achieve this? Were I a Christian I could seek sanctuary, labouring safely behind the walls of some great foundation; yet the protection of Christians is now more dangerous to me than the swords of those other hunters. No doubt King Henry has offered a king's ransom for my words, preferably accompanied by my head, and the Pope has good reason to offer more: a martyr's ransom perhaps!

'I would travel south to Aquitaine, for Queen Eleanor has always been kindly disposed towards me and fears neither King nor Pope, nor, I believe, the Devil himself; yet I feel that in her pride she may overreach herself, and that safety in her lands may prove to be an illusion. King Louis of France would protect me, as ever he has, but he is a staunch Christian and may no longer look upon me with favour.

'No, it is to my own that I must turn. In some way, by constant movement from place to place, by the care of good men like my present host and other Brethren who will hide me, I will set down the truth if it be the last thing I do upon this earth.

'I pray that in time's fulness I may close my eyes and no longer see the sword of Mauclerc twisting in the riven skull, scattering brains and blood, that King Henry, no less than the earth, may live. And by God's Will, by the two faces of Mary, by the blood of the Bull and of the Son who died, I pray that what I write concerning the life and death of Thomas of London may be safely hidden and thus preserved from those who would destroy truth.

' "I would hear and I would be heard. Amen.
' "A mirror I am to thee that beholdest me. Amen.
' "A door am I to thee that knockest at me. Amen." '

The writer is William of Colchester, a name which is mentioned by few of his fellow chroniclers, unsurprisingly perhaps, since his references to them are invariably far from flattering. He was born at Colchester in 1119. Nothing is known of his parents or his youth, except that he was given a good education which eventually took him to Paris where, in 1138, he met Thomas of London, Thomas Becket, a fellow-student and fellow-admirer of the great Abelard.

Only now and again does he make direct comments concerning himself, but they are always revealing, and the attitude to him of others, particularly of that remarkable woman Eleanor of Aquitaine, coupled with the fact that Thomas valued him so greatly as a friend, tells us a great deal about the kind of person he was.

His appeal to God's Will, the Two Faces of Mary, the blood of the Bull and of the Son who died, whatever its exact meaning to him, certainly had the effect he desired.

9

Three years ago, while researching his book on Joan of Arc, Adrian Garner visited the wonderful private library of the Château de Varende, some thirty miles from Poitiers. He had heard that the Degency family possessed certain documents purporting to have been written by Joan's old friend Jean de Metz, dealing with her supposed reappearance at Orléans after her execution.

He found that the documents were not genuine; he also found, in the vast cellars under the library, many miscellaneous pages of a far older text concerned with Henry II and his Archbishop, Thomas Becket. Luckily this subject is outside his period; as luckily, we have known each other for many years, and he is all too well aware, from innumerable midnight conversations, that I have an insatiable interest in these two extraordinary men and in the inconsistencies of their accepted historical relationship.

I was given permission to make a further search and, after seven weeks of exhausting and exhaustive rummaging, I emerged from underground with what seems to be the whole of William of Colchester's manuscript. How long it had been there, or indeed how it reached Varende in the first place, is anybody's guess; but one should not forget that Poitiers was once Eleanor of Aquitaine's capital city.

The pages, carefully mounted for preservation, were sent to Matthew Fairleaze, the celebrated expert on medieval Latin. He found the document fascinating and agreed to complete a rough translation. Following this, my own part in the undertaking has been small. Our chronicler was no classicist; much of his writing is racy and far from impersonal. Therefore I've tried to echo something of his 'modernity', which would have shocked, and been meant to shock, his more scholarly colleagues like John of Salisbury; I haven't attempted any imitation of 'medieval writing', which could only come between the reader and William's own distinct style, and I have not made any footnotes. However, it might avoid some confusion if I point out here that a 'clerk' in those days was a lay member of a Christian establishment, not to be confused with a 'clerk in holy orders' who was a priest.

The theory that Henry and Thomas were not Christians but heretics is certainly not new; neither is the suspicion that both may have been 'gods' or 'devils' of an older religion. The importance of William of Colchester's manuscript is that for the first time we have proof that the theory may be true; at least it makes good sense of many things which have hitherto seemed to be erroneous when not purely nonsensical. Even after the first few pages it is easy to understand why the chronicler had to hold himself in check regarding certain secrets which he, like his fellow 'Brethren', had sworn never to reveal; and which they never did reveal, not even when submitted to unimaginable tortures, not even when the flames finally began to hiss around the stake.

Part one

You are the king who would come, and there is great glory for you. Do not fear any trouble in your soul before two times the sacred number, but go forward in strength to do the many things that must be done.

Joan of Winchester, December 1154

I

Anyone who has ever met King Henry II of England knows that he acts upon his own will and intuition, and always has. He led an army when he was fourteen, married at nineteen the greatest heiress in all Europe, eleven years his senior, who had but a few weeks previously been queen to the French king, and seized, at twenty-one, the crown of England.

Yet we are asked to believe that within days of his coronation this unbiddable and violently tempered youth accepted as his Chancellor a stranger, an unknown clerk, one Thomas of London, possessing no noble connections of any kind, and that he did so merely upon the advice of Theobald, the elderly Archbishop of Canterbury, and of three other equally old but less intelligent bishops.

He who believes this would believe that pigs fly, for in addition to his inherited Angevin characteristics Henry, being what he is, would rather base a choice upon the entrails of a chicken, in Roman fashion, than upon the word of any Christian, however worthy.

The historians have, as usual, glossed over what they are unable to explain. Here is the truth.

In the year 1151 Thomas of London and I were in Auxerre, some hundred miles south of Paris. We had been sent there by our lord the Archbishop, in whose court we both served as clerks. I will be more correct, and say that Thomas served the Archbishop, having in fact created for himself a unique position as Theobald's private secretary and general factotum, whilst I served Thomas. He was indeed the most brilliant of the young men surrounding the Archbishop, envied, disliked, respected but not loved. I was his shadow and his friend. I was about to write his only friend, but of course there was to be one other who outshone me in every way: Henry II, King of England. From that other friendship came great power and wealth, some happiness, much sorrow, and death.

But in June of 1151 we were two clerks in our early thirties studying civil and canon law at Auxerre. Law in all its forms fascinated Thomas. He appreciated its necessity, delighted in its absurdity, and at all times in later life took advantage of its shortcomings. At Auxerre he played games with it, throwing up glittering towers of argument with a force which, alone, seemed to hypnotize any listener. His words, as always, were gold: even if on more than one occasion he had to turn to me for the actual legal point, which I would supply. In words of lead.

Even in those days I kept the day-book which was to grow, as Thomas's power grew, until it became a secret unofficial document of great importance, and finally a danger to both our lives. From it, I see that on the evening of 23 June while I was sitting in the cloister trying to digest my supper (the food at Auxerre was most inferior), Thomas came to me, excited, and said, 'Pack, Will, pack! We leave for Paris at dawn.'

I do not like Paris; it is a prehistoric rabbit-warren, crowded with students who babble and shout all night as well as all day. I asked why, pettishly no doubt.

'Because,' he said, 'our future lord attends the King and Queen of France. Particularly the Queen.' Thomas had a small quick smile, as though what he had said was not worth much in his own opinion. He was at this time a handsome elegant figure: tall and slim, brown-haired, pale-skinned, his dark eyes always alight with intense forethought.

Looking back, it is odd to think that we were even then acting as traitors, not only Thomas and I, but godly and respected Theobald of Canterbury himself.

In 1151, Stephen ruled (if that is the word) England. The land had been laid waste by futile civil war between this uncertain and unkingly King and Matilda, that tiresome and overbearing woman who could not forget that she had once, as wife to Henry V of Germany, been an empress. The skirmishing of these two grabbing for the crown, each with a cohort of nobles, are not part of what I have to tell here, for which God be praised. Or at least only insofar as this journey we were about to make from Auxerre to Paris was instrumental in bringing an end to chaos and in restoring peace and prosperity to England.

Henry, the young Duke of Normandy, and his father, Count of Anjou, had been summoned to Paris by their liege-lord, King Louis VII of France, to pay homage. The King, who had recently returned from a less-than-successful crusade, was a quiet man, brought up in the cloisters of Notre-Dame, where he would willingly have stayed had not his elder brother, returning on horseback from the hunt, been tripped up by a pig and died of it. His mild blue eyes and sometimes hesitant manner formed a convenient mask for a quiet man's determination and sly patience. Others despise Louis; I admire and understand him, for if kingship had ever been thrust on me, he is the kind of king I would have had to be myself.

As for the rulers of Anjou and Normandy, he needed the friendship of both, since their lands drove an ugly wedge into the centre of his own domain.

Thomas and I reached Paris without incident. The roads of France were as dangerous as the roads of England, the one having been given over to disorder during the King's absence in the Holy Land, the other rent by civil war. We travelled, I'm happy to say, with two knights and a group of their liege-men, fellow-Normans on their way home.

Let me say here that I was not always privy to Thomas's plans before they were put into execution; I think he suspected that I do not hold my tongue too well after a glass or so of wine, and this may be true. I was surprised, therefore, after we had fought our way through a rabble of students and a muck of refuse to the Ile de France, that we were admitted immediately into the palace, and taken to the apartments in which the Angevins, or Plantagenets as they sometimes call themselves, had been comfortably installed.

This was not my first meeting with Geoffrey of Anjou, who was to die in September of that same year 1151, and I confess to being bored by his noble looks and manners. I find his habit of wearing a spray of broom (Genista, hence Plantagenet) in his cap or helmet a perfectly flamboyant symbol for the whole man. But perhaps, plain of feature myself, I am merely jealous.

His son, Henry of Normandy, I now met for the first time. I found a heavily handsome youth with reddish-gold hair, his figure at that time well built but still trim. I also noticed with some surprise, for there is a winning roughness about him, that he was unusually well educated, and courteous : this last a virtue not always found in princes.

It was clear that he and Thomas had met before. I don't know where, and I was never told. Already it seemed that they took pleasure from each other, as I did from their company. Yet I admit that my unadventurous blood cooled considerably when I realized the purpose of our meeting. The door was opened by the same self-effacing manservant who had admitted us, and Queen Eleanor swept into the room, dominating it at once.

Her beauty has not been exaggerated, nor her pride of bearing. Her physical courage had never been in doubt; she accompanied her husband on his crusade, and by all accounts enjoyed it more than he did. She is one of those rare women who move easily among men as their equal; anything less is not to her taste. Thomas, whom she had not met before, but of whom she had obviously heard, was presented. She received him graciously, but I thought, even then, with a kind of cool appraisal, not wholly won over by his charm. When I was brought forward she raised her eyebrows. Duke Henry said, 'Thomas of London claims that this good man is his right arm.'

The Queen nodded, accepting me without enthusiasm, and saying to no one in particular, 'We should not wish Thomas of London to go without his right arm, should we?'

Neither of us missed the light threat in this rejoinder. It was to be a long time before Queen Eleanor came to trust Thomas, long after I myself, in unlikely fashion, had become her fascinated but somewhat fearful confidant.

At the time of her marriage this woman, as Duchess of Aquitaine and Countess of Poitou, held possessions wider than those of King Louis himself, spreading from the High Auvergne to the ocean and from the River Loire to the Pyrenees. Within this ancient kingdom she had been born to a life full of song and lazy sunshine and courtly dalliance, a life more civilized than any other in Europe. By contrast her husband's city of Paris, though just as ancient, had seemed to her an overcrowded barbarian pigsty; in truth the only real delights that the city had to offer her enquiring mind lay in the schools, and she often ventured forth to hear the great masters at their discourse.

As for her marriage, which had so far given the King and France two daughters in fourteen years, her own remark, 'I thought I was marrying a king, I find I have wed a monk,' says all that need be said.

This remarkable woman now did something which shocked me as much as anything that has happened in my whole life; she drew from her sleeve two objects, a book and a small cross carved of light wood. Her limpid green eyes dwelt for a moment on each of our faces before she handed the cross to Thomas. I don't think he was as shocked as I, but he looked at it for a long moment before breaking it into small pieces which he thrust out of sight into his pocket. More surprising yet was the book: nothing less than the rock upon which our faith is built, the Acts of Blessed St John, the Beloved of Christ. It was not until I had considered the matter afterwards that I came to understand that only this one woman could have used it in such a way without affront.

One must remember that her grandfather was William IX of Aquitaine, close friend of the Conqueror's son, King William Rufus of England; and, as all the world knows, Rufus was a self-confessed 'pagan', to use the Christian word, who openly mocked the church and who died in the year 1100 as Divine Victim of the Old Religion: by the arrow, under the sacred oak-tree on the morrow of Lammas, one of the four great 'pagan' festivals. And it was this same Duke of Aquitaine who also held the title Count of Poitou and was the first of the Troubadours – the evangelists, one might say, of our religion.

Certainly it can have been no surprise to his grand-daughter that we four men were not Christians but, each in his own way, followers of older and more profound religions. Thomas and I had long been of the true Cathar faith, which had started in her own lands, among the men of Albi, before sweeping across the world like a cleansing flame. The Angevins, I had heard, held to even more ancient beliefs. Do not let this surprise you; at the time of which I write at least thirteen of the crowned heads of Europe adhered to one or another of what the Christians are pleased to call 'the heresies', while in the deep countryside of their domains the great majority of ordinary people still worshipped the old fertility gods with the old rituals and dances. Sometimes their priest joined them, sometimes not; either way they would go to church on Sunday, their heads full of their own prayers, for the Mass was in Latin and none understood a word of it.

All this Queen Eleanor knew better than any woman, but she could not have been privy to the mysteries of our faith, for these are revealed only to men.

After we had each kissed the Book, herself excepted, a most extraordinary thing happened; young Duke Henry made the Sign of the Lion, the origins of which are lost in time, connected with the god Mithra whom the Roman soldiers carried with them to every corner of their empire; we imitated him as a matter of politeness, but of a sudden the gesture made me uneasy, and I have never forgotten it; for in this I saw a first outward indication of the spiritual gulf which separated him from Thomas.

Now I must explain this difference between the two men, for it is the very lynch-pin of what I have to tell, and the reader must not believe that, though both were by Christian standards 'heretics', there was the slightest similarity between them. Henry's gods were pagan, to us as to Christians; they were the dark gods under the hills, and the horned god of fertility, and the Sun which is also Mithra, and the Moon which rules the flux of all the world. For Henry, Christ the son of God did not exist. For Thomas, Christ (though not the Christ whom the Christians accept: here I must walk warily) was the living symbol upon earth of God's knowledge and light; and Christ's love for John was the love of all mankind, without which we are less than beasts, and without which we cannot know the universal love of God.

It was not in Henry to be a believer as Thomas was a believer, though later he pretended to belief for political reasons. Our true Cathar faith demanded too much of him, as, alas, I confess it does of me. Only a man such as Thomas could discipline himself inwardly and thus attain Perfection.

More of this later, but while I am on the subject I should add that there was nothing in the least unusual about the fact that we two 'heretics' were clerks to the good Archbishop of Canterbury. I assure you we were not alone; all men must worship God as best they may. To the uninitiated, our religion seems to follow that of the Christians quite closely, though in fact the likenesses are purely superficial and for us the Mass has many secret meanings of which I may not speak. However, we cannot in all conscience pay respect to the Cross. What sane believer in God could possibly worship the instrument upon which the Son of God was hideously tortured and killed? But then Christians are inconsistent in most of their tenets and philosophy.

I must say that I thought that the demands being made upon our secrecy were becoming somewhat too dramatic. The Queen changed my mind for me hastily by saying, 'Well, I have consulted men wise both in theology and law, and also some who profess to know the King's mind which he does not know himself. All agree that a separation is possible, and that the King might welcome the idea once he gets used to it.' And, smiling, she took young Henry's hand.

The events arising from this remark are now part of history, and it would be tedious were I to write here the conversation which followed. Within a few months she and Louis were legally separated on the always convenient grounds of consanguinity; shortly afterwards she and Henry, Duke of Normandy, were married. He was nineteen, she thirty-one.

I had the opportunity of observing the royal pair during the first years of their union, and I am forced to conclude that a large part of their motive was indeed mutual love – even more rare among princes than politeness.

Politically they were joining territories which ran from the sea-coast of northern France to the borders of Spain; a kingdom to be reckoned with. The rest, the great prize, still lay across the water, but it now became clear that their eyes were already fixed upon it.

Gazing fondly at the young Duke, Queen Eleanor said, 'Thomas of London must be very sure of himself or he would not be in this room now, he and his right arm.'

Henry smiled. 'You do not know Thomas as I do. If he says a thing is impossible he means that it may be done. If he says it is possible, he means that he will do it. If he says that it is probable, you may be sure it's already finished and done with.'

The Queen nodded and turned to us. 'And this question of England belongs to which category?'

I think that only Thomas would have dared to answer her, 'Quite impossible, my lady, but with God's grace I shall accomplish it.' Her smile was as brief as his own. He continued: 'His Holiness the Pope does not love King Stephen . . .'

'The Pope! Are we then to have endless shilly-shallying and politicking? I had thought to hear of armies.'

Duke Henry said, 'You shall have armies too, my love.'

Geoffrey of Anjou smiled. 'The British weather is inclement. I doubt if you will wish to go riding as an Amazon again.'

It is said that there was at one time a close relationship between Queen Eleanor and this handsome father of her husband-to-be. I do not know the truth of it, but the smile she turned on him was not like the one she had shown Thomas. As for her Amazonian exploit, I believe that on a certain occasion connected with the crusade she and some of her ladies rode bare-breasted in imitation of those female warriors. She said now, 'The army was encouraged, recruiting was doubled.'

Henry gave a great shout of boy's laughter, taking her hand and kissing it. But it was not a boy's voice which said, 'No lady of *mine* goes to war.'

She nodded, not meekly, and turned back to Thomas. 'Tell us in detail what you propose to do, and how; and what this fledgling statesman . . .' she tightened her fingers on Henry's hand, '. . . has promised you by way of recompense?'

Bowing, he replied, 'My recompense lies in the service I perform for you, for my master, and for England.'

The green eyes glittered. 'Oh, Thomas of London, you must learn to speak our language.' There was no telling whether the 'our' was spoken of herself in the royal sense, or of herself and young Duke Henry who again laughed, boyishly.

I now understand this laugh better than I did then; if his plans matured correctly as, with the buoyancy of youth, he was sure they would, the language that both these strong-willed people would be speaking before long would be his own.

The reader might be forgiven for assuming from Thomas's words that it was he alone who was planning and working for the accession of Henry of Normandy to the English throne. I must admit that he tended a little towards self-aggrandizement in those years before he gained power. Perhaps it was his intense ambition, then unfulfilled, that demanded an attitude altogether uncharacteristic of the real man; or am I so intensely partisan that I write this to excuse him? Either way he would forgive me; one of the most endearing things about him was that he always stood a little apart from his own behaviour, mocking or criticizing himself a long time before others did so. Also let no man forget that there were two Thomas Beckets one inside the other, and had not the hidden man been so sure of his own spirit, the visible man could never have achieved the things he did.

As for the ousting of Stephen of Blois from the throne of England and the replacing of him by Henry Plantagenet, the chief power and wisdom behind all of it was that of our master Theobald, Archbishop of Canterbury. During the terrible years of anarchy which Stephen unleashed upon England due to his squabbles with Empress Matilda, when the great lords ran wild, taking advantage of civil war to fight their own land-grabbing feuds, building castles without permission, turning churches into improvised fortresses, burning towns and crops and forests; during these years Theobald towered above all others, not only the leading Christian in the land but its only statesman.

The chroniclers say that he groomed Thomas to be Chancellor in order to preserve the interests of the church against a new young king who promised to disregard them. It is however just as likely that the wise old man knew that both young Henry and Thomas were, as he would have put it, 'heretics'; I think it possible that this is why he chose Thomas, for the very opposite reasons to those given by historians. Better that the King be advised by a forward-looking and intelligent 'heretic' (one, moreover, who owed everything to Theobald), than by a Christian to whose every word the King would be deaf.

In the autumn of 1152 while Henry, having married Eleanor, was spending a passionate and politically advantageous honeymoon in Poitou and Aquitaine, accepting the homage of her countless fiefs, Thomas was sent to visit the Pope. The Christians were at this time undergoing one of their frequent periods of dissension and muddle; there were in fact two Popes. Thomas and I attended the nearer of them, Eugenius III, who was not only the more friendly towards England and Normandy but also the more intelligent. Our mission concerned Eustace, son and heir of King Stephen who, knowing that the boy was as unpopular as he was himself, wanted to ensure the succession by having him crowned immediately. Thomas easily persuaded the papal court that the House of Blois had no rights whatever to the English throne, and the Pope forbade the coronation.

This threw King Stephen into a black rage; he accused the Archbishop of treason, quite correctly, but even those who agreed with him could see that his power was tottering, and took no action. In any case, more urgent matters were soon pressing. Although she did not accompany her husband, being already pregnant with their first child, the ex-Queen of France was now given her armies. On the morning of the holy day which the Christians call Epiphany in January 1153, Henry landed in England from thirty-six ships with a force of 140 horseman and 3,000 foot soldiers. King Stephen rode out to meet him with those barons whom he imagined to be loyal to him, though many were not.

There was then a deal of skirmishing and trumpet-blowing, much bandying of threats between heralds, which effectively gave the people an impression of armed liberation from the tyrant's yoke; but the true business of prising the crown from Stephen's head was a matter of the law and a judicious application of threats: what Queen Eleanor would doubtless have called much 'shilly-shallying and politicking'.

The Archbishop had underwritten a fine legal training for Thomas and myself, and Thomas now put this to good effect, forcing King Stephen into a corner from which he could find no escape. Even then, the King's capitulation was probably achieved as much by the will of God as by any man-made machination. Prince Eustace, visiting Bury St Edmunds where he intended to appropriate illegally certain properties, choked himself to death while consuming a dish of eels.

It is clear that all men, and princes in particular, should never underestimate the power of God's humbler creatures. A sow put Louis VII on the throne of France, and an eel cleared for Henry Plantagenet the path to the throne of England.

Saddened by his unattractive son's death, cornered by Thomas's legal barricades, there was little fight left in King Stephen. Henry now brought pressure to bear on those of the King's wavering supporters who held properties on the other side of the Channel, implying that these might melt away if they did not change sides; for whether they liked him or not he was their liege-lord in Normandy and beyond.

And so at last, by hook and crook, an agreement was reached. Stephen would be allowed to rule for the rest of his life, and at his death Henry would succeed to the kingdom. There is no doubt that Thomas had played a large part in this victory, and had indeed accomplished the 'quite impossible' task of which he had spoken to Queen Eleanor in her erstwhile palace on the Ile de France.

Already, a year before he became their King, the common people of England had shown how they would take Henry to their hearts. As for him, I have never ceased to marvel at the attitude of this impatient and intractable man to the exigencies of the mob. Dismounting, throwing aside sword and cloak, he would move among them at complete ease. I have seen him buffeted this way and that, clawed at and kissed, even caught up shoulder-high and carried by a phalanx of excited peasants under whose feet, had he fallen, he must surely have been trampled to death. Not only in youth but even in his later years, he never failed to have time for them.

Of course they recognized in him the blood of the Conqueror, but the Conqueror was a harsh man, unloved by these English whom he conquered. Why then the adoration?

Now, with hindsight which I wish had never been granted to me, I know the answer. It was another king whom they saw in this boy with his red-gold hair and his workaday clothes; for though he was a clean man and his clothing was always of the finest quality, he eschewed bright colours, rich materials, royal trappings, and habitually seemed little better attired than the best of these country people. It was William Rufus, Henry's grand-uncle, whom they saw – another Red King come again to save them from the depredations of the nobility and the ravages of civil war, another king who might one day die for them as Rufus had died, to make the earth rich again with his sacred blood, and to atone for their sins against the dark gods under the hills, thereby ensuring a fair spring for sowing, the right amount of rain in summer, and a rich and mellow autumn's gathering.

This is what they saw, and he knew it; 'pagan' himself, how could he not know it? And he used it. And this knowing and using led him at last into a terrible trap from which there was only one unthinkable escape. Yet to Henry Plantagenet anything that is expedient is never unthinkable.

Before returning to Normandy, where his lady, Eleanor, was now brought to bed with the child, Henry summoned Thomas to a secret meeting. Their relationship was punctuated by a series of such meetings, momentous beyond the seeming of the moment; some of them are unknown to any chronicler saving myself, while others, though known to all the world, have been misinterpreted already by worthy men, John of Salisbury, Alan of Tewkesbury, Herbert of Bosham, William Fitzstephen, because they lack knowledge of the central secret which is the key.

The day-book, which Thomas had already adopted as an unofficial record of his acts and, to a lesser degree, of his thoughts tells me that early in the morning of 3 December 1153 he woke me up with a finger to his lips. He had come directly from Henry and wanted me to take note at once of what had been said. The Duke of Normandy had rejoined his army, and the meeting had taken place in a barn by the flicker of firelight. I honestly believe that this man who was so soon to be our king preferred to sleep in straw than in a king's bed, just as he preferred to move unless it was essential for him to stand still. Many stories are told, and I suppose I will add to them, of how he suddenly decides to ride just when his court is settling down for the night, or of how he will just as suddenly decide to sleep, tumbling into the hay of some remote barn while the great lords surrounding him squabble, and even fight, for the shelter of a bracken-bed in the hollow of a tree. How often have I thanked God that I was Thomas's servant and not his, for I would have been long since dead and buried.

In the small hours of that bitter December morning, Thomas said, 'Henry of Normandy has been received into the Cathar church.' I remember that I stared at him before setting my chilled fingers to the page; it is, as I well know myself, easy to be received into our church, less easy to discipline oneself to its demands.

Pacing my small cell, keeping his voice low in order not to arouse nearby sleepers, he described how the very air of Aquitaine, where all men of education adhere to our faith, led Henry to ask questions, led him to perceive that the 'pagan' belief of his ancestors was but a poor substitute for our truth. He was taken to one of our masters and talked with him several times before deciding to become an initiate.

I stopped writing, and said, 'He did so to ensure more closely the loyalty of his southern realm.'

Thomas laughed softly. 'His motives are not our concern, William. I do not ask how often you yourself have renewed the Spirit, nor how often you have curbed lust or given your body to the healing lash.' My expression, I fear, made him laugh again; he was in high good spirits. 'I do not even care how long Henry holds to the tenets of our faith, I only care that he holds them now. We are one, Will, *now*, when it matters.'

It seemed that the great master whom Henry had sought out near Poitiers had applauded the fact that Thomas of London was to be the young ruler's spiritual adviser.

'But there is more,' Thomas said, coming back to sit opposite me beyond the wavering flame of the taper. 'Henry said, "I shall need you by me, Thomas, for when this thing comes about I shall be lord of an empire, and I can be in but one place at one time." '

Thomas asked what position he could possibly hold, he, a mere clerk, a merchant's son and a failed merchant at that. To which

Henry replied, 'A high position. Let us give it a name when it exists.'

He stood up then and held out his hand. Thomas thought for a while after I had penned this; then he said, 'I knew that he expected me to drop upon one knee and kiss it as any of his feudal lords might do, as he himself must pay fealty to King Louis of France, like it or not.'

'And you did not do so.'

'No. I took his hand, standing face to face with him, and I saw his surprise, for he is too young as yet to hide what he feels. I took it in the secret grip, which you know well; then he, remembering his recent conversion, smiled and returned the pledge with his fingers.' He nodded to himself. 'But I see that one does not so easily better those Angevins. Searching my face he said, "Thomas, are you my man?"'

'I said, "My lord, you know I am."'

' "My man unto death, Thomas? By God's will and the two faces of Mary, by the blood of the Bull and of the Son who died?" '

As I have said, it was icy cold in my cell at that hour of a December morning, but I think I would have shuddered had it been an afternoon in July. Thomas saw everything: 'You think I was wrong?'

'Who am I to say? You know the heart of it, I do not.'

'I answered him, "I would be united and I would unite. Amen." '

My quill was poised over the parchment, yet it seemed that I could not force it to move. I looked up, and found no humour now in Thomas's eyes; they pierced me with anger. 'If you cannot write, then speak! Are you not my friend?'

'You swore allegiance to death and beyond on our most sacred oath; upon the Book itself.'

'How else,' he demanded savagely, 'can I achieve what must be achieved?'

I know that I glanced away from his eyes before I replied, 'I am in no position, spiritually or practically, to speak as your conscience.'

'You have set yourself that task, it seems.'

For answer, I forced my quill to the parchment and began to transcribe what he had said; but to my amazement Thomas wrenched it from my fingers and flung it aside: 'No, chronicler, this time you shall not take refuge in the written word, you shall speak!'

Angered myself by this churlishness, I said, 'Very well, my lord, *what* must be achieved?'

He was silent. I continued, 'The Duke of Normandy is well able to take the crown of England with no more help from you; we may leave the rest to history. Therefore when you say, "How else can I achieve what must be achieved?" I understand that you have sworn your life away in the cause of your own ambition.'

'Is ambition then a sin?'

'You know better than I that it is not; but if you have sworn more than you are willing to fulfil, then you betray not only the oath, not only Henry, but yourself; therein, I think, lies the greatest of all sins.' I paused for I had not wished to speak thus and hoped that he would refute my words with some subtle twist of argument; but he remained silent for a long time, then, in a very different tone, said, 'But what of the *nature* of that ambition, for it is in their nature not in their existing that all things must be judged?'

'Each must answer that for himself.'

'It shall be answered, it must be answered.' I could sense in his tone many future hours of meditation and prayer; then he sighed and looked up at me directly, considering my features with interest and a trace of surprise. 'I have never considered why I wished you for a friend; we have ever been close, and thus I accepted it. Now I begin to see much in you that I perhaps took for granted.'

He held out his hand and I grasped it, saying, 'Thomas, it is your friend and chronicler I wish to be, not your conscience, for I could never match the one God gave you.'

He nodded, but absently, and said, 'We parted, Duke Henry and I, upon the Kiss of Peace. He is of course a high enough lord to imagine that he gave it to me, his servant.'

I remember that I stared in astonishment, assimilating the depths of this remark. Only after some thought did I perceive that it would be Thomas, senior in our faith and recommended by a great master as Henry's spiritual adviser, who would give the Kiss and Henry who would receive it. I said, 'He did not understand?'

'Not then. Not yet. One day perhaps.'

Brilliant and wily Thomas of London! But oh, the repercussions of that midnight oath and that Kiss of Peace; and the lack of peace it would bring to all of us!

So much for the official statements of the chroniclers, who can seldom forbear to invent when they do not know the facts; and so much for the 'mystery' of Thomas's sudden promotion to the post of Chancellor only a few days after Henry's coronation.

The pact was made and sealed in a barn, by firelight, some ten months before Henry was called to the throne. That Archbishop Theobald had prepared the way for it no sensible man would ever doubt, but that he could have stopped it even if he had wished to is an impossibility.

I would be united and I would unite. Amen.
A place I have not and I have places. Amen.
A temple I have not and I have temples. Amen.
A lamp am I to thee that beholdest me. Amen.
A mirror am I to thee that beholdest me. Amen.
A door am I to thee that knockest at me. Amen.
A way am I to thee a wayfarer. Amen.
Now answer thou unto my dancing. Behold thyself in me who speak, and, seeing what I do, keep silence about my mysteries. Thou that dancest, perceive what I do, for thine is the passion of the manhood I am about to suffer.

Oh Thomas, my Brother, my friend!

3

King Stephen died on 25 October 1154.

Thomas did not tell me why he considered it so vital that he himself should be among those who brought the news to Henry. If I were asked to hazard a guess, I would say that he held vital information concerning the loyalty or otherwise of all the powerful lords in England; there were also rumours of a certain plot to ambush Henry soon after he landed on British soil and to murder him. Whatever the reasons, I am sure that the Archbishop knew of them or he would not so swiftly have given his permission; only ten days before, he had appointed Thomas Archdeacon of Canterbury, and there was much work for my lord to do at home. On the other hand, Theobald suspected, and Thomas knew, that on Henry's arrival he was going to be offered a higher post yet, and any work he began as Archdeacon would only have to be delegated to someone else.

Fast travel on urgent missions has never been to my taste; roads are dangerous, and the sea even more so. I kept a mouse-like stillness, but of course Thomas noticed it, with some amusement, and shouted, 'Come, William, to horse, to horse! We are the makers of history.'

Our escort consisted of Randulph de Broc, he who was eventually to become one of Thomas's most persistent enemies, and eight of his men; we left Canterbury within a few hours of hearing of the King's death.

The streets were buzzing with extraordinary tales. One of particular interest, because it showed that the English were not unaware of the legends surrounding their future king and the Angevins in general, was that Satan's daughter had flown into the King's chamber and literally torn his soul from his body as if it were an ill-fitting shift. Long ago it is said that a certain Angevin ancestor returned from some journey, probably warlike, with a bride of surpassing beauty. This lady, however, possessed one unusual trait: she would not stay in church for that part of the Christian ritual known as the Consecration when, in the form of a piece of bread, the body of Christ is supposedly offered to the worshippers. Again and again she departed before this moment, showing it seems to me a certain intelligence, for who but a dolt, or I suppose a Christian, would see the body of Jesus in a stale crust? However, the habit worried her lord, who arranged that on a certain occasion those near her would step upon the hem of her dress, holding her where she was. Upon seeing the sacred titbit the lady gave a scream, slipped out of her clothes in one elegant movement and flew out of the window of the church. She was, it seems, none other than this same Melusine, the Devil's daughter, who had made off with the late King's soul.

She had of course borne several children to her Angevin lord, and it is said that her blood still runs high and fast in their veins, explaining the extraordinary rages which possess them all from time to time; I have witnessed more than one in Henry, and they are truly demonic.

Imagine my horror, upon arriving at Dover, to find that Thomas intended to cross the Channel that very night. It is treacherous enough by day, and I was certain that the captain of our smack would tell him as much; but no, not at all, it was generally agreed that advantage should be taken immediately of what they called 'the calm sea', and within the hour we had swallowed down a meal and were loaded aboard, sails set for Wissant.

Since nothing in my whole life has ever matched the horror of our return journey, which I will describe in due course, I can say with hindsight that this was indeed a calm crossing. We did not reach Wissant of course, but then sea-captains seem to be constitutionally incapable of reaching the actual port they are aiming for; in fact we landed in thick fog not far from Boulogne, instantly took to our horses and headed towards Rouen where Henry and Eleanor had taken up residence in the capital city of the Dukes of Normandy.

Of the many important things that had happened in the earlier months of that momentous year, the one to cause most furore was the birth of Eleanor's child. After being married to Louis VII of France for fourteen years and in all that time presenting him with nothing more than two useless daughters, she had, within nine months of marrying Henry Duke of Normandy, presented him with a fine boy. Louis's opinion is not recorded. Henry was boisterously delighted, and his lady, prescient as ever, was about to be repaid with the crown of England, which meant that she and her young husband would reign over an empire larger than that designated Holy and Roman. As for Louis, though he remained their overlord his own possessions would be completely dwarfed by this unruly and unfriendly giant of a neighbour.

Pausing only to snatch the most meagre of refreshment, we rode on to the borders of Henry's domain; and here, while changing horses, we learned that he was not at Rouen with his court but once more in the field, leading an army to settle some dispute on the borders of the Vexin, that most disputed plot of earth dividing Normandy from Paris.

We found him sick, unable to hold any food in his stomach and consequently very weak; we learned that he had set out from Rouen in this condition, against everyone's advice; and in this condition he would willingly have returned to his capital city, gathered up his wife, his son and an army, and set sail immediately for England. Luckily almighty Providence had other plans, for at the beginning of November there sprang up a season of furious winds which made such a course impossible, and which also, it seemed to me, saved the life of Henry Duke of Normandy. Had he attempted the journey sick and fevered he must certainly have died before reaching his new kingdom. Or am I underestimating the infernal energy of the man?

Within two weeks his court had gathered at Barfleur, attended by a gaggle of Christian prelates and a swaggering host of knights and barons, some from beyond Henry's domain who owed allegiance to Louis VII of France rather than to the future King of England.

However, as November crawled by, the chances of our ever embarking upon a crossing seemed to grow more and more remote. Never had so violent and continuous a series of gales been known in those parts, and I suspected that there would be many in England who would see in this a heavenly portent unfavourable to the Angevin cause. Nor was Henry unaware of the fact.

Thomas and the Duke spent much time together, making plans. On the only two occasions when I was personally summoned into the presence, the Duchess being also in the room, Henry immediately referred to this vexed subject, appealing to me at once for an opinion of what might be happening on the other side of that stretch of stormracked sea. I said, 'There will be certain high lords who will already have begun to rattle their swords, defying you, particularly after a glass or two of wine.' This made his lady laugh, and for the first time she flashed me a glance of some approval.

'Name them,' said the Duke; and I did so, knowing that Thomas must have called me thither for corroboration.

Henry began to pace about the room, his furious impatience seeming to spring from him like a supernatural force so that one felt it almost physically. I remember thinking that in the past year he had put on the semblance of five years, while Eleanor had lost as many, as if to confound those who had suggested that she would never bear a boy-child if, indeed, she was young enough still to bear any child at all. These critics would certainly have kept their mouths shut had they known that she was to bear him seven more, four of them boys.

Her late husband, King Louis, had decided after due thought to make a pilgrimage to Compostella in Spain where he would ask the advice of James, that city's own Christian saint from whom it gained many economic advantages. It so happened that his route upon this pilgrimage led through the Spanish court where he was able to examine the Princess Constance; he found her healthy and of a child-bearing constitution, and so took her with him to France and married her. If St James of Compostella had any influence at all in the court of Heaven, Louis might now expect a son in due course.

Day after day, week after week, the storms bombarded Barfleur, while I thanked God and warmed my feet at the fire. At intervals the Duke, accompanied by mariners and captains, would battle his way against the gale into a position where the heavens might be consulted for some change of weather. There was none, and I must confess I began to have serious qualms as to whether our master in Canterbury had the power to keep England at peace for much longer.

And then, on 7 December, the unspeakable took place. I heard, without believing, that the Duke's patience was at an end and that he intended to *set sail* into this maelstrom. 'Whatever happens,' he had said, 'I will go to England, I will be crowned before Christmas and hold my Christmas court in London.'

I am unable to describe my horror, and I saw many braver men than myself change colour when they heard the news. Moreover, Henry being Henry, there was to be no loitering once the decision was made; hardly even time to pack one's few belongings before we were all being herded, heads down against driving rain, towards the port.

Here was a scene of utmost confusion as men and animals, each as terrified as the other, were packed into the bucking ships, while the gale screamed in the halyards and the timbers thudded at the quays as if to shatter themselves instantly rather than face what lay outside the shelter, if that is the word, of the harbour. I remember how serenely the Duchess Eleanor boarded her vessel, nurses and ladies around her, carrying in her own arms her precious son William, who merely gazed all about him with wondering eyes at the majesty of nature gone mad and his father gone even madder.

We set sail; and almost at once the ships began to separate, now seen, now obscured by violent squalls. The trumpets sounded bravely, but all too soon their little voices were swallowed up by tempest, and the ship's lanterns, glimmering faintly, were lost to sight. Nothing remained under the iron sky of driven cloud but vast hills of water up which our gallant vessel climbed laboriously, reaching at last a white crest where the spume was whipped away to reveal yet another vast valley of water on the other side. I have never before and never since heard the name of God called upon so continuously and with such fervour by so many people in one place at one time; no, not even in the great church of Canterbury during the Mass; for there was not a voyager who did not recall the story of the famous White Ship which over thirty years before had disappeared without trace in these same waters, taking with her the heir of the first Henry, also named William.

At last we were told by the seamen to note how the waves were relenting; unimportant news to we landsmen who would feel them lifting under our feet for days to come. It was however true that after a whole twenty-four hours of this nightmare we had reached some creek not far from the port of Wareham in Dorset.

We in our faith do not share the Christian enthusiasm for miracles, yet I feel inclined to borrow the word in its Christian sense when I report that not one of the ships that left Barfleur was lost in the storm; all ended up at different parts of the English coast and met with welcomes of varying enthusiasm according to the popularity of the Duke of Normandy in that particular region.

No one was surprised to hear that many nobles, taking advantage of Henry's continued absence, had rallied armies of their own, and I believe that had we not arrived when we did, the anarchy of Stephen's reign would have broken out threefold within a few days. But it must be remembered that the storm had not abated

35

by one iota, and it was the unfriendly elements which proved to be his true friends, for when these renegades heard that the heir to the throne had suddenly appeared out of the tempest they were at first disbelieving, and then, as the certainty of the news grew, filled with fear and awe; some naturally reasoned that none but the Devil's progeny could have crossed that raging sea and survived.

Whatever the reason, it is a fact that as the different bedraggled bands of Henry's retainers headed for Winchester they were not even met by a token show of force. Castles and watchtowers stared at us silently and kept their peace. God (or the demon-ancestress Melusine) guarded us all.

The people of England showed none of the reticence of their lords. Caring nothing for rain and gales, which are a part of their everyday lives, they came forth cheering from hovels and villages to welcome the king who was to be 'theirs', true successor to William Rufus, a Red King again at last. Moreover he had come to them before Christmas, as they had known he would; for it must be remembered that 25 December, day of the winter solstice, birth-day of the Invincible Sun, had been held sacred for many years before the Christians appended it to their own calendar, working on the principle that one must absorb what one cannot destroy. Had not the ancient god Mithra been born in a cave on that day, and been worshipped by shepherds who had been tending their flocks nearby. How many hundreds of years before the birth of Christ? Nobody knows; it is all lost in the misty shadows of antiquity. Long lost, and yet remembered as if in the marrow of men's bones.

We found Henry at Winchester before us, his ship having come to rest in the lee of Hengistbury Head below the great forest of Hampshire in which Rufus had died by the arrow. He was in good humour, delighted by the number of noble lords who had already come forward to support him, and by the notable inactivity of those who had not; delighted also by the acclaim of the people who be-sieged him at his every appearance, hailing him as King though he was not yet crowned.

I noticed immediately that the ties between himself and Thomas were in some way strengthened, as if welded on the anvil of that monstrous sea-crossing and the uncertainty of what lay ahead. The

Duchess Eleanor had also subtly changed her attitude towards Thomas; I would not go so far as to say that she now seemed to trust him (it was a long time before she trusted him), but she at least showed acceptance of him as the remarkable, and remarkably useful, man he was.

Henry had sent riders ahead towards London, wanting to know the temper of the people there, which is invariably different from that of the rest of England, inclined to tetchiness and swift changes of direction. One of them now returned with a young lord whom they had met upon the road, heading for Winchester with the self-same news that the Duke desired. He was a handsome young man, richly dressed, so that when he knelt low in front of Henry he looked like a prince falling to his knees before some well-to-do farmer.

Henry said, 'Well then, is my capital city to be my friend? Will it bow like you, or will I force it to that position?'

The young man replied, 'Sire, already the bells are ringing and they are hanging evergreens from every house to greet your coming.' And then, before anyone could move, he had whipped a dagger from within his splendid clothes and was lunging upwards at the man who stood above him.

It was the first time I had seen the Duke, as it were, in war, and I do not know where he found the speed with which he reacted. For by the time the knife had reached the level of his groin he was no longer there, but a good four feet back, from which position, and as the dagger reached its useless zenith, he kicked out with all his great strength, his boot finding the man's face as if it were some ball thrown to him in play. The knife fell and the man flew backwards, hitting the wall and bringing down the tapestry so that it enveloped him in its folds. Nor, by the time others in the room had freed him, was he a sight for human eyes, his face all blood and the jaw hanging awry.

Henry said, 'I shall take the advice of Thomas of London and approach London cautiously.'

He spoke lightly, seeming to dismiss the matter, but this was only a public attitude; in private he brooded upon the incident like any other man, which is why Thomas came to me later, after supper, and bade me go to a certain house and bring to the castle a woman called Joan who lived there. I had visited her twice before with Thomas, who, as is well known, put much trust in such people. Some would say too much trust.

The Duke had retired to a small chamber, for it was a cold night, and sat with his legs stretched out to a roaring fire; his lady had withdrawn a little from the heat and was bending over the cradle where their son lay asleep. Thomas met us on the stair, motioned others to stay outside, and took us into the room.

Henry examined the woman's face with interest; and indeed it is an interesting face, parchment-coloured and without age: she could be thirty or sixty, with eyes of so pale a blue-grey that they sometimes seem to fade into the white. She bowed to the Duke and to the Lady Eleanor, and only then, for the tapers were not many, did her strange eyes fall upon the child in his cradle. Near to her, I heard a faint hiss from her lips, and her body was seized by a stillness like the stillness of death.

I don't think Henry noticed her reaction, but his Duchess had certainly done so. He said, 'Come, Joan, you know I am such a one as you can trust, by the Bull and the two faces of Mary.'

'I know that, my lord.'

'Then tell me, what of London? Shall I be crowned there and how soon?'

'All London awaits you, sire. The king who was no king is forgotten, and no other man shall turn his hand against you.'

One could see that the Duke was surprised by her knowledge of the attempt upon his life, for all who witnessed it had been sworn to secrecy; but he expected such things of these people, and so smiled. 'And the crown, Joan?'

'It shall be yours, in the appointed place of your forefathers, before the day of the winter solstice and the sun's birth. You are the king who would come, and there is great glory for you. Do not fear any trouble in your soul before two times the sacred number, but go forward in strength to do the things that must be done.'

'What else, Joan?'

'I have seen nothing else; my sight grows weak perhaps.'

'What, after the eight years?'

'I see no further, my lord: only the four and the four, and that is blessed.'

Henry nodded; then gave her gold and dismissed her.

She bobbed him a curtsey and, keeping her eyes away from the corner beyond the fire where the child lay in his cradle, hurried towards the door. I opened it for her, while the Duke said to Thomas, 'Let us not look beyond eight years, Thomas, it is a world of time.'

I do not know what Thomas answered, for suddenly the Duchess Eleanor was at my side. 'Stop her,' she said in a low voice. 'Stop her before she leaves the castle; and hold her; and send me word where you are.'

She had moved so swiftly, and the tone of her voice being such that it demanded an equal swiftness from me, I easily caught up with Joan and the servant escorting her before they had reached the great central courtyard of the castle. When I told her that the Duchess would speak with her, she nodded and looked away; then sighed with a kind of resignation. I took her to a small chamber next to the guard-room, and sent word to Eleanor as instructed.

She came quickly, wearing a plain cloak over her rich clothes. She did not have her husband's easy manner with ordinary people, indeed she had none of his roughness, but she had been born to rule and, failing sympathy, spoke as a ruler – yet also as a woman to another woman. 'Mistress Joan, what was it that you saw in my son?'

'He is but a child, your grace.'

'Answer me. I am strong for any answer.' And, since the poor woman hesitated: 'Was it death, Joan?'

'Yes.'

Eleanor turned away. I felt great pity for her, but it is not in me to be able to offer comfort to such a woman. After a time she said, 'How long?'

'Not long, my lady. I . . . I see no further than two years.'

The Duchess nodded, then looked at me. 'No word of this, William, no word from either of you, for only the two of you know, and if there is talk I shall not have to look far for the mouth that spoke. And to Joan: 'I am with child again.'

'I know.'

'It will be a boy?'

'I cannot say. I think so.'

'It will be a boy.' She stated it now, not questioning. 'Will he live to be king?'

'He will assuredly be crowned, my lady.'

The Duchess did not perhaps notice that the answer had been to a question she had not precisely asked; or perhaps she did not wish to notice. In any event she appeared satisfied enough. Her unusual green eyes flashed from one to the other of us. 'No word,' she said again, and to me: 'Not even to Thomas of London, William. The Duke will go forward without *this* care upon his shoulders.'

Such is the power of the woman that it never entered my head to speak to Thomas of what had passed; I think it was the only secret I ever kept from him, and, though I know it to be an unworthy thing, I will confess that I gained an odd warmth from it, knowing how much he withheld from me.

I will note here, out of context, that within three months Eleanor had indeed given birth to another boy, the young Henry upon whom so many hopes were to be placed, and that her first-born was indeed taken from her before two years had passed.

It was only when these two occurrences came about as the woman of Winchester had foretold that I began to apply my secret knowledge to what she had said to the Duke: 'Do not fear any trouble in your soul before two times the sacred number.'

As the years passed and approached the eight of which the woman had spoken, there was no mistaking the signs of impending disaster which multiplied around us; and if the 'troubles' which she had prophesied as afflicting Henry's soul were of his own making, as ever they were, those that beset Thomas of London were no less self-inflicted if one knew, as I did, their deepest cause.

More than once, and less in mockery than he pretended, my lord referred to me as his 'conscience', so that the memory of our argument upon that chill December morning was never allowed to leave us. 'Ambition' was a word that haunted him, sometimes seeming a natural state of man, sometimes synonymous with evil. At times he could justify all that he was to make of himself; at others I truly believe he stood to one side and gazed in horror at that self, seeing it as a mockery of every spiritual value upon which he based his life.

He showed little of this to the outside world, some would say nothing of it, but then as a 'heretic', adhering to a religion which might or might not be in danger of vicious persecution, he was adept at hiding his feelings. I believe that I am in a position to say that in Thomas of London we may see true greatness based upon a doubt, and thus understand how little minds, certain of too much, never even achieve the shadow of greatness.

As for the future, I have never wished to know what it holds, and I thank God I know nothing of it now.

Next day, Henry took note of the royal treasure, part of which is held at Winchester, and left for London. No one who had witnessed the arrival of each of his weary and battered ship-loads at the city gates during the past days would have recognized the splendid procession which now set forth in a panoply of armour and banners. Each clarion-call of trumpets summoned further crowds of country folk to cheer the Duke's passing. As ever he was easy with them, offering a jocular and carefree face to all and sundry; but I knew that the quick grey eyes would be noting how, on every side, lay the evidence of futile civil war; whole villages showing only blackened timbers to the winter sky, and many of the sodden fields still grey with the ash of burned crops. Such wanton waste made even my mild blood boil, I dared not think what it was doing to his.

Now that he was making his entrance into the great public arena of his new kingdom, Thomas had advised the Duke to change the outward look of his entourage, surrounding himself with English nobles (which is to say Normans who had been some generations in the country) and choosing to ride at his side the Earl of Leicester, a good man held in high regard by all estates of people. Those lords who had recently crossed the Channel with him rode close before and behind so that their 'honour' should not be offended, the nobility being as particular of their 'honour' as a demure but loose woman of her virtue.

It was part of this processional plan that Thomas should retire from the centre of things – the 'honour' of the great lords had already suffered serious affront because this mere clerk had seemed too close to the future king. So we rode with a raggle-taggle of Christian bishops and their courts, each as intent as any penurious nobleman on securing for himself a financially rewarding position under the dispensation of the new regime. At Windsor we left the Duke's company, bidding him a secret farewell and taking faster horses straight to Canterbury to acquaint our master the Archbishop of Henry's plans.

The royal palace of Westminster had suffered considerable damage and looting during the useless civil war into which those two egotists, King Stephen and the Empress Matilda, had plunged England. It was thus partly the fault of his own mother (for Matilda had married Geoffrey of Anjou following the death of her first husband, the Emperor) that Henry was forced to inhabit an older and unsalubrious residence further down the River Thames at Bermondsey.

From here, on the Sunday before Christmas of that year 1154, the Duke of Normandy and his Duchess went in procession to Westminster Abbey, which also showed signs of war and depredation, and were crowned by our Archbishop of Canterbury before an assembly of Church and State that promised the new King a massive majority of support in the great work of reorganization which faced him.

Henry's burly youth, his strength and his princely bearing commanded the respect of all who saw him. The more perspicacious were also aware of something in him both reserved and mysterious, which tended to put them instantly on their guard and their best behaviour. Those of us who knew that he was not a Christian understood the source of this intangible which so troubled the souls of others.

As for Queen Eleanor, she was already a legend in her own right, and none can have failed to be impressed by her beauty and by the gracious ease with which she dismissed her thirty-four years; yet there was about her too a strangeness, a sense of belonging elsewhere. Indeed some of the regality invested in these two people stemmed directly from the fact that they did not belong to England, not even to Norman England, and in some ways never would.

As they left the Abbey there could be no doubt that the people of London, even those of Saxon blood, had taken them to their hearts. Their triumph seemed already to be healing the wounds of war, the evils of anarchy; and their Christmas court, which they held in that city, was a merry one.

At this same court, to the envy of some and the plain fury of others, an unknown clerk from the household of the Archbishop of Canterbury, calling himself Thomas of London, was appointed to the high post of Chancellor to the King – an event which, as I have described, left critics and chroniclers alike chasing after reasons like children after snowflakes.

A few weeks later the Queen was brought to bed and delivered of her second son, the young Prince Henry.

Thus, to the joyful sound of bells and a cheering people, King Henry II led England into the year 1155.

4

Now began the noble seven years during which the King laboured with his Queen and with his Chancellor to hold together and make strong the wide Plantagenet empire, challenging any intruder who would destroy what he was building, and bringing the sanity of law and prosperity to all his people; for this, whatever men may say of him, is a great King, and none, not even those who have good cause to hate him as I do, should forget it.

The plain facts of what he achieved during those years, and is achieving still, may be found in every chronicle, and I have neither the heart nor the time to repeat them yet again. As my reader must now understand, I have a different thing to tell, a chronicle within the chronicles, a pattern that lies behind the battles and truces, the courts of law and the conferences. For if these 'plain facts' are all that is set down upon parchment, no one will ever know of the forces that created them, in secret and sometimes in shame. This is my matter, and so I make no excuse for touching the 'facts' only when I can illuminate them from within by the light of secret knowledge.

Immediately after Christmas, and even before the birth of his second son, Henry flung himself upon his new domain like a watchdog upon an intruder, his inhuman energy shocking and then exhausting those he commanded to accompany him; and this entourage often consisted of two hundred people and more, pack-horses, mules and carts carrying everything – documents, chapel, kitchen, clothing, gold – that might conceivably be needed for practicality or to impress.

'We wear out our garments, break our bodies and our beasts, and never find a moment for the cure of our sick souls,' groaned my illustrious colleague, Walter Map, who also considered that the King moves like 'a common carrier'. Poor Map, he must indeed have been in a sorry state if reduced to thinking of his soul!

All men, from the greatest lord to the humblest porter, suffered the same agonies of exhaustion, of sudden departures before dawn, sudden changes of plan or direction in the middle of the night. King Henry would descend upon this bishopric or that castle just when the incumbent had calculated that he was going in the opposite direction, scenting out malpractice or a whiff of incipient treason and punishing them forthwith, dismissing one man and replacing another, destroying a bailey here and appropriating a castle there, sitting in judgement on half a dozen law-suits, rooting out a marauding band of robbers left over from the war, holding a meeting of the Council of Wallingford and, next day, descending on Nottingham Assizes to see what passed for justice in the Midlands.

In all, perhaps this sense of justice was his strongest flail, and the balm most needed by a desperate people who had all but forgotten the meaning of the word. Map, still panting along behind, observed that 'whoever has a good case is anxious to try it before him; whoever has a bad one does not come to him unless he is dragged'.

The Queen joined him as soon as she was able. Unlike Walter, she was not heard to complain of the conditions, but then she had known rougher journeying in harsher climes; she accompanied her lord in good spirits, attracting the wonder of all, full of curiosity and the wisdom of a woman born to rule a people more practised in tricks and deceit than even the Norman English. Her eyes, as quick as the King's, noted every wavering glance, every evasion, every tale a little too glib.

As for Thomas, the Chancellor sometimes travelled with this scurrying royal entourage, or joined it at given places for one purpose or another, usually of a legal nature, or stayed in London to execute the King's will in matters of state. Of their private relationship I will speak later.

In one year of prodigious effort Henry changed not so much the ravaged face of England – it would take time and the seasons and growing prosperity to do that – but the spirit of the country. He threw open every door, some of which had been bolted for many years, to admit God's sunlight; he swept his new kingdom clean and repainted it with hope so that even the humblest man could look to the future, see it more clearly, and not be afraid of what he saw.

Much ink has been wasted in exclamations regarding Thomas of London as Chancellor; it is perfectly true that there had never before been a Chancellor in the least like him, but then there had never been a King of England like Henry II. This King did not ask Thomas to be a clerk of the exchequer, he asked him to be a prince, the spirit of absent kingship. Now I will never deny that my lord enjoyed his state, though there have seldom been princes who acted with such self-restraint; and let us remember that Thomas of London, although he came of well-to-do Norman stock, was the son of a merchant; let us remember too that his father's fortunes failed, and that the merchant's son had to make shift to earn money at once as a mere accountant. It would be a rare man indeed who did not take pleasure, and show it, in finding himself equal to the noblest lord in the land and a great deal more powerful.

If there are to be exclamations, let them reflect the fact that though the Chancellor made for his pleasure a splendid palace full of rare and beautiful things, he himself remained modest and in all ways a true servant of the King. His table was always set for a feast as far as his guests were concerned, and dressed with the finest silver and gold; yet he himself ate sparingly and drank seldom, if at all: and, though there was always talk and laughter and music in this Chancellor's house, no loose woman ever entered the door, not even to please the King himself when he demanded it.

Greatest of all exclamation during these years derived from the

45

fact that the Chancellor was known to be celibate, but the men who exclaimed at that were certainly stupid indeed, for the wiser ones must have known that he belonged to the Cathar faith and was one of the elect few who were able, by strength of character as well as by inborn inclination, to attain what we call Perfection. Some men are possessed by strong lusts of the flesh, and King Henry was such a man; others have weaker desires, and I betray no confidence, since Thomas has admitted it to others in my hearing that fleshly desire did not trouble his blood overmuch.

Now, our religion has been criticized on several counts, some of which are impossible to answer because, by doing so, one may disclose the most holy of our secret mysteries. But I shall reveal nothing if I agree with those who claim that a religion excluding women may tend to attract sodomites; of course this is true, and it is also true of the monastic orders of the Christian church, and of armies, and of all conditions where men must hold together; but it is not true of all men; no generalization is true of all men.

The love of a man for a woman, and his desire for her, is a state of nature and therefore of the will of God. Our true faith would be no faith at all if it envisaged a world denuded of children and finally of human life; but the way to Perfection is another way, and it cannot be followed by any man, not even by many, like myself, who once wished to do so. In this, as in other things, Thomas was an exception.

You shall see in a short time where this leads.

In January of 1156 Henry left for his own country of Anjou, embarking upon an exploit of which one can only claim that right was on his side if one is thinking in terms of empires and dynasties and not, as lesser men like myself tend to do, in terms of broken promises and breaches of faith.

On his father's deathbed he had sworn to cede to his younger brother, Geoffrey, certain parts of Anjou, and this he had faithfully done. I think, to grant Henry a little due, that Geoffrey was now of a mind to push the agreed frontier here and there, giving himself more space, but the fact of the matter is that it suited neither Henry nor his Queen to have a younger brother ruling lands which separated Maine from Poitou, for north of Maine lay Normandy and south of Poitou lay Aquitaine, and brother Geoffrey stood like a wall between them. Thomas accompanied the King upon this expedition, partly because a legal solution would suit those concerned better than fratricide, partly because the King demanded his constant company, both in work and leisure, so that their friendship was the wonder of all.

During this absence the Queen sent for me to Bermondsey. Excluding others from the chamber, she said, 'You grow plump, William of Colchester, but then I hear that the Lord Chancellor lives in some state up there at Westminster.'

I had heard many times that the Queen was not at all contented with her lot, and I could not blame her. I said, 'He keeps but a small house, my lady, few rooms indeed compared with this great palace.'

'Few but good, eh, William?'

One must admit that the situation was all very well for King Henry; somewhere in Anjou at that very moment, it would matter little to him whether he was about to spend the night in the great ducal palace of Angers or in some woodcutter's hut surrounded by his army. But Thomas had told me that the Queen was once more with child, and she had no reason to be content with her lodging nor with the enclosed life that winter and circumstance were forcing her to lead.

Certainly London was unlike any other city she had seen upon her many travels: a thriving, rich city inhabited by a red-faced and prosperous people forever intent on business transactions, a city resounding with the chink of gold and silver. But I suspected that long ago she must have grown tired of the bustling river beneath the palace windows, the coming and going of ships from many lands, the Strand, raucous with fishwives and wherrymen, the busy bridge weighed down with shops and houses, however fascinating she may at first have found them. She was used to her own southern high places, sunlit even in winter, luxurious and scented with flowers.

She watched me at my thoughts for a few seconds, and then laughed. 'You are an honest man, William. Your face is mirror to your thoughts.

'I have seen,' she added lightly, 'something quite new to me, an experience which grows more gratifying with every year that passes; I have seen boys sliding on the frozen fields with the shin-bones of animals strapped to their boots. They go at great speeds and take great tumbles, and I wish that I might join them.' She sighed, thinking as much of royalty no doubt as of the child in her womb. Then, suddenly sharp: 'What of the King and your master, the Chancellor?'

I stared at her, thinking, What of them?

'What feeling do they bear one for the other, William?'

I said, 'I cannot speak for the King, but Thomas is his most loyal subject and loves him well.'

'I can speak for the King; he trusts Thomas completely. And loves him well.' She was gazing out of the window at the steel-grey river, frozen a little at the edges. 'What,' she asked me softly, 'is the nature of that love?'

You will see now why I have written as I did of our religion and its critics. The Queen continued: 'Don't forget that I come from the birthplace of your faith, and that many of my family adhere to it, I know of a hundred friendships formed in its name, some worthy, some not.'

I knew at once the source of this disquiet, for I had heard some rumours myself, and it would have been unlike this woman if she had not heard them too.

When in London, the King was in and out of his Chancellor's house at all hours of the day and night. Just as his kingship never came between himself and the ordinary people of England, so it never entered his head not to throw his arms around Thomas, nor to wrestle with him if his energy demanded it, nor to play boy's jokes upon him and be disappointed if Thomas did not reply in kind; and more than once the King grew drunk, and his exhaustion when it came being as tremendous as his energy preceding it, he had slept where he was, once in the most literal sense, falling down in front of the fire whence none could move him, so he was covered with furs and left there.

It is always pleasing to me when the great behave in a manner which shows that they are genuinely capable of forgetting their greatness, but one does well to remember that not all men are so minded and that greatness, to some, is only there to be picked at and soured by the acid of their own small minds.

I am seldom brave and very rarely angry, but on this occasion I found much to my own surprise that I was both. I said, 'Majesty, your servant Thomas is but a merchant's son raised to a high position, which he carries with greater honour than could any other man in your kingdom. If he is dazzled by the friendship of a King, is that strange? I too have heard the loose talk of gossips, which they direct at all who are raised above them and at everything they are too petty to understand . . .'

'I must rouse you to anger more often, William, you begin to speak well.'

'I grant you, it is a fierce love that Thomas bears for the King, and God help the man who stands in its way. But God will never help the man who has said that they know each others' bodies, for it is a foul slander, and even I would draw a sword to it. Thomas would willingly die for the King, and that, I beg to think, is the highest love known to the human race.'

She nodded absently, so that I was forced to add, 'And since your majesty already knows so much of our faith, I will tell you in all confidence that Thomas of London is what we call Perfect.'

At this she turned on me a flashing green glance. 'He wears the cord around his body?'

I did not think she would know of this, but since she did: 'Yes, your grace, he wears the cord.'

She left the window, shaking her head and spreading her hands. 'I was a fool ever to have allowed this maggot to have entered my brain. I know the King too well, I wonder what slut he beds tonight. It doesn't matter, I can forgive, and it saves a world of torment to forgive what you *must*. God knows, there are worse things than a lusty husband.' She stood before me and held out her slim hand, which I took awkwardly. 'As for what you have told me regarding the Chancellor, I will not speak of it, just as you did not speak of a certain subject when I forbade it.'

As I left her presence she added, 'You are a rare man, William, you set my mind at rest, a miracle that few accomplish. I shall call upon you again.'

Let me say at once that I had purposely diminished in the Queen's eyes the state which Thomas held at Westminster; moreover that wise and perspicacious woman had known that I was doing so and had kept her peace, having a true regard for loyalty.

She knew as well as I did that with the King still occupied abroad, and with Thomas acting as ruler of England, all the great men who came to London upon matters of state, or indeed for mere pleasure, turned their steps towards the house of the Chancellor. If the Queen was visited at all it was as a matter of courtesy, and I hope that I have portrayed enough of Eleanor to indicate that she would not for long bow to such a secondary position. I mentioned my suspicion to Thomas as soon as he returned from Anjou. There was much business for him to deal with, and I think he pushed the matter to the back of his mind.

In France the campaign had gone well. The King's brother, Geoffrey, for whom I cannot but feel a certain sympathy, was brought to heel by means of siege, and 'returned' to Henry the sentinel castles of Chinon, Mirabeau and Loudun, thus setting Henry's Anjou cheek by jowl once more with Eleanor's Poitou. Later in that year 1156, Henry, who had always kept his weather eye upon Brittany, moved an army into that ocean borderland to 'settle a feud' between local lords. He settled it to such effect that upon his return Brittany was found to have become mysteriously subject to Norman power; Louis of France, the rightful over-lord, remained silent, and Henry installed Geoffrey there as a watchdog.

Eleanor, though now within a few months of childbirth, had written to her husband complaining with some savagery of her living conditions, and it was not long before Thomas had to re-trieve my warning from the back of his mind and take immediate action. So explicit had been Eleanor's words that the palace of Westminster was suddenly covered with workman like bees upon a swarm. This was at Easter. Seven weeks later, at Whitsuntide, a transformation had taken place, and the Queen was presented with a new palace at almost exactly the same time that she presented her lord with his first daughter, named Matilda. She moved into the palace immediately and set about bringing a vestige of southern civilization to this city of northern merchants and anglicized Norman barons.

The flood of artistic ideas which began to pour forth from the Queen's palace upset many good and learned men as well as the usual puffed-up hypocrites, yet many of the seemingly frivolous things which she encouraged were to stand her adopted country in good stead. The old flowery *chansons de geste* were now, it seemed, out of date. Romance was fashionable, particularly such stories as that of the love of Tristram for Yseult, but it was Geoffrey of Monmouth's fairy-tale *History of The Kings of England*, already re-edited and dedicated to Eleanor, which was to have the most far-reaching effect; and a certain part of it, that dealing with the legendary King Arthur and his court, became so popular that it spread all over Europe and even to Byzantium. All poets and writers took up the 'Matter of Britain', making Arthur one of the great heroes of the world.

Some, of a wily disposition, suggested that in this there lay less of art and more of typical Plantagenet political cunning, for presently the legends of Arthur began to eclipse even those of Charlemagne himself; and Charlemagne was not only the first of the Holy Roman Emperors but also a very special 'ancestor' of King Louis VII of France.

However that may be, new manners followed hard upon the heels of the Queen's new artistic ideas. In order to gain entrance to her presence it was no longer merely enough to hold a great title, for she would suffer no roughly dressed lord, smelling of his country estates. Fine clothing and frequent bathing of the body were required, not to mention eating habits that befitted a royal establishment.

Now the visitors to London thought twice before heading for the house of Thomas the Chancellor, for the attractions of the Queen's palace went far beyond fine food and informed conversation. And even the great lords, in imitation, were forming their own bands of actors and singers.

Of course the gossips were hard at work inventing petty jealousies where none existed. The Queen was merely acting as the world expected her to act, for was she not Eleanor of Aquitaine? And the Chancellor's time was now more than ever given up to affairs of state which were not only his business but his delight.

There is no need for me to state that Thomas loved power, for it is self-evident and he readily admitted it, and there is no law of our faith which forbids power or pomp or indeed the ambition which gives rise to them. In this it is the Christians, with their usual false humility, who fail to understand that nothing matters in the outside man providing that it does not run contrary to what he guards most sacredly within his soul. And thus, as we already know, ambition was for Thomas the wily enemy with which he was forced to wrestle, sometimes for a blessed while victorious, sometimes locked in wearying battle, sometimes utterly subjugated and at his wits' end.

Once, at this time, my lord sent for me in haste. There was a cluster of troubled servants hovering at his door, as well as one or two important men awaiting audience on matters of state. Only I was admitted.

I found him on the bed in the inner chamber, and was stricken by what I saw. Of course I knew that as one Perfect in our faith he regularly submitted himself to the scourge, but on this occasion I do not know what had possessed him, nor why those who exacted the penitence did not refuse to go further; his back was a mess of blood, and the face he turned to me was that of a sick man in extremity.

Harshly, commanding no pity, he said, 'Well, Conscience, we agree my ambition is too great, yet I will cast out that devil. But what of my pride and my love of show? What of my gold and my banquets and the alms I'm so famous for giving, aye, and my daring in the lists? I mock my boasted Perfection, do I not? I mock our whole faith and the truth I claim to bear. Answer, Conscience! Is my immortal soul in danger of damnation?'

Shocked, for his tone, his very words, were as lacerated as his body, I stammered that his parlous condition and the questions he asked were all the answer his soul required; I knew that I made little sense and that what I said would never satisfy him. To my horror he struggled from the bed despite my protestations and gripped me with hands of iron, for he was very strong in those days, and shouted:

'Do not mince mindless words with me, William. The one man I can trust. Answer ... !'

I thanked God that a sudden spasm of pain preserved me from

answering what I could not; he fell against me, and I realized that he had lost consciousness.

I laid him on the bed and sent one of his men, whom I knew to be trustworthy, for a certain Daniel of Southwark, who was of my lord's household: a necromancer, some said: others, an alchemist: certainly a man wise in herbs and healing.

He was lean and dark-bearded, silent and ever ironical. Upon seeing Thomas's back, he sighed and shook his head, and sent his boy for certain unguents. To me he said, 'In order to defy devils must one pretend that devils have ridden on one's back? I find little "perfect" in this.'

I said, 'From a Hebrew one expects understanding, not mockery.'

'One can only mock what one understands, my friend.'

The boy returned, as dark and quiet and lean as his master. Deftly the lacerated back was cleansed and smeared with some country-smelling concoction, dressed with clean linen and lightly bound. I sat beside my lord's bed until he awoke some hours later; the eyes that looked into mine were no longer glazed by mental or physical anguish. After a time he said, 'You sent for Daniel.'

I nodded, and gave him the draught which the Jew had left; he drank it, put down the goblet and took my hand in his. 'I love the King,' he said. 'I serve him with body and soul as ever I swore to do. He is my friend and pays me great honour. I cannot before Heaven ask for more.'

'Then do not torture yourself with what Providence has seen fit to give you.'

He closed his eyes, and I thought that already the drug had claimed him; but presently he said, 'Providence wears many faces and must be watched.'

I stayed by him until I was sure that he truly slept.

I must state that from this day a deep uneasiness possessed me. As my lord grew in grandeur, becoming one of the greatest and most respected figures in all Europe, the more did this worm of dread nibble at my innards. If the reader discerns it here or there in what follows I beg him to excuse it and to reserve his judgement for the turn of events upon the eighth year after the wise woman had spoken at Winchester.

Not long after this incident the King made one of his swift and sudden descents upon London. I remember how he laughed when he saw what Eleanor had accomplished, and how he boasted that now even he, King Henry, had a palace as fine as that of his Chancellor; but, as I have said, his preference was always for the talk of learned men, and so he was as often to be found at Thomas's table as at his own. I think the Queen suffered no more on this account.

What her thoughts were at the death of her first-born, as foretold in Winchester, I do not know. Henry suffered a little grief, but for so outward-turning a man of only twenty-three grief passed quickly. Had he not another fine boy as well as a daughter? And early in 1157 was not his lady again with child which, God willing, would prove to be a prince?

It seemed in this time that the King's mood of optimism, as well as his presence of such lusty good health, was like an epidemic. All England buzzed with prosperity and peace like a well-set beehive, and London was fast becoming not only the richest but the most fashionable city of Europe.

As for the great domains beyond the sea, even though the Vexin was an unhealed wound and the southern lords of Toulouse promised unrest, yet the way was set and the great empire was beginning to take shape.

The King and his Chancellor were as one; tongues might wag with evil, yet no one could insert the keenest knife-blade between the two men, so closely did the common interests of government, and their mutual love and respect, bind them.

5

At Oxford, in September of the year 1157, Queen Eleanor gave birth to her fourth child, and, almost as though King Henry in the full glory of his power and success could command all things, it was another prince, Richard. He was immediately proclaimed the Queen's personal heir, the future Count of Poitou and Duke of Aquitaine, and she was to love him more than all her other children.

I had then, and can vividly recall now, a sense of time beginning to move faster. Great events were in the making. England had settled into the pattern of lawful peace which Henry had devised for it; therefore he, his Queen and his Chancellor felt free to spend more time in the great continental domains where their presence was more urgently required, and to that end they made repeated crossings of the Channel as if it were no more than a ford across a shallow stream.

The King, moving with his usual demonic speed, resting hardly at all, reduced the castles of those lords who spoke against him, rebuilt his own and Eleanor's capital fortresses, set watchtowers to guard roads and rivers. Forever building, repairing, enlarging, he stamped his mark upon citadels from Rouen to Chinon, from cool Argentan to burning Ventadour: and stamped it also upon the minds and memories of men. At this time Eleanor revisited her southern lands of Poitou and Aquitaine, finding that she liked, a little too much perhaps, the hot hills and green valleys of her youth. How she bore such journeying I do not know, for she was soon with child yet again; an extraordinary woman indeed, now nearing her fortieth year, and this was to be by no means her last confinement.

Even for me the Channel and its vicissitudes were becoming commonplace, and I am happy to say that my lord would leave me, with his documents and his clerks, in whatever city or stronghold seemed a possible centre for the King's whirlwind activities. Thus I became familiar with the great Castles of Angers, Chinon, Le Mans and the like, and I soon felt more at home in these places that I had once called 'foreign' than ever I had in London or Canterbury. I led an idyllic life of great comfort, and had it not been for that malaise which constantly fed upon my soul, these would surely have been the most contented days of all my life. Yet I was always edgy, and too often blunted that edge with wine; also I confess that with my lord away and my religious pretensions all but abandoned, I found more than one comely woman of a decent age to lighten my hours of laziness, for I worked but little and had at my fingertips any documents the Chancellor might need.

It speaks much of my mood in those days that I was even pleased when Thomas broke in upon my fretful peace, appearing suddenly at the door of my office in Rouen, and crying, 'Pack, Will, pack! We go once more to Paris.'

Much had indeed changed since that evening in Auxerre, seven years before, when he had interrupted my indigestion with almost the same words. Then, as dusty clerks, we had been glad of the company of two tattered knights returning from the Holy Land. This time . . . By God's name, I do not know what to call our state upon the journey we were about to undertake!

What had occurred was of vital importance to the Plantagenets. After some years of trial and error, Constance, Queen of France, had finally become pregnant. For months her husband and indeed all France had been breathless in anticipation. Now, in the spring of 1158, she presented them with yet another princess, Marguerite.

Thomas saw in this a chance for which King Henry had long been waiting. They met Louis upon the borders of Normandy; Henry knelt humbly before his overlord, whom he could, at that time, have defeated in the field with but half his army, and suggested that there might be profit in the matter for all concerned if this new-born child were affianced to his own son and heir, Prince Henry, Count of Anjou and Maine, now aged three.

Louis VII, who may himself have begun to despair of ever producing a male child, knew very well that the English King was gambling upon the hope that by this marriage his son might one day wear the dual crown of the two countries; yet, rather than offend Henry, this was seemingly a gamble Louis was also prepared to take. The Kings agreed, but the French people were another matter. They would protest vehemently at this union, having good reason to dislike and mistrust the Plantagenet and, even more, his Queen; they must therefore be placated; they must be impressed; they must be entertained.

Thus, at Rouen, her green eyes afire with malice and laughter, Queen Eleanor joined in the game of placating, impressing and entertaining the French, among whom she had passed fourteen wearisome years. 'Monkeys!' she cried.

Thomas asked, 'Are there not enough monkeys in France already?'

'One to each horse, wearing little jackets of gold.'

The King laughed. 'Embroidered perhaps with the lilies of France. Would King Louis take that as a compliment or an insult, do you think?'

Well, the monkeys' coats carried no fleurs-de-lis when we rode out of the gates of Rouen, but they were made of golden cloth, and the collars and chains around their necks were also of gold. We numbered in all 210 on horse: knights, noble squires, clerks, stewards, men-at-arms and -in-waiting, all wearing bright new dress, glittering with gold and precious stones. Eight huge wagons bore the Chancellor's personal belongings, followed by others containing his kitchen, his chapel, tapestries and furnishing in case he were to lodge in rooms not splendid enough for the representative of the King of England. There were grooms, each leading a pair of fine-bred hounds, hawkers carrying on gloved arms the finest birds. The pack-horses carried his treasure, his documents, gold and silver plate, and each was led by a groom and attended by fierce mastiffs. A further 260 men went on foot, before and behind wagons laden with great barrels of beer, a beverage of which the French were ignorant; these men sang the songs of England as they marched. Finally, attended by noblemen, as befitted the occasion, came the King's great Chancellor. He was also attended by myself, cursing the high collar of my fine new tunic which chafed my neck. I worried nearly all the way from Rouen to Paris about the precious gifts which were my particular charge, wondering, like a mother at Christmas, whether we had left anyone out.

Arrived in Paris there was no place large enough to hold this assembly but the vast residences which the Knights Templar had recently built outside the city gates. Thomas distributed his gifts to nobles and prelates and the King himself, while his every appearance in the streets was accompanied by largesse: gold for any students of English birth, vats of ale to gladden many feasts.

It was clear, even to the doubting Parisians who share many characteristics with their London counterparts, that here indeed was a great man who must represent the greatest King in Christendom. The image of the Countess of Poitou, who had slighted the fair name of France, was forgotten in this shower of wealth – ironically, since she herself had played so great a part in organizing it.

And the object of our embassy? That thorn in Henry's side, the Vexin. What else?

I sat with tablet in hand while Thomas, smooth as silk, using delicate threats as small and quick as mice, and flattery as soothing as warm oil, coerced Louis into giving his infant daughter the cursed Vexin as a dowry. But Louis had lost none of his old cunning: of course his daughter should carry the Vexin – on the day of her marriage. He reasoned that with the bridegroom still three years of age, it would be a good span of time, even by the marriage customs of dynasties, before the wedding would be celebrated.

A few weeks later King Henry went quietly to Paris and collected the little girl who would, by custom, be brought up within his domains, but not, Louis stipulated with some vehemence, at the knee of Eleanor of Aquitaine. Henry agreed without demur. Never before and unfortunately never again were the two Kings to appear on terms of such amity. Louis may have protested gently concerning Brittany, but Henry paid no attention; and when Eleanor bore him yet another son later in the year the boy was christened Geoffrey after his brother who had died childless. In accordance with his father's plans, and in the fullness of time, this child was to become Duke of Brittany.

I have recounted these events before describing what befell me on our return procession from Paris. It was generally believed, with some jocularity, that I had lived a little too well during our visit to King Louis' capital city, and that when I fell from my horse, speechless, I was but paying the price of it. This may be true in part, but there was more to what ailed me, and that more was a matter of the spirit not of the body.

Only a few leagues from the city gates I suddenly perceived, if I may use the word in its deepest meaning, the gaudy show and panoply of our appearance. The hawks and stag-hounds and snarling mastiffs suddenly seemed to my sun-dazed eyes merely the finest specimens in our whole vast bestiary. On all sides I saw red-faced men who bore some similarity to humans, but very little; the glitter of their gold and the multi-coloured flames of their brilliant silks and velvets seemed to blind me, while the songs that the English foot-soldiers still continued to bellow as long as they were upon French soil, beat upon my eardrums like the very sound of Hell itself. I seemed to be falling, and perhaps was, long before I actually fell; and in these extended moments it was the monkeys, perched so solemnly each upon his horse, which seemed to me to be the rulers and leaders of our obscene rout. Finally, and it must have been at the moment of his seeing me fall, my lord Thomas turned to me, in alarm no doubt, yet all I saw in this great man who was shaping dynasties and building empires was yet another gibbering ape wearing the Chancellor's robes. Then the flames leapt up to engulf me and I was burned to death and darkness upon the dusty road.

Thus did the maggot of dread, which first bit into me as I sat by Thomas's bed after that inhuman scourging, have its final way with me upon the earth of France; and yet I think that what happened there was seeded at a still earlier time: in my cell of a cold December morning when my lord so blithely told me of what he had sworn away in the name of the future King and of his own ambition.

His was the face I saw upon regaining consciousness: thoughtful, kindly, full of concern. I was lying on a clean bed in a humble room, and we were alone together. I know that I wept because his gentle hand held a fine kerchief to my eyes. 'Sleep,' he said. 'All is well. Sleep.'

Later it was night, and I awoke to find Thomas still in the room. He had sent the great procession rolling ahead of him, knowing that he could overtake it within an hour or two. He came to the bed and felt my pulse with light fingertips, his eyes searching mine. 'What ails you, Will? You babbled in your sleep of apes and power and four upon four years, making eight for the blood of kings, and Heaven knows what else!'

I said, 'My lord . . .'

'I am not your lord here, I am your friend as ever I was and will be.'

I wept again, for I was quite unable to control my emotions, and said, 'Thomas, it were best that I leave your service; too much troubles me.'

He replied drily, 'I have witnessed that too much troubles you, dear and good William, but you shall not leave my service, for I have need of you and you of me.' He sat down, leaning close. 'What is this ferment in your soul? All is well with us, never better. We live in great times, we go forward to greater yet.'

I shook my head. 'Great times and greater times are for such as you, Thomas, but not for me; perhaps it is this very greatness which ails me.'

He smiled gently. 'Does my ambition frighten you so much?'

'No, no.'

The smile faded. 'You . . . foresee?'

'I foresee nothing. I am a small man and a coward in life. I fear too much greatness, too much power, too much show.'

'And thus you allow that . . . fool's carnival to make you sick.'

'It was an outward sign of . . .' I shook my head, lost for words, bewildered.

'Of inward folly.'

'I know not. Forgive me, Thomas. You see how useless I am to you.'

'I know how useful you are to me. For look: you say you fear too much greatness and power, yet you have no greatness and power; therefore you fear for me. How many men would fear thus deeply for a friend?' He shook his head and took my hand between both his. 'You need courage, Will; and to those of our faith courage comes through the Spiritus alone. What ails you is a lack of that holy spirit which is your own greatness; I think it has been long since you called upon it.'

'I lapse, I am not worthy.'

'A wench here, a wench there! You are but a believer in any case, and you are a good man. I strive for Perfection and even wear the cord, yet I am far from Perfect; but the striving gives me leave to lay hands on you if you would have it so, William of Colchester.'

I felt, as I have felt before, power flow from his hands to mine, and for the first time in many months, nay years, I sensed a possibility of peace within myself. I said, 'My good lord and friend, I would have it so.'

Then Thomas knelt beside the bed and closed his eyes and was still, and all care slipped from his face, leaving it smooth and full of light. I may not write of the words and actions he then used, but I believe that before he had even finished the sacred things I was, if not asleep, lulled into a state of trance which presently led to sleep. I remember that before he left he said, 'This house is owned by a good man, honest. He and his wife are well paid to look to your needs. Rest here, William, for in truth you chose a good place to fall; then return to me in strength, because I need your friendship.'

I slept, long well into the afternoon of the next day, and when I arose and had eaten some simple food, I went out into a golden evening and saw that Thomas's words had been true. My host was a tenant farmer of some substance, and his lord a good one; his fields stretched down to the verge of the River Seine where giant willows and poplars shaded the banks. I spent some days there, sleeping in the shade or lying awake to watch the birds and animals of the place or, on occasion, fishing with enough success to supply for all of us a fine supper.

Too soon I knew that my body had caught up with the strength which Thomas had already given to my soul and spirit with his healing hands; but when I returned to Rouen I found that my lord and friend had already ridden southwards with the King's army.

Their concern was the great southern province of Toulouse, reaching to the shores of the Mediterranean Sea. A glance at the map shows how convenient would have been its addition to the empire over which King Henry and Queen Eleanor already held sway. But principalities may only be stolen for a good reason, and the reason in this case was not good enough: Toulouse had once belonged to the Queen's grandmother, Philippa, who had married that same Troubadour Count of Poitou whom I have already mentioned. But these two worthy people were long dead, and the province had slipped into other hands.

This was only the first of the stumbling blocks, and the least suspect, for none could deny that Queen Eleanor did indeed have some justice on her side. King Henry had none; the province belonged to the King of France, and Henry as Duke of Normandy owed him allegiance and had no right to appropriate what was his. This difficulty was compounded by the fact that King Louis' own brother-in-law was now holding the capital city in his name.

However Henry was determined to have Toulouse, and he commanded Thomas to find some excuse which would at least give a semblance of legality to his intention. My lord had exercised his usual cunning, but it was a well-nigh impossible task, and the gambit which he finally conceived was a dangerous one.

It rested upon a certain Count of Barcelona, who was at that time claiming that Toulouse really belonged to him. He must have been as surprised as was the rest of the world to hear that Henry II of England was about to ride to his 'aid'; surprised and, if he were a wise man, alarmed.

So the King set forth in full panoply, some indication of the size of the army being given by the fact that Thomas himself rode at the head of a private force of 700 horsemen and 12,000 mercenary foot-soldiers. As a Perfect in our faith he was forbidden to kill any man, so that for every minute he spent in the field he was in imminent danger of death; that he held rigorously to this tenet and yet survived shows, I think, that God must indeed have been at his shoulder.

Heaven alone knows how King Henry would have dealt with the Count of Barcelona had they taken the city and the province; it was providential for the Count that they did not do so, and the reason that they did not do so was extraordinary indeed. For once King Louis of France was roused from the patient torpor in which he appeared to spend his days, and found that he was angered and affronted by all this marching and double-dealing, with the result that when at last they drew up in a thunder of hooves and a rumbling of siege-engines before the red walls of Toulouse they found that King Louis himself was ensconced within.

Henry had been known to break his word upon occasion, but this situation bound him hand and foot; he was surrounded by lords who owed him allegiance, and he knew that several of them did so unwillingly. To attack Louis, his own liege-lord, was to invite disaster within his own empire; and so, in a rage, he withdrew from the city and contented himself with ravaging the surrounding countryside, until winter put an end to the whole unheroic proceeding. The Chancellor took off his armour and donned his lawyer's robes, which proved a more effective guise; he swiftly negotiated a 'peace' which strengthened King Henry's borders and enabled him to withdraw without undue loss of pride – and this he could have achieved in any case, army or no army.

So they returned to Normandy, reaching Falaise in good time

for the Christmas court, at which I was reunited with my lord: a merry enough occasion in spite of the King's brooding face. He would not forget Toulouse.

After a few weeks Queen Eleanor made a journey to England in order to fulfil royal business, and doubtless to see if the English nobility were continuing to pursue the arts and the habit of washing themselves with the required regularity. She travelled all over the realm, showing herself to both lords and people.

Now this woman had been born to a great house of rulers, and had been married to two kings, so that there is no wonder in her sense of duty and heredity; the wonder, to me, is that she continued to carry out her royal duties long after Henry's treatment of her had become the gossip of all Europe, and that she did not sooner turn upon him in open rebellion.

There is no doubt that her love for him continued long after his love for her had withered, but it must be said on his behalf that when a woman is eleven years older than a man, the passing years do little but widen the gulf. The Queen found herself in middle age when her husband was in the prime of his young manhood, and it is well known that when he approached one of his liege-men's castles during those endless journeyings, comely daughters, young wives, and even cherished maidservants were forthwith hidden away, their absence being explained by a visit or a fever.

My day-book tells me that Thomas and I crossed and recrossed the Channel constantly in the year of 1160, but I myself seem to have little detailed recollection of our travels; my notes tell me that we attended to the King's business in Rouen and Angers, that we waited on the Queen at Westminster, Bristol and Northampton, as well as representing her in certain legal matters at Poitiers. We also spent time at Beverley in Yorkshire, where Thomas still held the provostship, visited his estates at Berkhamsted and at Eye in Suffolk, and paid our respects to Archbishop Theobald at Canterbury, finding him in poor health. But mostly we were in France where Thomas could keep company with the King, who never grew tired of his presence. In a long life I have never known two men to be of such a single mind, in work and in pleasure.

Henry would not leave his continental domains. I believe that the defeat, for such it was, at Toulouse had roused in him a dogged

Angevin determination to have revenge; he meant to be the ruling power in Europe, and it was no part of this plan that pious Louis VII of France should make him look ridiculous.

None could see it then, but in the autumn of the year 1160 came the first tremor of the landslide which was to sweep us off our feet. Death was abroad, and birth also, and neither boded well.

As soon as Henry heard that Queen Constance of France was again brought to bed with child, he quickly sent word to Eleanor in England, summoning her to his side and bidding her bring the young Prince Henry and Princess Matilda. Upon their arrival, some weeks before the French Queen was due to give birth, he had the Prince pay homage to King Louis near the borders of their two lands. This ensured the boy's position *vis-à-vis* France should Queen Constance now produce the long and feverishly awaited male heir. Princess Matilda, barely four years old, was held in readiness so that if this heir materialized she might at once be affianced to him. Thus, whatever came to pass, England and France would in some way be allied.

In the event, poor Constance presented her distraught husband with yet another girl-child, and then, the strain of the world's attention finally proving too much for her, died while delivering this catastrophe into the feudal battlefield of kings. Evidently Louis had not come to terms with St James of Compostella; perhaps his gift to the shrine had not been sufficiently generous.

He now possessed four daughters; if he failed to get a son, France might possibly pass into Plantagenet hands, and war would certainly break out concerning the succession. The French King, at his wits' end, behaved with the most uncharacteristic haste. Constance had been in her grave less than one month when it was known that he intended to marry again. For generations his family had feared the power of the house of Champagne, and Louis had long since sought to ameliorate this situation by betrothing one of his daughters to them. Now, ignoring consanguinity, he took as his third queen Adèle of Champagne, sister of his future son-in-law. Thus, Henry of England saw, lining up against him, not only the King of France, not only the lords of Champagne but also those of Blois, to whom Louis was allied via yet another of his daughters. The latter in particular were unlikely to forget, ever, that it was only Henry's intervention regarding Stephen of Blois which prevented them from occupying the throne of England.

Somewhere in this hasty rearrangement of the pieces, Henry perceived upon the great chessboard where he was continually playing for power, a way of changing the situation to his own advantage. Taking care to act with extreme legality, Thomas advising them on every point, the King and Queen of England arranged a marriage of their own. They dispensed with the formality of inviting the father, King Louis, to the ceremony; indeed they never even informed him of it – he would surely be much too busy with his own courtship. So at Neubourg in Normandy, young Prince Henry, heir to the throne of England, aged five, was wedded to Louis' daughter Marguerite, aged three, in accordance with the agreement which Thomas, escorted by monkeys, had made in Paris some years before.

At last the Vexin was Henry's to hold and guard as his three-year-old daughter-in-law's dowry. He descended upon it with his army and annexed the whole small but troublesome territory.

By the time King Louis looked up from his own wedding arrangements it was all over and done with. Thunderous protests were launched from Paris and from the houses of Champagne and Blois, the latter two preparing to take the field to punish the King of England for a bare-faced breach of his allegiance to France. But Henry had timed his actions to a nicety regarding the seasons. Winter now fell, hard and sudden, as if in league with the English King. He and his wife drew back into their own undisputed and heavily fortified lands to spend a joyous Christmas at the great castle of Le Mans.

There seemed good cause for the rejoicing that ensued. The Angevins had shown their hand, directed the course of affairs in Europe, and proved that they were the power above powers which all men must now reckon with. Those first tremors, as I have said, had passed unnoticed, and now nobody even felt the ground beginning to slide beneath our feet.

6

In the early spring of 1161 Theobald of Canterbury lay dying; when he knew that there was no hope for him he sent urgent messages both to the King and, more particularly, to Thomas. Neither went to him.

It is hardly surprising that Henry did not tear himself away from the demands of his continental kingdom to attend the deathbed of the Archbishop, though in my opinion it would have looked well in the eyes of the rest of the world had he done so. Without the old man's support, his way to the throne would have been many times more difficult. Feeling was harsher against Thomas in this matter, and loyal as I am I cannot but agree with his critics. I write this with a clear conscience, for I urged him to go to Canterbury, not once but many times. That he was of the true faith and Theobald a mere Christian is not excuse enough. If the Archbishop had not taken Thomas into his household, raised him up to a high position, educated him in the great schools of the law, and taken him on many of his journeys, even visiting the Pope, Thomas, however he had appealed to Henry, would never have had the knowledge to accept and hold the great position of Chancellor. He owed everything to Theobald, and he was wrong not to drop all business and hasten to the deathbed of his friend and patron at Canterbury.

It was as though his death, and the absence from it of both England's rulers, cast a blight upon that country. The winter had been harsh all over Europe; we in Normandy had been glad of it because passions at the French court regarding Henry's actions of the autumn and his seizing of the Vexin, had been cooled if not frozen by it. But our spring when it came was a true season, while on the other side of the Channel it was false.

To begin with things seemed well enough; but then as May passed to June there was no cooling shower to refresh the earth, and as June passed into summer all things began to wither. The little streams and ponds where the cattle and sheep had taken their water dwindled away, and the people were forced to carry from the deep springs and wells. But as August came with the full heat of the sun, even the deepest wells failed and springs which had always given abundantly within the memory of the oldest people began to run dry.

The animals died or were slaughtered; the crops crumbled to dust in the husbandman's hand; and then the people too began to starve, particularly those bound to lax or absent lords who had made no provision for years such as this. There was much grievance in the land, and many said that it was because their King, their Red King, stayed away too long; not only that, the Archbishop was dead in Canterbury and no one had come to take his place. For it must be understood, in fact it is vital that it be understood by all who read this, that in the minds of the common people, since Saxon times, the King and his arch-priest were one, indivisible. Nor did it matter in the least that the King was a pagan, worshipping (if he worshipped at all) the ancient gods of earth and sky, while his Archbishop worshipped God the Father and Christ the Son. If the people looked to the King and failed to find him, they turned instinctively to the Archbishop. So it had been; so it was; so, as I write this chronicle to tell, it was to be in the future.

I will not say that England's hardships did not often occupy the thoughts of King and Chancellor; both were touched very closely, not only by natural pity, but because they knew that political discontent would be certain to follow. They postponed many of their plans in Normandy, Anjou and Aquitaine, and set great sums to relieve the suffering; but neither had seen this with their own eyes, and the sums were too small and came too late.

However, Thomas had thought upon a way to ensure that the nobility of England might be reminded, in spite of discontent among the people, that they owed allegiance to the Plantagenets and to no other. The young Prince Henry would be seven years old in February of 1162; what better than that he should be taken to England and officially presented to his English lords as heir to the throne; and to lend maximum weight to the occasion, what more fitting than that Thomas himself, the great Chancellor, should escort the boy, conduct the ceremony and be first to bend the knee in homage?

The journey was planned to take place in May when, by God's

good grace, the earth would have flowered into a prosperous spring, erasing from the minds of the people the disasters of 1161. It was certain that they would associate this rebirth with the appearance amongst them of the youthful Prince, thus transferring to the son some of that ancient religious awe they felt for the father.

It was a wise plan, and bore the imprint of Thomas's deep understanding of such matters, yet it was not to fall out in accordance with his hopes; for now the time had come, and the eight years since Winchester were whittled down to but a few days. Now, as after some great pageant when the labourers set to work dismantling all the splendour, brocades and cloth of gold and rich tapestries falling away to reveal the rough timber that held them, so the years of my lord's glory were revealed in their true worth.

It sprang, as such things will, from an idle word: in January of that year, when Thomas and I were about the King's business in his Norman capital of Rouen, we were visited by the Prior of Leicester, an old friend from our days at Canterbury and one of the few Christians whom Thomas trusted completely. I have said that King Henry put great faith in the Earl of Leicester, and it must in some way have been from this powerful source that the good Prior had gleaned what little information he had. Little, but enough! He said, 'And what of this news that the King would have you as Archbishop of Canterbury?'

Thomas was as adept as any man I have ever known at hiding surprise, and this was the only time I ever saw the faculty desert him. Seeing his expression, the Prior burst out, 'In God's name, what have I said? You knew nothing of it!'

Thomas said, 'My dear friend, you do not know the King. This is the kind of trick he relishes; he will wait until we are surrounded by all kinds of company and then spring the news at me like a hawk. Thank you for your warning; now I shall see to it that his hawk strikes at air, and I shall send it fluttering back to his wrist in a fine rage.'

Such is the smoothness of his tongue, and so quickly had he recovered himself, that the Prior was at once calmed and amused, though Thomas warned him severely to speak of the matter to no other person. But he was deeply disturbed, and as soon as our guest took his leave he began to pace to and fro furiously.

I knew better than to speak; indeed I had no wish to speak, for I was too amazed, not by what the good man had said, but by the fact that of a sudden all the uneasiness and dread which had tormented me for so long seemed to flow out of me like pus from a wound that is upon the turn and will henceforth mend. What we had been told was indeed dreadful in its implication, and was to prove more dreadful in fact, yet it was at last reality; and I beg to think that mankind may better live with reality, however harsh, than with an easy falsehood.

Thomas now paused in his pacing and stared at me. 'So, William. Why do *you* think the King has never spoken to me of this?'

'I think,' I was able to answer with honesty, 'that he is unsure in his own mind and has not you to advise him upon the matter.'

'He would do well to be unsure.' Yet something in my tone made him examine me more closely, ever quick to appraise the mood of others. 'You are calm, Will, in view of what we now know.' The dark eyes searched my own. 'Was this your maggot, my friend? Was it for this you fell fainting from your horse? Was this your fear of too much greatness, too much power?'

As typically, he gave me no chance to reply, but brought a fist crashing down upon the table. 'So I am to take the young Prince, the heir, and present him to the country in state; and shortly after that I am to be made Archbishop, high priest of the realm!' I noticed that a goblet had overturned, emptying a few drops of wine, blood-red, upon the board. 'And after that, what? Eh, William? What are my lord King's plans for me after that?'

The question was rhetorical; I was not required to answer, and I could well appreciate the bitter anger.

Thomas said, 'By God's blood, he'd better think twice, or I'll throw that hawk back at him and it shall have his eyes!'

Part two

When you forced me to become arch-priest of
your kingdom, you would have done well to ask
me whether I wished to die for you.

Thomas of London, June 1163

There is a legend, which most of the writers of history have followed in their chronicles, that the King did not speak directly to
Thomas concerning Canterbury until the hour of his departure for
England with the young Prince; that is to say at the castle of
Falaise during the Easter court. A little thought might have warned
these writers that the King would hardly wait until such a man as
his Chancellor had one foot in the stirrup before bringing up so
momentous a matter. The implication that the two men spoke together for less than an hour, that during this time Henry over-
powered Thomas's objections, and that Thomas rode away having
accepted his lord's ruling, is absurd, and I do not ask the reader
who has followed me me thus far to believe a word of it.

At the time of the Prior of Leicester's visit to Rouen the King
was at Angers; he journeyed from there into Brittany to try the case
of a baron who had plotted against him. It was the beginning of
March before he returned, and on the very evening of his return
he supped at the Chancellor's table and spoke openly of the matter
before three others who were present, myself included.

'Canterbury,' he said, 'can no longer be left vacant. We are
making enemies there, who say that we merely use the see and its
empty bishoprics to finance wars and the building of foreign castles.'

'The which,' added Thomas, 'is true.' He betrayed nothing of
what he knew, but was his usual easy, slightly sardonic self. Only I
could read the glint in the dark eyes.

Henry said, 'I am not concerned. What does concern me is that
we have created a legal system which fails to work for one reason
only; because any guilty man with the wit of a titmouse can evade
our courts and have himself tried before the courts of the church,
which have no legal system worthy of the name. That practice will
stop.'

'And who,' enquired Thomas, pouring more wine, 'will stop it?'

I think, so well did these two men understand each other, that something in Thomas's tone warned the King that his thoughts were not as secret as he had supposed. 'Why,' he replied, smiling his warmest smile, 'the new Archbishop, who else?'

'Ah! Who else?'

'We must seek and find a man of power, a man with some knowledge of the church but not tied slavishly to its demands, a man of vision and, most important of all, a King's man.'

They eyed each other appraisingly for a long time in silence. Thomas said, 'A hard task.'

'Think on it, my friend. Sleep on it. The hour is late and we go hunting at dawn.'

'I fear,' said Thomas, 'that I shall not have time to sleep on it long enough for inspiration.'

It was a cold and wet March that year. Rain came driving in from the western ocean and spoiled their day's hunting. Sitting beside the fire in a woodman's cottage, stretching steaming boots to the heat, King Henry said, 'Did you think on Canterbury?'

'I did.'

'Will you take it?'

Thomas, in dictating this to me, said that he toyed with the idea of feigning shocked surprise, but abandoned it as unworthy and replied, 'No, my lord. Saving your grace, I will not.'

The King then expounded with enthusiasm the perfection of his plan: Thomas, Theobald's most trusted clerk, well-known at Canterbury, aware of the church's demands: Thomas, the Chancellor, even more aware of the counterdemands of the state: Thomas, the brilliant lawyer trained in the greatest schools: Thomas, the King's man, Thomas, the King's friend. Working closely together within this combination of Chancellor and Archbishop, they would reorganize England's legal procedures and put the power of the Christian church in its place once and for all.

Thomas said, 'I value your friendship more than this honour. I will not be Archbishop.' He spoke nothing of the hidden reasons; he admitted to me later that he could not tell, dared not believe, that they even existed in the King's mind. 'He loves me, William. I cannot, before God, accuse him of such thoughts.'

I asked whether the King had accepted his refusal.

'No. He said we would speak of it again later.'

I recall that he then went to the fireplace and kicked the logs into flame, staring thoughtfully. I said, 'If he wants it, Thomas, he will command it.'

He nodded. I knew that I had read his thoughts. I began, 'If Henry Plantagenet commands . . .'

'If he commands, I shall obey. He is the King, I am his servant.'

Coming from another man this might have sounded like resignation and subservience; coming from Thomas it did not. I knew then that he was already planning ahead, and that his acceptance, if it ever came to that, would not be what any of us, the King in particular, expected.

Twice more before the Easter court at Falaise Henry tried persuasion. On the second occasion I was present; I think because both men desired a witness who was not a Christian, and I was the most secure choice. King Henry pursued his argument doggedly, with a passion which held only a trace of the rage he would have turned upon any other man, until at last Thomas burst out in something like anguish: 'Oh my dear lord, you are right in all you say, but it breaks my heart that you desire so much to lose me as a friend.'

The King appeared stunned by this. Then: 'By God's blood, I lose no friend, I simply gain an Archbishop who will not fight me at every ditch.'

Thomas gained control of himself, and then said very quietly, 'You ask me, my lord, whether my love for you is greater than my love for God.'

Henry pounded his knee with a red fist. 'You're not a damned Christian, don't pontificate like one!'

Thomas said, 'Do you not understand? It is the same God.'

'It is *not* the same God.'

At this I was stabbed by a pang of memory. Eleven years before, at that meeting with Queen Eleanor in a room of her palace on the Ile de France, young Henry Duke of Normandy had surprised me by making the Sign of the Lion, half-forgotten Mithraic talisman. Had I not sensed at that moment the spiritual gulf which separated the two men? Now, more dangerously, it gaped between them again.

Thomas said, 'Forgive me, I know more of such things than you. It is the same God, however different the religion, and I love him more than I love you. Do not ask me to make a choice between you.'

'I do. I shall.'

'Then,' said Thomas, 'command me, and I shall obey.'

King Henry stood up abruptly, seized by some unusual agitation. He paced about the room, biting his lip; then said, 'Never. I will never command you.'

'Then I will never become arch-priest of England.'

I understood then why Thomas had not touched upon the deeper thing that lay behind this whole argument: the showing of the Prince, the homage, the becoming of Archbishop; he did not in his heart believe that Henry would ever force him to it, and he was giving his friend every possible chance not to cast the die.

Queen Eleanor, knowing and loving the King as a woman and a wife, not as a friend, had no such illusions. I understood that she sent for me because, having bared her heart to me once on the dangers of the relationship between Henry and Thomas, she felt me to be a reasonable person, and perhaps the only one, to whom she dared speak concerning the imminent destruction of that relationship. She wasted no time in preliminaries. 'The Chancellor must on no account accept this offer.'

'But, your grace, if the King commands ...'

'He cannot command a man who is not there.' I was amazed – she knew that Thomas would never take flight – amazed and then alarmed because, knowing it, she could yet advocate it.

I said, 'He won't leave the King's side.'

'Make him. Tell him that the King *will* command it; we all know what disasters may arise from that.' She came nearer, her eyes holding me. 'I do not love your Thomas; I cannot find it in my heart to like him overmuch, but I know a great man and a good man when I see one. Without him the King will be lost; none can curb that temper except Thomas.'

'From time to time.'

'That in itself is a miracle.'

'You ...'

'I was able to hold him in check as long as he loved me.'

I glanced away and she took my arm, turning me back to her.

'Yes, you see how urgently I feel, or I would not say such a thing, even to you. If the King is not curbed he will over-reach himself on every side. He needs Thomas more than he knows.'

'My lady, the Chancellor does not take advice from me.'

'Tell him that I will make urgent legal business for him. In . . . Angoulême. He must ride there at once. Meantime I have friends here who will press other names upon the King for Canterbury; half the bishops in England pant for it.'

'They are not Thomas.'

'No, but at least three are less Christian than they appear, we both know that, and one of those shall have the see and do the King's will there.'

'You know his will, my lady?'

'I know that he has dark thoughts, William. He is not Christian and neither is he Cathar. He will return to the old ways of his fore-fathers, and the fact that it is expedient politically will convince him that it is right.'

I need hardly add that Thomas listened to no word of this advice; and I need hardly describe the heaviness which fell on my heart when I realized that the Queen had all but paraphrased the very words that I had written long before in my day-book, and repeated here upon another page: 'To Henry Plantagenet anything that is expedient is never entirely unthinkable.' Perhaps because I did not love him as Thomas loved him, I saw this more clearly. It seemed to me, as it did to Queen Eleanor, that the Angevin, being the man he was, would inevitably take the final, disastrous step.

True, he hesitated until the very last moment, when Thomas was about to set out from the Easter court at Falaise for Barfleur and England, escorting the young Prince who had already been his ward for over a year. I think, even then, that Henry almost let the moment pass, the moment that would change history, but some demon in the Angevin blood would not allow him to do so.

He took his Chancellor by the arm, and said, 'Thomas my good friend, I have listened to your advice for many years, I owe you many debts for the many times you have been right and I wrong, but in this one matter I *know* that I am right.'

Thomas said nothing.

The King continued, 'It is my will that my Chancellor also becomes Archbishop of Canterbury.'

Thomas bowed. 'Your grace does me great honour.'

Those who stood apart noticed that the two men looked at each other for a long time in silence. In that time, though it would take many months for the outward signs to show, their friendship died. Love is harder to kill. Incredible as it may appear, in view of what was now to happen, their love survived; imprisoned, tortured, maimed, it sought and found a deep hiding-place, and stayed there for many years; yet it did not die.

If in the telling of my story I have one worthy thing to say, it lies in the matter of this love: a gift greater than mankind deserves, and perhaps the only gift which he cannot destroy at will.

2

Our crossing was fair, with a calm sea. For much of the time Thomas sat alone in deep thought, smiling only when the young Prince ran to him with excited news concerning the ship and the men who sailed it, listening gravely but absently to the commissioners whom Henry had dispatched with him for the purpose of completing the ecclesiastical transactions and arguments regarding Canterbury.

When the English coast appeared as a dim grey line of menace upon the horizon, he summoned me; the smile with which he greeted me was ironical and weary. 'Well, William, my Conscience, are you of a mind to chide me for the pass to which my wicked ambition has brought us?'

He knew that I could not bear to be mocked at such a time upon such a subject, but I would not let him draw me out; I said, 'My lord, I can live with your ambition more easily than ever I could before, now that we know its true worth.'

'*Do* we know its true worth?'

'We are nearer knowing, are we not?'

He shrugged, looking towards England. 'I think perhaps you mistake our lord King's estimation for the truth, and though he be great he is not God: neither God with a capital G nor god with a small g, for that is a title he wishes upon me. As for my ambition, it is possible that the erstwhile enemy may now prove to be my friend.'

He looked to see if I had understood him, and I said, 'Does it not change its name, becoming spiritual?'

This made him smile. 'In me, I am afraid, it may ever remain ambition, but I think it may now sit with us at table and not offend you.'

Again he looked towards the grey strip of land which was our destination and our destiny, and when he spoke again all lightness had left his voice: 'We are alone now, Will, as we have never been alone before.'

'We have good friends, my lord, both in England and in Normandy.'

'Let us count them after I have defied the King.' He nodded, seeing that I did not deny that he must, sooner or later, defy King Henry and then went on to speak of my day-book, his concern surprising me, for it had until then been as ordinary to me as the habit of washing my face each morning. 'At all times it will be locked in the strongest of secret hiding-places; you apart, it will now be the only witness to what I truly think and do.'

He looked with some affection to where my colleague, Herbert of Bosham, sat in deep discussion with some bishop. 'We shall no doubt be surrounded by various chroniclers, many less honest than our good Herbert. They must write whatever history they wish, according to what they imagine they hear and see; but mark well, William, that you write the truth, lest even we ourselves forget what it is.'

At Southampton we were met by many lords and prelates, who mattered less than the bad news that this year promised no better harvest than the one before. Then it had been lack of water; now, when the country people had scratched up the iron ground for a difficult sowing, torrential rains had washed the seed away, and floods had destroyed many of those poor houses which had not, the previous summer, cracked and tumbled down before the searing heat. King Henry's hope that Thomas might present his son to the nobles against a general background of satisfaction and the prospect of a fruitful year was not to be.

Our party divided soon after landing, the Prince, some lords and prelates riding with us to Winchester where the ceremony of allegiance was to be held. The others, Richard de Luci, his brother the Abbot of Battle, the Bishops of Chichester, Exeter and Rochester, headed for Canterbury. Watching them go, Thomas smiled and said, 'Rather our work than theirs, my lords,' for he knew that they would meet much opposition and undergo many violent and wearying arguments before he was accepted by the Christian churchmen as their leader and Archbishop.

There is no need to enumerate here the things which the lords of that church held against Thomas the Chancellor, but he had won many cases for the King against them, appropriating funds and levying taxes which sometimes halved their revenues; moreover he had never surrendered the archdeaconry, and his failure to come to Theobald's deathbed was still, and would always be, held against him.

It was dusk before we entered the great courtyard of the castle where, eight years before, I had stopped the wise woman so that Queen Eleanor might question her. I do not know what Thomas's feelings were, but I was uneasy, full of foreboding; and that night, against my principles, not even telling my lord, I went to the edges of the town and sought the woman at her house, for I felt an urgent need to use her strange gift, to learn something of our future, good or bad I did not care. But she was dead and her house was deserted. Few wish to live in the places where such as Joan have lived with her secrets.

So, as you may read in any chronicle, Thomas went about his work at Winchester, convening all the King's lords to pay homage to the boy Prince at Whitsuntide; as usual he prepared everything down to the last detail, even to the fitting of the tiny coronet which young Henry would wear, coaching his ward in words and deportment while at the same time conducting many affairs of state which awaited his coming or that of the King.

Meanwhile, at Canterbury, the unhappy commissioners fought heroic battles of debate in order to convince the chapter that King Henry's choice of spiritual leader was the very one they themselves most wanted. The chapter resisted with spirit; as far as they were concerned Thomas of London was a politician, which made him an excellent Chancellor but not an Archbishop.

The majority of them were not to know that even though he was no Christian, Thomas knew more of spiritual matters, and had suffered more in their name, than any of the men who sat in judgement upon him. There was, however, a minority, for as I have said our true faith has many adherents within the Christian church, and it was possibly as much upon their recommendation as upon fear of the King's anger that Thomas was eventually accepted by the monks of Canterbury, though with reservations.

At Winchester the ceremony of allegiance proceeded as planned. Thomas was the first to approach the little Prince, solemn upon his throne, and bend the knee in homage. He knew full well the meaning of what he did; knew that Henry had so ordered this ceremony that all England, all Europe, could now see and understand that the great Chancellor, who was to become the great arch-priest, was acting in place of the King and had therefore become the King.

Now you will understand why I have emphasized the ancient bond between King and Archbishop, and the fact that in the eyes of the people they are interchangeable. Henry, who had loved and valued my lord so much in life, was giving a sign to all who understood such things that he would value him as much, or more, in death. What the King could not know was that even though Thomas was acting upon the royal will when he bent his knee to the young Prince, he resolutely refused within his heart to accept the royal intention.

Perhaps I alone understood this, and thus I alone trembled to see him pay homage at Winchester. He smiled as he did so, but the smile concealed a tightly sealed cauldron of hidden rage which, in time, was to explode, shaking the foundations of all Europe.

On 2 June at Canterbury, watched with varying degrees of suspicion by all his monks, he was ordained priest. Next day, the Christian festival of the Blessed Trinity (do not ask them to define this; they are disagreed upon the matter), he was consecrated Archbishop of Canterbury by Henry, Bishop of Winchester.

Thus far King Henry's plans had matured with their usual success. What Thomas did next was not, however, part of the royal rearrangement. He resigned the Chancellorship. News of this crossed the Channel that very night and, next morning, threw Henry into such a rage that he fell screaming to the floor and chewed the rushes scattered there.

Thomas had said to me of my day-book, 'Mark well that you write the truth, lest even we ourselves forget what it is.'

I suppose that nothing illustrates his meaning more clearly than the panegyrics which you may read on every side concerning the 'change' which took place in him upon becoming Archbishop: 'a transformation', 'a delayed spiritual awakening', 'a rejection of splendour and an assumption of the most humble simplicity'. They are so ridiculous that they do not deserve comment. There was no change whatsoever in Thomas; he had always been celibate; always offered himself to scourging, always given alms with great generosity, always fasted at given times, always prayed far into the night. By God, to read these idiots one might think he had kept, as Chancellor, a court full of loose women, and spent his years in that high office lying abed with his face buried in a wine goblet. Nothing could have been easier for a man already Perfect in the Cathar faith than the puny asceticisms practised by an Archbishop of the Christian religion.

As for the practical matters of reorganizing and ruling the see and all its estates, these were but a farmyard compared with the empire over which he had presided for the past years.

Sometimes when I glance at other chronicles I feel that I have suddenly gone mad, yet at second glance I see that what they are relating is indeed *a* truth, and it is not their fault if what they have to tell is as meaningless and as circumscribed as the view of a small boy peeping through a hole in a wall. Armies may pass, but he sees only five or six men at a time; battles may be fought and a thousand men killed, but it all happens a little to the left of the chestnut tree which is the boundary of his vision.

Then, contrarily, when these poor chroniclers are at last vouchsafed a whole view of what is happening, they lack the secret knowledge to pick out, not at the centre of the picture but somewhere towards its edge, the little detail which reveals everything.

I had thought my telling of this history to be difficult before, but now I see that the true test lies in what is to come. I can only surmount it by in some way comparing the two visions, superimposing one upon the other: the first, which all men think they know, is a great tapestry of courts and councils held at high-sounding palaces, Nottingham, Clarendon, Montmirail, where nobles and bishops and papal legates gesture and thunder in a flamboyance of robes and banners, trumpet-calls and the glitter of jewels: the other, which no man knows, is the ugly truth behind the public history-making, and it lies with two men only, who fight silently and savagely in the dusty darkness behind that tapestry: Thomas and Henry locked in a struggle which, as each well knows, must end in the ritual death of one of them.

3

The King's mandate to his new Archbishop had certainly not included instant resignation of the Chancellorship; but I was present at their meeting in Rouen, and wrote of it directly afterwards that Thomas had said, 'It is the same God, however different the religion, and I love him more than I love you,' and therefore Henry should not have been surprised that immediately after being ordained he began to right the wrongs which had been committed against Canterbury, setting his house in order, using all his energy, his knowledge of law, his charm and, if need be, the ruthlessness which had made him so valuable to the King. Even as a 'heretic', Thomas considered Canterbury and all its possessions to be God's property. In our religion we have a slightly larger view of the Almighty than that of the Christians: for us there is but one God, though he may show himself to different people in different ways; to the Christians there is only the Christian God, a 'jealous' God as their holy book rightly but inhumanly pronounces, and no other.

The new Archbishop now commanded the Earl of Clare to come forward and pay homage, and taxes, to Canterbury for his tenure of the castle of Tonbridge; he also reclaimed Rochester castle, occupied by one or other of the warring parties in King Stephen's civil war; and he sent his knights to retrieve the property of Eynsford, seized by a certain William de Ros following the death of Theobald.

Naturally all these actions reached the King's ear and increased his irritation against Thomas; but, though he sent the infant Princess Marguerite, now aged five, to join her seven-year-old husband in Thomas's household, where both children loved to be, he did not come to England himself.

I remarked on this one evening as we walked in the cloister. Even though he now habitually wore the black gown of an Augustinian monk instead of the rich velvets and furs which he had so much enjoyed during his days of worldly power, the look he turned upon me, irony edged with anger, was more that of the Chancellor than the Archbishop. 'Have you not done your counting, William? The King will come, he *must* come, early in the new year of 1163.'

Now I admit that I had raised the subject only to find out if my lord's thoughts still ran in the same line. Hearing that they did, my heart sank and I fell silent.

Thomas smiled. 'Have no fear, Will. I was wont to beat him at chess five times out of six, even when he knew my game. But this is a different game upon a different board, nor am I the same opponent.'

In January of 1163, once again defying a terrible storm which had held him at Barfleur longer than he liked, King Henry, with Queen Eleanor, landed at Southampton. They were met by the usual congregation of nobles and prelates, most of whom had not seen their monarch for four years, and many of whom were bursting with complaints against the new Archbishop. Upon the moment of the royal disembarkation you may be sure that all eyes were glued to the royal countenance and all ears turned to catch the manner of the royal greeting.

Young Prince Henry ran forward to welcome his father and was seized up in a rough embrace, unaware that the steel-grey eyes were searching over his small shoulder among the men who stood upon the harbour, their robes and cloaks billowing in the gale.

Henry greeted the elderly Bishop of Winchester, brother of the late King Stephen, and took the hands of the lords of Leicester and Southampton, while his eyes passed clear over Thomas.

'Where,' he said, 'is my lord Chancellor?'

Nobody knew what to make of this, but Thomas stepped forward and knelt, saying, 'Here in the heart, your grace.'

'Disguised?'

Those who had come to press complaints began to look uneasy, seeing that the King was disposed to be merry, whatever his inmost thoughts. Laughing, he raised Thomas and held him and they exchanged the Kiss of Peace; at which the faces of many present fell into lines of deep disappointment, while my heart at least began to beat again with qualified regularity.

Of course it was not possible that Henry was pleased with Thomas's conduct; in fact I don't think I ever admired his self-control, knowing how foreign it was to him, nor his statesmanship more than I did on this occasion. My thoughts turned to Queen Eleanor and, my eyes following, found her own fixed upon me; she nodded, not at all by way of greeting, but as if to say, 'Yes, William, we have things to say to one another, you and I.'

I have not spoken of my new position in the Archbishop's household since it differed little from the one I had held under the Chancellor. In my way I was to Thomas what he had been to Theobald when he had first gone to Canterbury, a kind of private secretary. It was generally understood that I was too busy with my new duties to continue as a chronicler, and I encouraged this assumption in the interests of secrecy.

Thomas had nominated Herbert of Bosham as his personal historian, chiefly because of Herbert's addiction to mountainous verbosity. 'Let him,' said Thomas, 'cloud every issue with words, the more the merrier, for he understands nothing of the truth, and God be praised for that.'

The King and Queen had decided to rest at Southampton for a day, but Thomas was summoned to attend the King in private council on the evening of their arrival. He insisted, much to my apprehension, that I should accompany him; when I suggested that my presence could only aggravate the royal irritation he replied, 'Not at all. You are still my right arm, and the King trusts you. Besides, the Queen has personally requested your appearance.' The dark eyes were amused. 'I hear that you once spoke to her in anger on my behalf; I have never thanked you for it, and she has never forgotten it.'

On entering the presence I was immediately reminded of that other occasion at Winchester; another gale bombarded the thick walls of another castle, and the King once again lolled before a blazing fire, while the Queen sat back from it a little with, of all things after the stormy crossing they had completed only a few hours before, embroidery upon a frame.

The King now took Thomas to task for everything he considered to be a breach of the faith between them, beginning with his resignation as Chancellor and ending with his recent excommunication of William de Ros, who had proved intractable over the matter of Eynsford. 'In all,' he said, 'you have acted like a Christian, which you are not, and you have not acted like a King's man, which you are.'

Thomas said, 'I am a man of God, you made me such.'

Queen Eleanor sighed. Thomas said, 'William here has a copy of our very words at Rouen and at Falaise. Will you hear them?'

'God's death, I remember them, do you think I'm senile? And no Archbishop, not even a Christian one, has power to excommunicate a royal tenant without permission of the King. Learn your law, lawyer!'

Thomas bowed. 'I stand corrected.'

'What's more, and worse, you have allowed Tom, Dick and Harry to be tried in the courts of the Christian church, when you know, better than I, that the civil courts *which we created* should have judged them.'

There was silence. The gale howled, stirring the tapestries upon the wall. The Queen's needle plucked at her canvas.

Henry shouted, 'Do you deny that?'

Quietly, Thomas answered, 'I deny nothing.' I wondered whether he was going to mention that the year was 1163, and thrust upon us the real reason which lay behind this meeting, but I guessed from his guarded words and watchful expression that he was waiting for Henry to take the first step. I think that Henry was aware of this too. He studied my master's face for perhaps a full minute in silence; then threw himself back in his chair and turned to stare into the flames. I found it difficult to remember that he was only thirty years of age; he looked forty, and a rugged, weather-beaten forty at that. Thomas, so many years his senior, seemed at this time more like a contemporary.

Still staring into the fire, Henry said, 'There is great unrest in the kingdom.'

'My lord, do you wonder? First the sun and then the rain have laid waste the land. Many are dead, many starve, many are homeless. And believe me, there are certain lords who love you considerably less than you may think, and are ever prepared to use the situation against you.'

'What do you advise?'

'A fruitful year. A full season of crops; ewes lambing, heifers with calf.'

The Queen looked up from her work, first at the King, then at Thomas, then at me. She at least realized exactly what my lord had said and why. Henry only leaned forward and put another log on the fire. 'Regarding these nobles who would make trouble, it would be wise to enforce more strongly our hold upon the country. God knows how soon it will be before I must go back; there is unrest in Aquitaine; my lady's henchmen there have short memories.'

'Or long ones.' She said it sharply, not looking up from her work.

It was perhaps the first public indication that all was not well between them. I added it in my mind to the words she had spoken to me in private regarding their relationship, and was not surprised to see the King frown.

Perhaps to cover this moment, for he was always diplomatic, Thomas said, 'And how does your grace intend to enforce more strongly your hold upon England.'

Henry stood up and met his eyes directly. 'I think,' he said, 'that it would be well, following precedents in other lands, to convene all our lords and bishops at Westminster, where in full state we will crown my heir.'

I held my breath. The Queen's needle was poised for an instant. Thomas said, very evenly, 'I understand.'

'You think it a good idea?'

'Extremely clever.' There was no mistaking the tone, but the King did not hear it or chose to ignore it. 'Good! We will ride to London together; we have much work to do.'

Thomas bowed assent, eyes lowered. I noticed that the Queen

had not continued with her work; the needle was still poised above a blue silken flower.

Thomas said, 'Your grace will find the ride interesting.'

When we were private in our quarters, Thomas turned to me and gave a sudden shout of almost boyish laughter. I found it more unnerving than anything that had happened on that precipitous evening. 'So,' he said, 'now I am to *crown* the Prince! By the blood of the Son, how far will he go in this game before he declares his hand.'

I could only reply, 'You are in great danger, Thomas.'

'Oh no, not yet. Let us see how his majesty feels after his ride to London!'

The young Duke of Normandy's first journey from Winchester to London was but a shadow of what took place when, as King, he now set out from Southampton in the sacred year 1163. Everywhere along the road the country people came running from farmstead and cottage, from the half-ruined shacks and barns where the destruction of their homes now forced them to live. In the bitter January weather, many of them showing every sign of starvation, they knelt in the rimed grass, slipped on the frozen puddles, and even forced their way between the knights of the royal bodyguard, pulling at Henry's legs or grabbing his reins. In the towns and villages there was such a surge of people that time and again the whole cortège could not move.

At first the King was pleased with this adulation, which showed so clearly that even after four years' absence the English peasantry still held him in their hearts, but after he had been forced to dismount half a dozen times while the cavalcade was halted, shivering in the wind, Angevin irritation began to show. I do not know whether this was because he was always impatient of slow travel and interruptions of any kind, or whether the exact meaning of this adoration was beginning to dawn upon him, in conjunction perhaps with Thomas's words, 'Your grace will find the ride interesting.'

It was dusk before we reached the castle of Guildford, and Queen Eleanor let it be known that she was cold and weary and would go no further. The King took advantage of this to avoid another day's confrontation with the worshipping crowd, announcing that he would ride that night for London taking a handful of men, Thomas and myself included.

That the Queen would summon me upon her arrival next day I did not doubt, and though I was fearful of such a meeting, Thomas was delighted by the prospect on my behalf. 'You may learn much, Will; perhaps more than you're forced to tell. If possible lose your temper again; she evidently finds that entertaining.'

I had no need to answer these witticisms; the Queen herself answered them for me in no uncertain terms by arriving unannounced and in secret to see Thomas personally. Entering in travelling clothes she said, 'Do you think that the King is the only one who can ride ahead of a procession? Today the Queen is unwell and must be carted with her ladies in a covered carriage. I shall rejoin them before they reach the gates.'

Over refreshment, she added, 'You are surprised that I act in this way, my lord. Then know that I am watched even as you are watched.'

'There are certain good reasons why the King should spy on me, renegade Chancellor turned godly.'

'Turned god, you mean.'

I found her outspokenness alarming, but Thomas merely shrugged. 'I see that no secrets are hid from your grace.'

'On the contrary. All secrets are now hid from me.'

'You attended our meeting at Southampton.'

She sipped her wine and said, 'I am allowed to be privy to what I already know. Beyond that, I believe my lord the King even has it in his mind to . . .' She searched, as ever, for the correct phrase: '. . . . to keep me in some safe place where I cannot "meddle", I think he would say, as I am "meddling" now.'

'And from where,' Thomas added, 'you could not, if you so wished, raise Poitou and Aquitaine against him.'

At this she dropped all banter: 'He spoke of that to you while you were Chancellor?'

Thomas remained pointedly silent. The Queen nodded to herself,

'I think we must barter frankness, you and I, my lord Archbishop. Who shall begin?'

Thomas smiled. 'While I was Chancellor the King often voiced a fear that half his empire belonged to you, and held you nearer its heart than it did him.'

She thought about this in silence for a time; then, 'Obviously, from your words at Southampton, you know what is in his mind regarding this sacred year 1163; the exhausting enthusiasm of the populace yesterday showed him that they too understand the meaning of the year, the more so after the many disasters which have befallen them.'

'Do we barter, your grace? You tell me what I have seen with my own eyes.'

She leaned towards him. 'Well then, you may be interested to hear that he does *not* understand the meaning of the Kiss of Peace, seen by all and understood by many at Southampton.'

I knew how badly Thomas needed this information, and his voice did not hide it: 'Thank you. Uncertainty regarding that has kept me awake at nights.'

'Not so long ago I would have explained it to him, but . . .' Her gesture was eloquent of many things that were now lost between herself and the King, but she disclosed no emotion. 'Now,' she put down her wineglass and stood up, coming near to him, obsidian eyes searching his dark ones, 'you will recall that when we were first in Winchester you summoned for the King a wise woman?'

'Yes.'

She felt my concern, for she was coming near to the only secret I ever kept from Thomas, at her command; she turned on me a quiet look of complicity and lied smoothly: 'To you she foretold, give or take a week, the exact date of your break with the King.'

'She was a remarkable woman.'

'That is why I sent for her again that night, in secret, while you all busied yourselves with order of march and bodyguards and precedences. We spoke of sons. She foresaw that my first-born, William, would die within two years; also that the child I was then carrying in my womb would prove to be another prince, young

Henry. I asked her if he would be King, and she replied after some hesitation that he would be crowned.'

How wrong I had been to imagine that Queen Eleanor, of all people, would not realize at once that her question had not been properly answered. So in part she was not lying; she had indeed met Joan a second time.

She continued now, 'I told her not to prevaricate, and she then said that what she had meant but feared to tell was that though the child in my womb would be the heir and wear the crown, he would not live to rule the empire upon his father's death.'

'Which leaves your favourite son and personal heir, Prince Richard.'

'Yes, Richard will be King.' There was a fierce pride in this; we were in the presence of a power to be reckoned with, and Thomas, as was his way, urged it into showing itself yet more plainly: 'All being contingent upon whether the woman, Joan, was correct in her predictions.'

'She was correct concerning you and the King, concerning the death of my first child and the sex of my second, still in my belly. She is not yet proved wrong in anything she foresaw.'

Yes indeed, a very fierce passion; I could see that Thomas was already assessing its possible use in the future. He said, 'Is it my turn to barter, or your grace's?'

'Mine. The King has commanded you to crown Prince Henry. Do you intend to do it?'

Thomas did not answer at once; I knew from long experience that he was judging how far he might trust her upon the basis of how far she had already committed herself to him beyond redress.

Queen Eleanor said, 'If you do, my lord, your life is in danger.'

'I would phrase it differently: if I do, I ask for death.'

'Men have asked for death before now; it is sometimes the ultimate gesture of power, and you are interested in power. Are you not? Also, forgive me, a certain familiarity with death, even a desire for it, lies at the heart of your Cathar faith.'

If she intended to anger him, and she did few things without intent, she was successful; a little too sharply he said, 'You are asking me not to crown young Henry, is that it?'

'Yes. He will never occupy the throne, and a coronation can only complicate the issue for Richard, who will.'

'Have you thought, as I confess I have myself, that if I refuse the King may command others to do it?'

She smiled. 'My lord, I know a little more about the deciding factors than that. It must be your power, your splendour that falls upon the child, followed by your death, or nothing is achieved and the King need never have raised you to your present high position.'

Thomas considered for a moment before replying, 'You have my assurance that I have no intention of dying for a long time yet, and therefore no intention of crowning Prince Henry.'

Surprising woman that she is, she now held out her hand, not for a courtly kiss, but in a man's gesture of agreement. Thomas took it between both his and bowed his head. The pact sealed, she said, 'Thank you, my lord, I too shall sleep better tonight. Now I must rejoin myself in that jolting cart before it reaches the palace of Westminster.'

4

Outwardly, even to those who wished to see a break between Thomas and King Henry, they seemed during the early months of 1163 to be as close as ever they had been in the past. The Archbishop attended many meetings of the Council, and indeed appeared to be acting as Chancellor, so that a number of people wondered why he had resigned from that position. After four years' absence from England, Henry found that there was much work to be done, and for most of it he required my lord's assistance. But this does not for one moment mean that he forgot his heir's coronation; he wished to announce the date of it as soon as possible, for it was planned as an affair of high state, and all would be required to attend it.

Thomas now acted against the King, using the kind of wile which had served Henry so well and for so long when he had been his Chancellor and not his Archbishop. He knew that in September of 1162, while he had been setting Canterbury in order, Henry had for once joined peaceably with King Louis of France in order to meet the new Pope, Alexander III. This had been a state occasion, a mere matter of diplomacy, for Alexander badly needed the support of these two kings if he were to hold office against the claims and enmity of the anti-Pope, a pawn in the hands of the Holy Roman Emperor, Frederick Barbarossa. Thomas knew Alexander well, for he had studied law under him, as Rolando Bandinelli, at Bologna.

Quite contrary to Alexander's true character, for he was a wise man, both courageous and practical, Thomas represented him to Henry as being extremely touchy and careful of his rights, adding, 'Why not, when his position as Pope is in itself so insecure?' And he convinced the King that this man would be highly indignant if the coronation were to be announced before papal authority had been requested and legally granted.

So cleverly did my lord handle this matter that not even Henry Plantagenet, ever alert against trickery, realized that he was only playing for time. The fact was that Thomas had already heard that Alexander intended to summon a council at Tours in May, and that presently he, Thomas, would be called upon to attend it. Meantime, the King never mentioned the deeper meaning of the coronation, and Thomas continued to wait for him to take the lead, anger growing inside him. I have often wondered whether Henry took my lord's knowledge and acceptance for granted, or whether he too was playing a waiting game until the trap was set and sprung.

The Pope's command came in April, and Thomas pretended great surprise and delight. 'Ah,' he said, 'here we have the perfect opportunity. I will obtain a private audience of my old master as soon as the opportunity presents itself, and I will request the coronation in person. We cannot fail.'

I trembled to see the games and tricks which my lord played upon the King, for I alone knew the hidden anger that gave birth to them. Moreover I believed that Thomas played them with a kind of reckless delight as, I have heard, committed gamblers delight in a wager which may ruin them entirely.

The vitally important bishopric of London had lain empty for some time, and it was Thomas himself who suggested that the Bishop of Hereford, Gilbert Foliot, might fill it, despite his knowing that this ambitious and venal man was chief among his enemies. Henry, of course, cared little one way or the other, and Foliot was duly appointed; also to be the King's personal confessor, which naturally delighted the pompous fool – but then he didn't know that Henry was 'pagan', rarely confessed at all, and when he did invented the whole rigmarole.

Yet all this was dangerous, and if Thomas in his anger enjoyed it, I certainly did not. Foliot could, and was to, turn upon Thomas at the first opportunity. And as for the game he played at Tours, that was all but suicidal; but so he wished it, and when a man gambles with his own life there is little that a friend may say.

In the first place the council had been called to consider the matter of 'the heresies', our own true faith foremost among them; Thomas derived some amusement from professing horror at these 'daggers pointed at the very breast of the mother church'. He was much applauded for that phrase. He spoke, as always, with wit and brilliance, and the Pope was greatly taken with his old pupil's success, eminence and possible usefulness; for Alexander badly needed King Henry's assistance against his rival, the papacy still being split.

The Council lasted from 19 to 21 May. Little was achieved by it. Thomas was in no great hurry to return to England, and we visited friends and Brethren at Le Mans and Falaise on our way home.

At Southampton where we landed we were met by feverish messengers from the King. Thomas was summoned at once to the palace of Woodstock near Oxford; I was by no means unhappy when my lord sent me directly to Canterbury to attend to our affairs there.

The first of the two most fateful private meetings between King Henry and his Archbishop took place on the afternoon of 9 June 1163. Thomas dictated an account of it directly upon his arrival at Canterbury next day.

They embraced, the King chiding Thomas for his delay in returning to England; then he said, 'I hear that you had many private talks with your old friend, and aroused the jealousy of all at Tours. So we have his permission and may announce the coronation at once?'

'No, your grace.'

The King stared in amazement. 'He *refused* to give his permission?'

'I never requested it.' And before the King could explode into rage, he added quickly, 'When you forced me to become arch-priest of your kingdom you would have done well to ask me whether I wished to die for you.'

Henry leapt to his feet, eyes wide, his face becoming that dark red which so frightened other men. Thomas did not move; but to give the King time to compose himself, as he had often done before, he said, 'You've experienced the mood of the people; they know the meaning of 1163 as well as we do: nine times the sacred seven since William Rufus gave himself to them as the Divine Victim. There have been two years of disaster; sun and rain have both betrayed them, and they fear that the old gods have withdrawn deep under the hills; they look for sacrifice as they always have. So, against my will, you make me assume the mantle of Archbishop and take his vows, which means that I am become a part of your royal body, just as we are both, in your royalty, part of the body of their god.'

Henry had regained enough self-possession to speak, savagely, without turning: 'Why repeat what we already know?'

'Because it is time we had this matter straight between us. King William Rufus sought the ritual death of his Archbishop, Anselm, but he failed. Do you think me a lesser man than Anselm?'

Henry turned to face him then. 'I think myself a greater man than William Rufus.' He came back to Thomas, grey eyes as steely as a sword. 'Long years ago we made a pact in a barn. I asked, "Are you my man unto death?" and you swore that you were; swore upon the most holy oath and upon your sacred book of St John. Did you not?'

'I swore as Chancellor. Archbishop was never mentioned.'

'You were not Chancellor until a full year had passed; neither was I King. You swore as man to man, or, if you will, as a clerk to a duke. You swore, and we took each other's hand on it. Since then, my lord Thomas of London, you have lived in higher state than any other prince in my domains; higher, I've heard it said, than King Henry II himself. Nothing has been too good for you and nothing has been denied you. Don't pretend you didn't know from the very beginning what lay in that!'

Thomas confessed to me that in this matter he had made one of the very few miscalculations concerning his entire relationship with the King; Henry fell upon his silence, pressing home the point: 'Will you, wise in all ritual, say that you never knew the Divine Victim is given all he desires, wealth, position, power, *until the appointed time*? Was it not always thus? Answer me, Thomas!'

'It was always thus.'

'Pope's permission or none, you will go forward and crown my son at Westminster.'

'No. You forced me to become Archbishop; you shall not force me to die for you.'

At this the King laughed. 'Then, my lord Archbishop, you made a great mistake at Southampton upon our meeting there.'

'How so?' He feigned the question; he knew what was coming.

'You let me give you the Kiss of Peace. In this year 1163, all saw and understood the meaning of *that*.'

'All,' said Thomas smoothly, secure in what Queen Eleanor had told him, 'saving yourself.'

The King stared, frowning, mystified. Thomas then told him the secret thing which he had held close for so long; it was ten years since he had spoken of it to me following that fateful meeting in the barn: 'I am your senior in the faith, I was appointed your spiritual adviser when you joined it; all who know anything know that. What they saw at Southampton was that I, not only your senior but your arch-priest, gave *you* the Kiss of Peace. If there is to be a ritual death, you, not I, will suffer it.'

Henry continued to stare, finding no words.

Thomas said, 'This is why I did not ask the Pope's permission to crown your son, my lord. Were I to do so, all your people would look to you for divine salvation; and even though you have no such kindly thoughts regarding me, your . . . friend, *I* do not wish to see *you* dead.'

He knew that there could be no more talk. He had defied Henry Plantagenet, who was probably at that very moment recalling how his people had surged around his every appearance, worshipping. All that Thomas could now expect was the full onslaught of the royal rage. He bowed low, and left the room without asking permission; left the King standing in the middle of it as if struck dumb.

The writers of history, wholly occupied with their argument concerning King's court and Bishop's court, confine themselves to stating that the first sign of open contention between Henry and Thomas occurred a month later at Woodstock during the first week of July when the King convened a Council there. Certainly Thomas disagreed with him over a matter of unofficial payments to sheriffs, which the King wished to regularize; but my lord's argument was such a sensible one that Henry agreed to it with no more than a shrug. There was also an argument over a certain canon of Lincoln, accused of killing a knight; he had been judged at the Bishop's spiritual court, which of course annoyed the King who demanded that he be tried again by a King's court.

This may indeed have been the beginning of the public battle between the two men; if so it was mild by Henry's previous record, and I think it more likely that the roots of the thing lay in what was said when Henry again summoned my lord to a private conversation, again charging him that it was his sworn duty to crown the young Prince and, if the people willed it, to die in the King's place as the Divine Victim.

Impatiently, Thomas replied, 'Your grace does not seem to understand the meaning of the Pax, the Kiss, which I had thought I explained at our last meeting.'

'I do not accept that explanation.'

'It will be to you, not to me, that the people look.'

'What you're saying is that you have broken your sworn word, you are no longer my man.'

Angry now, Thomas said, 'I told you at Rouen, again at Falaise, and again since then: by forcing me to become Archbishop you forced me to make a choice between yourself and God. I begged you not to do so, I told you that I loved God better than I loved you; you would not listen.'

'And I told *you* not to behave like a Christian because you are not one.'

Again Thomas said, 'My lord, it is the same God. And in his name let us stop this argument before we both regret it; let us be friends as once we were.'

But the King was already pacing to and fro about the room, a sure prelude to the Angevin rage. 'I see now what I was too trusting to see then. Coward that you are, you intend to take refuge behind the skirts of the damned Christian church.'

Thomas snapped, 'Your grace would do well not to put ideas into my head.'

'I hardly think your colleagues of the true Cathar faith will be pleased by that.'

'They will find it very ordinary. Many have done the same; and there is not one, I think, who will question my loyalty.'

'By the blood of the Bull!' Henry was shouting now. 'I don't give a damn for your true faith, or the Christian faith, or any other hocus-pocus you may conjure up to counter me with. The Old Religion was good enough for my fathers, it's good enough for me.'

'You were received into . . .'

'I played with the Cathar faith to gain support from the Queen's southern lords, and well you know it!' He was unleashing his rage now, just as he had curbed it at their previous meeting. 'Damn you all, with your oaths, your blessed St John, your unnatural celibacy and all the rest of the claptrap. You're a traitor, Thomas of London; you not only betray your allegiance to me, you betray the friendship you're always prating about. To hell with you! My dogs are better friends! Henry Plantagenet owes allegiance to himself and to the old gods alone, that's why my people love me.'

'Then die for them both, my lord!' Thomas admits that he was as angry as ever he had been in all his life. What he would not admit, even to me, was the depth of the wound that Henry struck that day, a wound to the heart. He had always known that the King was no Cathar, that the faith was too rigorous for him, and that he would always worship the old gods; but the dismissal of their friendship hurt him more than he dared say, and this even though he knew long before that it was ended. Therefore, since none can be hurt by those they do not love, it was at this same moment that he realized the extent of his love for the King.

When Thomas had dictated this to me he paused for a while,

lost in thought. 'So,' he said, 'that is the end of my worldly ambition. I cut its throat there at Woodstock and threw it down at the King's feet. Whether it was friend or enemy I shall never know. Both, perhaps, since we are dual creatures all.' He glanced at me smiling. 'Will my conscience rest the better for that death?'

'It was your conscience that slew ambition at Woodstock, but only to take ambition's place.'

'Oh, Will, what bitter words you find to say, and how they echo in my heart.'

'I do not mean them bitterly, my lord.'

'At least I knew ambition's face, but only God can see the face of conscience and know it as friend or foe.' He pondered this so deeply, with such sadness in his expression that I cast about for something to break the mood I had created. I asked what else the King had said at Woodstock, but it seemed that he had said nothing, shouting at walls and kicking at tables, allowing the famous rage to carry him away from all reason. Purple in the face, he had screamed at Thomas to be gone. As the Archbishop left the room, two terrified barons rushed into it, and were met head-on by a heavy silver candlestick which all but killed one of them.

So, to the sound of shouting and the smashing of furniture, my lord walked away from his King. They would not speak together again in private for nearly three years.

Upon Thomas's return from Tours in June, King Henry had probably planned that the Prince would be crowned towards the end of July and that the Archbishop's death, however he foresaw it, would occur on or near the third of the year's great pagan festivals, the Gule of August, first day of the month. Failing this, he was left with the last of the sacred days, 1 November, which the Christians celebrate as All Hallows.

After their final argument at Woodstock on 6 July he must have known that he could achieve nothing by August, but his actions seem to indicate that he still had hopes for November. If he could not persuade the Archbishop by then, he had lost the power of the sacred year; words having proved useless, he now resorted to more forceful methods, hoping to show Thomas that without the King's support he was in any case doomed to fail as high prelate of England, and might therefore bow to an inevitable fate. There can be little other explanation for his convening, on 1 October a full Council of lords and bishops at Westminster.

The ostensible purpose of this meeting, that of settling the primacy between Canterbury and York, shows that from the start he wished to make Thomas feel insecure. As things turned out, however, the King was unable to withhold his true feelings, breaking into this dull and purely ecclesiastical discussion with a passionate outcry against his old vexation, the courts of the church.

He again demanded the delivery of clerks into his own courts at the time of their arrest, and not, if some bishop willed it so, after the church had made a prior judgement.

Thomas was careful to let other bishops answer, which they did with spirit, claiming that only a clerk already judged by them might, at his second offence, be handed over to the King's court.

Henry's temper had been mounting throughout the whole meeting, largely, I think, because Thomas had spoken hardly a word. Now he leapt to his feet, demanding a categorical answer: would all his bishops undertake there and then to observe the royal customs of his ancestors?

At this Thomas also stood up, speaking for all the bishops: 'We will observe the royal customs as Your Majesty demands, but saving the dignity of our order.'

Henry shouted, 'Is that a plain yes?'

'No, my lord, it is not.'

At this the King's rage overcame him, and he dismissed the Council, striding from the hall without even asking for the usual blessing. Then, of course, many of the bishops became alarmed and some even followed him to ask his pardon, saying that they would have agreed with him if the Archbishop had not commanded them to show a solid front.

During that night I think King Henry finally realized that Thomas did not intend to be intimidated, and that the heir was never going to be crowned during the sacred year, as he had planned. It must indeed be hard for any king to admit such a defeat, let alone a king as determined and as impatient as Henry II of England.

Next day he again summoned Thomas, who found him surrounded by barons and those bishops who had always opposed their primate – Gilbert Foliot, needless to say, foremost among them.

Henry said, 'My lord Archbishop, we do not think the manor of Eye nor the castle of Berkhamsted to be a part of Canterbury's domain.'

'No, your grace; they were mine when I was Chancellor.'

'You are no longer Chancellor; you will surrender these holdings to the Crown.'

'As your grace commands.'

'Also, we no longer consider it befitting that our son and heir, Henry, and his bride, Marguerite, be kept in the tutelage of Canterbury where, it seems, they may learn much that is not suitable. You will send them to the royal palace of Westminster into the keeping of the Queen.'

Thomas did not reveal by so much as the flicker of an eyelid how deeply this last demand hurt him, for he loved both children and they loved him; indeed his household was the only constant home they had ever known. As for Eye and Berkhamsted, the loss of their revenues was a crippling one.

I was alone with him at Canterbury some weeks later when the news came to him that Henry had summoned his Christmas court to be held at Berkhamsted castle, the Queen and their children attending him.

Thomas turned bleak eyes to the bleak winter sky and said, 'How fortunate that I wear a smaller size in boots than does the King.' He sighed and added, 'What next, Will?'

5

What came next, as any chronicle will tell, was the meeting at Clarendon, the King's hunting-lodge in Wiltshire. It would be wearying indeed to repeat all that occurred here, for it has been feasted upon by every man within the Christian church who can hold a pen. To give Henry his due, this council was truly a political one, summoned in all good faith so that the King might try to settle once and for all, not only the vexed matter of the courts but also the entire behaviour of the Christian church in England.

I can only assume that he was, at worst, suffering a fit of temporary madness or, at best, advised by idiots; for what king could ever control a powerful body which is itself ruled from outside his kingdom by another man altogether, in this case the Pope?

There was a great deal of wearisome talk, culminating in that ill-advised document known as the Constitutions of Clarendon. This was a purely Christian matter; since he was a Cathar, it was of little interest to Thomas personally, and if there had not been such serious repercussions, the sight of a 'pagan' king and an 'heretical' archbishop confronting each other on Christian matters would certainly have been ironical.

Though the King never missed an opportunity to ignore or to insult Thomas, Clarendon was not, like Northampton later in the year, a personal attack upon the man. Indeed Northampton might never have taken place if Clarendon had not brought forth its monstrous document; the Archbishop was weary of the talk and of a mind to agree with the King, until he actually *read* the Constitutions, when all his lawyer's training, as well as his commonsense, rebelled. 'Heretic' or not, he was certainly not going to involve the Christian church in England, of which he was willy-nilly the head, in so much out-of-date nonsense.

'So,' he said, waving the document, 'we are being asked to abandon all the work of the Gregorian reformers and go back fifty years to the days of the first Henry. If time is to be reversed, let us at least return to Roman Law, which was not only better written but more sensible. I will never, while I have breath, assent to these articles.'

He then bowed low to the King and swept out of the hall, those bishops with enough courage or conviction following him. News of this fiasco travelled swiftly across all Europe, and Thomas, to his own wry amusement and to the King's rage, was proclaimed a champion of the Christian church.

If there was anything that my lord's neat mind could not bear it was a muddle. He determined to go at once in person to the Pope and to explain the whole situation. Alexander was at that time at

Sens, not far from Paris, so that a short journey and a short conversation would unravel more swiftly than a multiplicity of letters the reasons why Thomas had been prepared to accept verbally what he refused to accept in writing. He also wanted to beg the Pope's pardon for having at any time agreed to anything which had occurred at Clarendon. 'For you see, Will,' he said, 'I begin to think the King was prescient when he accused me of seeking refuge behind the skirts of the Christian church; if things continue as they are, we may be forced to do exactly that. Let us therefore be sure that the Christian church is willing to protect us.'

In the event he was apprehended as we were about to take ship at Sandwich, and Article Four of the Constitution was read to him: 'It is not lawful for archbishop, bishop or beneficed clergy to depart from the kingdom without the lord King's leave.'

Thomas laughed in the faces of the barons who had been sent to stop him, though in truth the absurdity of it all brought him nearer to tears. He rode directly to the King, who was again at Woodstock. Henry received him before the court, Queen Eleanor also being present, and greeted him with the words, 'So now, my lord Archbishop, you find this country too small for both of us!'

Thomas replied, 'I find the public arguments between us not only foment unnecessary bitterness in England, but make us look ridiculous before all Europe and demean the realm in men's eyes.'

'If so, it is you who demean it, my lord Archbishop.'

At this there were shouts of agreement from those around the King, and certain voices called out for Thomas's resignation. Thomas, recognizing more than one of these, shouted back, 'When the King desires my resignation he will command it, with due deference to the Pope. Meantime I hardly think he needs the advice of turncoat knights who should by rights be serving the King of France, and bishops who owe their elevation to me in any case. As for the Constitutions of Clarendon, they are for the most part gibberish, and Pope Alexander will doubtless reject half of them.'

In this he judged Alexander correctly, for within a few weeks he returned the Constitutions to the King, accepting six of them and condemning the other ten out of hand. Henry allowed himself the luxury of one of his most famous rages and took to his bed for several days. Upon his recovering he began to make plans.

There was now an ominous lull. The spring of 1164 gave way to a fair summer, during which a constant stream of churchmen moved to and from Canterbury like ants to and from an ant-hill. All pleaded with Thomas to accept the King's demands upon whatever terms he wished, for the good of the whole church which was already cleft by the argument. They could rely on the Pope, they said, if Henry's demands became too impossible.

Thomas understood better than they did that Pope Alexander's position was as difficult as their own; without the goodwill of the King of England he would find himself, at that very moment, a Pope without power; so my lord listened to the pleading of his bishops and kept his own counsel.

The most unexpected of that summer's visitors was Queen Eleanor herself; she appeared with a full retinue, which meant that she had publicly come to Canterbury against the King's wishes and did not care who recognized the fact. She was on her way back to Angers where she now acted as Regent, a situation which well suited her if her appearance was anything to go by; she seemed to have been caught in a past moment of time and held there, so that only small details, a light line upon the hand or under the eye, revealed that she did indeed grow older like the rest of us.

After she had attended Mass, we withdrew to the Archbishop's private apartments and she said, 'Thomas, you are not famous for taking advice, but you would do well to take mine.'

He bowed, smiling. 'I think this is the first time your grace has ever used my name.'

'Perhaps because for the first time I find I like you enough to do so. Don't mistake me, I have always admired you and respected your talents. Liking is different.'

'So different that I must be bold enough to ask what caused the change?'

'Everything you have done since you became Archbishop.'

'It seems to me,' said Thomas, 'that I have *done* very little.'

'Which cannot have been easy for a man of your temper. Sharing your temper somewhat, I find that I might have learned much from you regarding my marriage. Be that as it may, I know from experience that you are not a man who evades situations by removing himself from them.'

'I sometimes wish I were.'

Eyeing him evenly, she said, 'Yes, I admit to finding Angers congenial. I am spared the royal rages and, worse, the repentance which follows them, and I am spared the boredom of having to look the other way in order not to notice the royal infidelities. More importantly Angers is not far from Poitou; I make plans to my heart's content.'

Eyeing her as evenly, Thomas said, 'You once begged me not to abandon the King because he needed me . . .'

'And, by God, time has proved me right!'

'He needs you also, my lady.'

'I am useful, as you were. And the Empire would find another son convenient. As for my husband, he has become a boor and a bore. If our business together were completed to the satisfaction of my interests, I would abandon him tomorrow.'

'Should your grace be telling me this?'

'Yes, because how shall I make you see, otherwise, that the time is past for your loyalty or love towards the King. He will never forgive you for not having crowned his son during the sacred year, just as I will never cease to thank you for the sake of *my* son, Richard.'

Thomas moved away; then turned back to her, spreading his hands. 'I am honoured by your grace's concern, and I take your warning to heart; but I have a duty here at Canterbury.'

'You will be forced to desert it.'

'That will become a different matter.'

'If you're not killed first.'

'That too will be a different matter.'

She turned to me. 'Does he always consider that he knows best?'

'Always, your grace.'

Thomas laughed, and she wheeled back upon him almost in anger. 'Believe me, I am not playing with words. The King means to destroy you.'

'He will find I am not easy to destroy.'

She eyed him in silence for a moment; then sighed. 'There is a point at which the values of men, loyalty, courage, all of them, become no more than the stubborn stupidity of a jackass.'

'And I have reached that point, my lady?'

'You are upon the point of reaching that point, my lord.'

If Thomas had been a different man he would have taken the Queen's advice, made his escape from England in spite of royal decree, and gone at once to the safety of the papal court; but he continued to preside calmly over Canterbury until, by October, the King had prepared his trap.

The charge against my lord is not worth describing in detail. It was a false charge, unworthy of King Henry II, based upon a fiddling piece of legal procedure by which Thomas was supposed to have 'unjustly delayed' a case brought forward by a certain John the Marshal. Since this individual was a baron and a member of the staff of the Exchequer, he doubtless considered it an honour to perjure himself for the King.

Thomas denied the charge and refused to answer the royal summons. The King thereupon demanded that he appear at Northampton before the Council on a further charge of feudal disobedience and contempt of the original summons. We therefore made our way to Northampton and lodged in the Cluniac priory of St Andrew. The King had found good hawking on his way north, and had paused to enjoy it; John the Marshal had found some business to attend to in London. The meeting thus began in confusion next day, the King having overslept and the Council being in disarray. It was, however, swift to dismiss Thomas's plea; he was found guilty as charged and fined five hundred pounds. Certain loyal bishops stood surety for this great sum, but no one would come forward to serve the sentence upon the Archbishop who was waiting in an outer room. Finally the Bishop of Winchester, that same good old man who had himself consecrated Thomas, told him of the judgement.

'So,' said my lord, to those of us who attended him, raising his voice that it might also be heard within, 'here we can see the King's "customs" as proposed at Clarendon. Mark well, my lord bishops in particular, that it was never the "custom" of any of the King's forebears to judge an Archbishop in their courts, they had more respect. I think our lord King already invents laws to please his humour of the moment. You will draw your own conclusions from that!'

Henry, hearing this from the other chamber, was furiously angry but contained himself, secure in the knowledge of what was yet to come.

Thomas now rose and went into the Council. The King then charged him with a further fine of three hundred pounds for revenues received from Eye and Berkhamsted at the time they had belonged to him.

Thomas said, 'As your grace knows, this money was spent in the royal service when I was your Chancellor. Also I am here to be judged concerning the matter of John the Marshal. Or,' he added, perhaps unwisely for he was angry, 'have the King's lawyers no case prepared on that account?'

Henry ignored this, and demanded the money. Again Thomas found men, barons this time, to stand surety.

The King then said, 'Do you then admit all these charges in good faith?'

'No,' said Thomas, 'I deny them, but bow to the majesty of your court . . .' He did so, making obeisance to the somewhat disconcerted assembly; and added, '. . . saving the dignity of my order.'

As you may imagine, that ended the first day's hearing. My lord was immediately surrounded by bishops urging him to moderation. I must say that I agreed with them. Who was at that time urging the King, and to what, I cannot say, but the following morning he dropped all pretence of a legal proceeding and set out systematically to ruin the man whom he had once called friend. He demanded huge sums as return upon two loans, one concerning his own ill-fated campaign against Toulouse, the other for 'various private enterprises' which Thomas was supposed to have undertaken at his own expense while Chancellor. Above and beyond these, he called for a full accounting for all the money which Thomas had received from vacant benefices and sees, and which he had used on the King's own behalf.

Thomas replied, 'My lord, you may remember that you personally granted me a formal discharge for all these moneys upon my agreeing to become Archbishop.'

Henry, cold as iron, said, 'A discharge for the moneys, yes; for the accounting of them, no.'

Of course it was quite impossible for any man to do what he was demanding. The demons of Angevin legend had utterly possessed him; we were witnessing the most prolonged as well as the most unreasonable of all his famous rages. Thomas, recognizing this, requested time to take counsel. The King agreed. And so, legally not owning a penny in the world, and not knowing what further impossible demands might be made of him, the Archbishop returned to the priory of St Andrew with his bishops. It was now understood by all that the King's purpose was a personal attack upon Thomas; yet, ironically, none knew the true meaning of the attack, for none knew of what had passed between Thomas and Henry regarding the Prince's coronation and the ritual death which was to have followed. This meant that all the argument which now ensued was based upon a cluster of false premises, and could help the Archbishop not at all.

On the following day, a Sunday, no meeting was called. My lord awoke with a fever; he wanted to join the bishops, who were once again locked in furious debate, but I prevailed upon him to keep to his bed, where he passed a whole twenty-four hours in sleep. For months now he had been under severe pressure and anxiety, though he was adept at hiding it as he hid other emotions, and I feared that he would be in no condition to face the King's rage for many days to come.

Yet on the Monday afternoon he awoke, saying that he felt refreshed; the fever had left him. He said, 'Will, this is the second turning-point of my life; the first was in that freezing barn when I pledged my life to Henry. Now I am in a cleft stick; I will not resign, for by doing so I admit that I am in error and hand myself upon a plate to the King's judgement, but I cannot fight his charges in law, for they are fantasies, and no law governs them. Besides, it would be contrary to all the principles I hold in our faith, and I think the King knows this and plays upon it.'

'What then, my lord?'

He rose from his bed, unsteady on his feet at first, and put on a robe. Then he said, 'I am in need of the Spiritus. Leave me, and let none disturb me.'

He prayed for five hours, and when he arose seemed like a new man, saying, 'All will be well. I know my course.' Then he drank a little broth, and fell once more into a deep slumber.

Next morning he was once again besieged by his bishops all clamouring like parrots; they had spoken with the King's counsellors, and now knew that if Thomas did not submit and resign his office, Henry intended to charge him with disloyalty and perjury. Thomas ignored them, and took me aside, saying, 'Stand close to me, Will, for the game we must now play is the most dangerous of all.'

I asked him what he meant, and he replied, 'The King leaves me nothing; I am stripped of all worldly power and goods, so now I must make use of whatever spiritual power I may possess, and I do not know what this may be.' Typically, he even managed to find a brief smile of self-mockery; 'A good time for testing, eh? We shall see whether I have been prating and pretending all my life, or whether I am truly strong in our faith. And since I'm head of the Christian church in England, let us try the power of that faith too. The King accused me of it many weeks ago; now I will follow his suggestion.'

He sent for his crossbearer, a man from Wales named Alexander. From him he took the heavy primatial cross and examined it closely as if for the first time. As I have said, we Cathars do not like this symbol of torture and death, and I could see that my lord was in some way forcing himself to accept it without repulsion, knowing its meaning for, and power over, most of the barons surrounding the King. At length he said, 'Well, it has a good weight, and would counter a sword-thrust.' He gave it back to the Welshman, who bore it before him into the church where, most of his bishops attending him, he celebrated Mass. I noticed that there were two others present who would recognize the Cathar meaning of its words at this moment of crisis, and was comforted by their presence.

Now, the Archbishop still wearing the stole under his heavy cloak, we took horse for the castle. The people of Northampton, knowing of the struggle between King and Archbishop, pressed around to receive his blessing; some of them no doubt expected to have a Christian martyr on their hands before the end of the day, and a few probably even looked forward to the eventuality, since martyrs are always good for business. Thus we came to the bailey of the castle. As we rode through, the gates were closed behind us; I did not like the sound of that clang.

Thomas dismounted calmly, as if unaware of the crowd watching him, as if unaware that the majority of them expected him to meet that day either a sentence of imprisonment for life, or death at the hands of the King's men. With the latter in mind, he refused to let Alexander bear the cross any further, but took it and carried it himself into the castle.

There is, at Northampton, a lower hall with a small room leading off it, where the Council had held their first hearings; above this is a larger hall, and the King had retired thither with his lords upon the Archbishop's arrival. Thomas now took up position in the small room below, attended by a few of his household, myself among them, while his bishops milled to and fro in the hall next door, bleating like sheep. The Archbishop of York and Gilbert Foliot were forced, greatly to their embarrassment, to pass within a few feet of Thomas on their way to join the King's party upstairs; what followed was of necessity punctuated by much scurrying up and down these same stairs, which were both too steep and too narrow for the purpose.

Henry had reverted to the matter of the Chancellor's accounts which, one would have thought, had been settled some days before. Thomas replied wearily, 'The King admits that he absolved me from all my Chancellor's debts; let us, for the sake of reason, since we shall none of us live forever, say that I destroyed all my accounts at that time. Alternatively give the King a stone and see if he can wring water from it.'

More running up and downstairs; then a somewhat bewildered lull from above; finally, setting the cat well and truly among the pigeons, a demand from the King that the bishops should now join the lords in order to sentence their Archbishop.

There was such a sound of renewed bleating from the lower hall that none, I think, could hear themselves thinking. Meanwhile, from above the voices of the King's party were rising higher and higher in anger against the confusion and indecision below.

Thomas sat apart in the small room, withdrawn, apparently lost in thought, his very stillness seeming to accuse his bishops of whatever they most feared in their own minds.

Now, as I had long ago foreseen, Gilbert Foliot came forward with a typically slippery suggestion. 'Let us,' he said, 'tell the King that if he will excuse us from pronouncing judgement on our Archbishop, we will appeal to the Pope ourselves, every one of us, accusing Thomas Becket of forcing us to be disloyal to King Henry against our wills, and begging the Pope to depose him.'

Most of the drowning bishops grasped at this straw. There was another journey up the stairs. Silence. Then the King spoke, and there was a gust of cheering from the barons. Henry had accepted Foliot's plan, which, I have heard it said and can well believe, was cooked up by the two of them during the time of Thomas's illness. The bishops, having betrayed their lord, were excused further part in the proceedings; they huddled together in the lower hall, some, it was clear from their faces, already regretting what they had agreed to in the cause of expediency.

The verdict was now being considered upstairs, accompanied by much shouting and stamping and repeated cries of 'Traitor!'

We heard later that the Archbishop was condemned on all counts and sentenced to imprisonment for life, but the deputation which came jostling down that wretched staircase, tripping over each other's cloaks, seemed ill-prepared to announce this sentence. Eventually the good Earl of Leicester, looking thoroughly ill-at-ease, cleared his throat and embarked upon a full account of the whole affair, beginning with the Archbishop's seizure of Rochester castle some eighteen months previously.

Long before he came anywhere near to the point, Thomas stirred and rose slowly to his feet. 'My lord,' he said, with a sigh, 'you are a layman, you cannot pass judgement upon me.' Leicester looked around helplessly, and the Earl of Cornwall took up the tale. He had not spoken more than half a sentence before Thomas moved his primatial cross and put it down firmly but gently between the two of them. My lord of Cornwall fell silent, gawping, then squared his shoulders and took a breath; then thought better of it and stepped back, crossing himself as he did so.

Hilary of Chichester was always equal to any occasion, and he now began to pronounce the finding of the court in his nasal and irritating voice. Thomas shook his head pityingly, and walked directly past him, out into the main hall and towards the door.

Now some of the King's men had come quietly down the staircase during all this, and others, hearing them shout, came tumbling down it more swiftly; all began to bellow, 'Justice!' and 'Traitor!', drawing their swords.

Thomas wheeled around on them, cross raised, and the floor about him cleared as if covered with cockroaches. Some were still shouting, but many more had fallen silent. Thomas said quietly to Alexander the Welshman, 'Go forward quickly. See that the gate is open!' and, as the man moved to obey, he pitched his voice more loudly so that there should be no chance of it not reaching the King in the upper chamber: 'I appeal to the Pope, I appeal to the power of the Christian church; and all you who have betrayed me here, whether bishops or barons or plain pig-farmers which I think you more likely to be, remember that I am still Canterbury, and can lay upon each and every one of you the hand of eternal damnation so that you burn in everlasting hell until the end of time.'

Then he swung around, the heavy cross scattering some who stood too near him, and before any of them had regained their voices we were out of the room.

Our horses were in the courtyard where brawling of some sort had also broken out; under cover of this the Welshman had managed to unlock the gate, and thus, incredibly, we all rode out from Northampton castle in freedom, scattering curious townsfolk as if we were soldiers and not men of God.

Reaching St Andrew's priory, Thomas immediately sent three loyal bishops to the King, begging leave for him to depart at once. Henry answered that he would think about it and give a decision in the morning.

Thomas was exhausted by the strain of that long day, for, whatever he may have said and however strong he may have felt spiritually, the fever still ailed him. He lay upon his bed and beckoned me to come close. 'Tonight,' he said, 'see that a bed is prepared for me in the church, behind the altar, as it was last Friday when I kept vigil. In the meantime I will speak to the Prior and ask him

for two strong men from among his lay brothers, adept swords-
men if he has any. After midnight, when you judge all things
quiet, come to me in the church; we will ride all night and all
tomorrow if necessary. Go now; see that our horses are fed and
rested.'

Before I reached the door, he added, 'William?' I turned to find
him smiling. 'In future time, you will never be able to say that
life in my service lacked interest. Or contrast.'

6

That evening a wind arose and grew quickly stronger, so that by
10 o'clock a wild October gale was beating upon Northampton,
bringing with it violent rainstorms. It was not a night that many
would choose to be abroad. Moreover such weather is abhorrent to
soldiers, since it causes great harm to swords and coats of mail alike.

A little after midnight I went to Thomas in the church and
found him ready to leave. The Prior had chosen as our escort two
strapping young men, Brother John and Brother Edward of the
Gilbertine Order who, I think, were perfectly content to leave
their humdrum existence enclosed within the priory and accompany
us on this perilous venture.

Knowing that the news of his disappearance would bring immediate pursuit, and that this would naturally turn south towards
London and Canterbury, Thomas rode north. Wind and rain were
making so much noise in the streets that none, I think, even noticed
our passing, and there was so much water overflowing the gutters
that it carpeted the cobbles against our horses' hooves. Someone
connected with the priory had a relative who kept the North Gate,
and we found it conveniently unbarred.

The ride which followed was indeed most uncomfortable, and in
more than one place the horses were into water up to their bellies,
but my lord's escape from what might easily have turned out to
be incarceration in Northampton castle, followed by the protection
of this storm, seemed to all of us God-given, and we in turn offered
our thanks for it. We rode forty miles that night, reaching the town
of Grantham a little before dawn. There was an inn, conveniently

upon the outskirts of the place, where a yawning and unwilling landlord found us something to eat and drink.

We left within the hour, before Grantham was properly awake, and continued northwards, the weather proving only a little less inhospitable by day than it had by night; but we did not complain, because the result was that there were few travellers upon the road, and those that we passed were intent upon their warm and dry destinations and showed no interest in us. Thus we rode another forty miles and reached the city of Lincoln.

Providentially, the sister of one of our Gilbertine companions, Edward, lived here; her husband worked in the cloth industry as a fuller, and the two good people opened their humble house to us without question. It was not of a size to accommodate four large men, and in any case the presence of so many strangers in one place could only have excited interest and speculation. Thomas stayed there, hidden, spending the best part of two days in sleep, while Edward, known by all in the neighbourhood as a relative, guarded him. John and I found a nearby tavern, and we all rested well.

Many stories have been invented over the years concerning my lord's journey south from Lincoln, and many monasteries have claimed, at a safely later date, that they gave him sanctuary. The truth is that word of what had passed at Northampton had travelled quickly from Christian foundation to foundation, and though there were a few willing to hide us, many more had been ordered by their bishops to betray the Archbishop the moment they saw his face. Meanwhile the King had commanded all ports to be watched and no man allowed to leave England unless he bore a royal permit; certain stretches of coast were even said to be patrolled, particularly in the south.

'Yet,' said Thomas, 'it is southward that we must go, for only in our own lands around Canterbury can we rely absolutely upon friends who will help us.'

This was true; and so we journeyed inland again, travelling to and fro across England, and never taking any of the roads which led directly south. Whether we went by day or night, we depended on the information of friends and Brethren; sometimes a valley would prove safe; sometimes we would take to the ancient upland paths; sometimes we would hide for a day. And so at last we came to Kent, to the manor of one whom I will call 'Ranulf', not a Christian, who hid us safely and proposed a plan for our escape.

As the day to start upon this dangerous venture, we chose I November, last of the year's pagan festivals, the very day, ironically, upon which King Henry had hoped that Thomas would, one year earlier, die for the people and Prince Henry's power over them. At dawn of this day we rode the seventeen miles from Ranulf's house to Eastry on the isle of Thanet. Here another friend, a good Christian man, hid us until it was dark. Then we made our way to a small cove in the lee of the North Foreland, habitual anchorage of fishing-boats. The early evening of winter had brought with it a light mist which aided us in reaching the boats and in boarding the one which Ranulf had long since chartered from a certain fisherman who had known Thomas's generosity in the past. We set sail at once, and the coast of England was lost to sight within a few minutes.

For that time of year the crossing was reasonably calm, due, we were told, to the fog which blanketed half the Channel. On the other side all was clear, and we landed by brilliant moonlight near Gravelines on the coast of Flanders.

Thus, on the Christian day of All Souls, 2 November 1164, began Thomas's long exile. He would not return to Canterbury, the eyes of all the world upon him, until the year 1170, ten times the sacred seven since King William Rufus had given himself to the arrow under the oak-tree as the Divine Victim.

Part three

I will fight you, Thomas, you leave me no
alternative; I will fight you to Rome and back, to
Hell and back, I know not where. And I shall win.

King Henry II, March 1166

Thomas of London had entered the household of Theobald at Canterbury in the year 1143, a young man of twenty-five. He had worked hard, made himself indispensable to the Archbishop, travelled with him far and wide, and been educated by him in learning as well as in life.

Eleven years later, in 1154, he became the King's Chancellor at the age of thirty-six. He had worked so closely with Henry, lived so closely to him, and acted for him so often in his absence, that one might almost say that he had known what it was to wear a crown. His return to Canterbury as its lord, though brief, had added greatly to what he had already learned of the Christian church, both in strength and weakness.

On 2 November 1164, when we landed on that bleak bare shore in Flanders, backed by a bleak waste of salt-marshes, he was indeed penniless and an exile, but he possessed knowledge and he possessed the experience to use it.

Firstly, though he never deviated from our true faith, and constantly renewed himself through it, he knew, as did all we Brethren, that its worldly power was nothing, except insofar as this or that powerful man might also adhere to it and so give assistance in secret, behind the world's back. Real spiritual power rested in the Pope, and if the Papacy had not been split at this time, if the Pope had sat secure upon St Peter's throne in Rome, things might indeed have been resolved more swiftly for my lord.

Alas, it was not so. As I have described, Alexander III held his position by the good graces of the Kings of France and England; he dared not anger Henry Plantagenet, and could order him only at his own risk and only then upon the safest ground. Indeed the antagonism between Henry and Thomas must have tried his patience and diplomacy to its utmost limit, and it is a certain sign of his great wisdom and courage that he was able to rule the situation in any way.

When Thomas had shouted at Northampton, chiefly for Henry's

hearing, 'I appeal to the Pope, I appeal to the power of the Christian church,' it was the word 'power' which mattered to both of them, for both knew that Thomas had no other.

The fact that these words were to send all the writers of history scurrying away in the wrong direction may also have been part of my lord's intention; for now more than ever he needed to be two men, the one a public figure, maligned and exiled Archbishop crying for justice, the other a secret shadow, a 'heretic' who must work out his own destiny in deference to his own true faith.

Proof of how well he succeeded in this double life can be summed up in one important incident. All the historians state that he did not meet Henry face to face until the year 1169 at Montmirail, but in fact, as I well know for I was present, they met a full three years prior to that, in 1166, and under extraordinary circumstances.

Let us then leave the history-writers to their history-making, which tends, at this time, to become a tedious and often inaccurate catalogue of appeal and counter-appeal – from the Pope to Thomas, from the King of England to the Pope, from the King of France to Thomas, from the Pope to the Kings of France and England, and from Thomas (or at least from his offices, directed by that prince of verbosity, Herbert of Bosham) to the Pope, both Kings and half Europe as well.

Let us also leave aside the legends: of how, when Thomas landed in Flanders, his delicate feet could not walk upon the rough ground, and of how we must needs find him a nag : of how a knight recognized him because he turned a knowing eye upon the man's hawk. Etcetera. *Ad nauseam.* Do they forget that my lord had been upon the hard road of escape for a full seven weeks, that he had once been a soldier and had never been a fool?

Let us to the root of the matter and its truths.

Upon landing we made our way carefully and on foot to an abbey near St Omer; four lay brothers travelling afoot or on horse were no unusual sight, and upon that same day we covered the fifteen miles from the coast without incident. On arrival, however, we found that King Henry's envoys, also hastening towards the Pope, were there before us. Alexander was at that time in residence at

Sens, southwards between Paris and Auxerre, where Thomas and I had studied and where this story began.

It will surprise none of my readers to learn that the King's embassy was headed by none other than Gilbert Foliot, Bishop of London, accompanied by Thomas's next most virulent enemy, Roger, Archbishop of York, by Hilary of Chichester, two other bishops and certain barons, chief among them my lord of Arundel.

We hid for a day in the marshes until this august assembly had ridden south, then made ourselves known.

It was indeed pleasant, after what we had been through since leaving Northampton, to rest for two days at St Omer knowing that we were not pursued, and my lord recovered greatly both in spirits and in health. We set forth from the abbey under conditions somewhat different from those of our arrival, bathed, freshly clothed, and escorted by the Abbot of St Bertin and the Bishop of Thérouanne, and thus arrived at Soissons some thirty miles from Paris. Next day, King Louis of France himself arrived at that city to welcome Thomas to his domains. Always a godly man, he showed the Archbishop great respect; of course, one would have to be simple in the extreme not to understand that the French King derived a great deal of sly pleasure in thus welcoming the man who had become chief enemy of the King of England, from whom he had suffered many insults. I should also add that in the course of time King Louis, no less than Pope Alexander, was to have his patience tried to its extreme by Thomas's presence on French soil and by his obstinacy of purpose; but the King, like the Pope, stayed always loyal. I cannot praise him enough.

With royal approval our state was once again improved, so that when the Archbishop of Canterbury rode from Soissons to Sens he was attended by a full retinue of bishops and clerks and was escorted by the King's own men. As we passed out of the city gates amid a cheering populace, for any enemy of the King of England was a friend to any Frenchman, Thomas caught my eye with the ghost of a smile half-hidden somewhere within his own. I wondered if he was recalling his words to me at St Andrew's priory: 'You will never be able to say that life in my service lacked interest. Or contrast.'

At this same time, we learned later, King Henry's eager envoys were not enjoying the happiest of receptions at Sens. Of course it would be too much to hope that Gilbert Foliot would have the commonsense, let alone the intelligence, not to cloud the issue with his personal dislike of Thomas. His account of the proceedings at Northampton swiftly deteriorated into a personal attack upon his Archbishop, so that Alexander was compelled to hold up a hand, saying, 'Gently, brother!'

Foliot, who obviously knew nothing of the Pope's liking for his ex-pupil, said, 'Well then, I shall spare him,' to which Alexander replied, 'I was not thinking of him but of yourself; I find that you lack not only charity but grace. Pray continue.'

It seems that this mild reproof, coming from his spiritual over-lord, so confused the Bishop of London that he was unable to recollect his argument. As ever in any situation, Hilary of Chichester was immediately ready to stand forward. No doubt panting to impress the Pope, he left himself too little time for thought, and his attack upon Thomas ran almost immediately into one of the best-known traps set for us all by the Latin Language. He found himself trying to conjugate an impersonal verb, much to the merriment of the assembly, and his speech broke up in a gale of laughter and more than one shouted comment.

I dearly wish that I might have witnessed this discomfiture of two of my lord's enemies one after the other before that distinguished company, and their anger when it was left to the Earl of Arundel, who spoke in French, to set King Henry's wishes before the Pope, firstly insisting that the King had acted justly in all his dealings with his Archbishop, and then requesting him to give immediate judgement in the case.

Alexander replied, 'I can hardly give judgement upon a case of which I have heard only one side, and that one side not even presented in proper legal terms. I refuse.'

'In that case,' said Arundel, 'King Henry commands me to beg of you a special papal legate who shall come to England and try the Archbishop there in person.'

This displeased Alexander even more: 'Does King Henry in his great nobility deem the trial of his *Archbishop* to lie within the province of underlings?' Then, rising to his feet: 'Until the matter is properly presented, and until I have heard what Thomas Becket himself has to say, there will be no more discussion of this case.'

He left the hall, and the English envoys were requested to remain no longer than was necessary within the Curia. They returned immediately to England, to Marlborough, where King Henry had summoned his Christmas court of 1164. The weather was not clement towards their crossing, nor do I suppose that they were in any great hurry to meet the King face to face. I will tell in due course how they were received.

As soon as they had left Sens my lord entered the city. We were greeted with warmth and sympathy. It would have been well for Henry had Thomas been presenting the royal case against some other person, rather than defending himself. He deployed all his old brilliance, charm and diplomacy, and only I could discern a new dimension: the steely purpose behind the penitent exterior. He knew that if he was to 'use' the Christian church and its power as he intended, he must needs move with care and humility. To this end he now did what he had sought to do before, and would have done if the King's men had not stopped him taking ship; he confessed that he had shown lack of faith and courage at Clarendon in surrendering to the King on any points, and he asked the Pope to relieve him of Canterbury for he was not worthy of it.

Alexander replied, 'Regarding Clarendon, you were under great pressure from King Henry and surrounded by bishops who did not support you as their oaths and duties demanded. You only agreed verbally and, seeing your own mistake as soon as you read the documents, you refused to sign. I consider that verbal agreement to be null and void.'

His pronouncement was received with enthusiastic assent by the whole consistory.

'As for Canterbury, your actions have proved beyond doubt that you are truly worthy of it, and I disbar the claims against you of York and London. Henceforth the Archbishop of Canterbury shall be primate of all England; that is my command, and letters confirming it shall be sent forthwith to the King and to both Bishops.'

He added that Thomas should have his full support in all that was to come, though he told him later in private conversation that this support would necessarily be of varying value according to his own predicament at the time in question.

These first political moves being made, we now looked about us for some kindly roof to cover our heads. With the help of King Louis and Alexander, and by the great generosity of the abbot himself, we were welcomed at Pontigny, a Cistercian abbey some thirty miles from Sens and thirteen from Auxerre. It was a prosperous foundation and, with assistance from the King no doubt, our small party did not strain its resources even when we were later joined by others, some useful and loyal, some neither.

By this time the august embassy sent by Henry to appeal against Thomas before the Pope had reached Marlborough castle and was in the process of wrecking the King's Christmas court, which had begun in great good cheer due to the defeat of the Archbishop and his flight into exile. Once again I must admit how dearly I would like to have heard the words with which Gilbert Foliot, Roger of York, and the ever resilient Hilary of Chichester tried to convince the King that they had not made asses of themselves before the whole consistory. I would hazard a guess that Henry told them to cut the cackle and get down to facts. Had they persuaded His Holiness to condemn Thomas? No. Well then, had Alexander agreed to send a legate so that Thomas might be tried by a papal court upon English soil? Again, no.

I think it would have been the Earl of Arundel who spoke out straightforwardly, admitting to the King that not only had the embassy failed dismally at Sens (I hope he included an account of Hilary's Latin imbroglio), but that they had also failed to gain the support of the King of France against Thomas. Henry had ordered them to request that he turn the exiled Archbishop away and offer him no assistance of any kind. I am sure that it had given King Louis the utmost pleasure to refuse; moreover he had expressed righteous indignation and horror, saying, 'I can only hope that my royal brother of England is at this moment upon his knees, begging the forgiveness of God.'

Ah yes, I think King Louis extracted every ounce of enjoyment from *that* encounter! But alas, it was all to end, as do so many excellent jokes, in tragedy. On the day after Christmas the Angevin rage burst forth in its most insane fury. First of all he commanded that all Thomas's family, however distant the relationship, be banished from England and sent into exile. Men, women, children, babes in arms, were all told to seek out the Archbishop and prove to him by their misery what he had wrought in England. Some of these unhappy people naturally found means to evade such extremes, begging secret lodging with friends in a far part of the country, or taking refuge with kinsfolk in Normandy; but many, less fortunate, did literally arrive upon the steps of the abbey at Pontigny with their children and the few belongings they had been allowed to take with them. The sympathy and open-handed hospitality offered to them by the abbey and by the people of France showed not only a natural humanity and grace but also a general dislike of the English King. And it would be absurd to pretend, as Henry has since done, that this action and those that followed did not greatly harm his reputation in the eyes of all men. Queen Eleanor had indeed spoken the truth when she said that without Thomas to restrain him Henry's temper and character could not fail to lead him inexorably towards disaster.

Having dealt with Thomas's family, he now fell upon all his friends and servants of Canterbury; all, down to the lowest clerk, were turned out of their houses and lodgings and, with their entire families including brothers and sisters, nephews and nieces, and even grandchildren suffered the humiliation of having their persons and their possessions put to bail at the King's pleasure. Lastly Henry turned to the Archbishop's estates, dispersing them among various local landowners.

Between the King of England, in his full grandeur as lord of the great Empire, and the monk, Thomas, at Pontigny, clad in the white woollen cassock of the Cistercians, there now lay a wide chasm; so wide that it seemed impossible for any bridge ever to be thrown across it.

2

At Pontigny, within the fixed ritual of the Order, my lord once more regained some inner peace, strengthening himself through prayer and meditation. He ate sparingly and received the necessary disciplines, but there was nothing new in that, and all in all the spiritual side of his life changed less than any other.

Thomas the Archbishop showed himself at this time to be so uncompromisingly Christian that all whom he wished to deceive were unconditionally deceived. Meanwhile the Thomas who had once been Chancellor kept his clerks hard at work, pouring out that flood of correspondence which I have already mentioned. He fought his case against King Henry in every way that his agile brain could devise, though the ordering of this mountain of words he delegated to good and loyal Herbert of Bosham, who was naturally in his element. The secret Thomas, of whom I have also written, moved more covertly, more often than not after dark, and not, I may add, wearing a white cassock. He knew that there were certain aspects of what I suppose I must call his 'mystical' life of which I disapproved, as did many another of his friends, John of Salisbury in particular. Indeed John, as far back as 1159, in dedicating his book *Polycraticus* to Thomas had cautiously, for he was always cautious, criticized my lord's leaning towards the magic arts.

In any case, I only discovered this department of Thomas's activities by mistake, in the following manner.

One evening in February of the year 1165 I was working late with Herbert upon a letter to the Pope. It was important, and we planned for a messenger to ride with it to Sens as soon as it was finished and signed. There was a rule that only I was allowed to attend Thomas in his quarters, and that night I did not dream that he would be awake, it being nearly the first hour, but Herbert saw that there was still a light at his window, so I took the letter and went to him for his signature.

The room was empty, the taper, forgotten, burning low. I extinguished it and returned, telling Herbert that the Archbishop had fallen asleep over the Scriptures.

Of course my lord knew from my face, as soon as he saw it next morning, that something was amiss with me, but he let half the day pass before saying, 'I asked you not to disturb me last night.'

'The letter was urgent. I saw the light at your window.'

He nodded to himself. 'I grow careless.'

It was a full week before he referred to the matter again: 'Lest you should think worse things of me, William, attend me after midnight tomorrow. Wear a dark cloak and be prepared to ride.'

As soon as I joined him, I knew that the Abbot was aware of his nocturnal journeying, though not, I am very sure, of his destination. Indeed there was such a coming and going of messengers and agents since our arrival at Pontigny that, though none could doubt the sincerity with which my lord followed the Cistercian disciplines, equally none could doubt that the monk was also a warring Archbishop, and I think it was the wonder of all that he found the time and the energy to fulfil both functions.

On this night we were escorted by Brother John and Brother Edward, who had chosen to stay in Thomas's employ rather than go back to Northampton. We set off in the direction of Troyes, not taking the road but traversing heath and forest rides which, I noticed, my three companions evidently knew well. There had been a west wind that day bringing rain, and the night though chill enough was not freezing.

The countryside of that part is wild and inhospitable, a wilderness of rock breaking from tangles of bracken and bramble, where it is not swallowed up by the forest. Some five miles from Pontigny there is a river, running between high banks; we turned south, following its course along a maze-like path for a further mile. Often I had to lay my face against my horse's neck to avoid the lashing of willow branches, and I was not sorry when we finally came to a halt at the foot of a rocky hillock, larger than others we had passed and surrounded by trees, stark winter branches against a sky of moon and blowing cloud.

John and Edward took our mounts, while Thomas led me into the grove, loud with the noise of the swift river; the moon gave but a shifting radiance under the trees, yet Thomas moved surefooted and I, following, felt that we were upon a well-trodden path which surprised me in the midst of that deep wilderness. Then a light appeared ahead of us, wavering uncertainly. An owl cried close above, and swooped, pale and seeming huge, out into the darkness. Something about the place was obscurely restless and alive, and I do not mean merely the rush of water, the wind in the bare trees, the suddenly startling owl; I mean that I was in no way surprised to find that it was a magic place.

The light was held by a young country girl, silent, unsmiling. She turned, and we followed her into a cleft between two rocks. Thomas took my arm and guided me now, for there were rough steps leading downwards, and I was aware that the cleft had closed over my head becoming a cave. The lantern showed water rushing by immediately to the right of the steps, deep and swift and dark. Then, but for its continual noise, it was gone. Light became brighter, and I saw what I must say I had by now expected to see. At the side of the cave, in a kind of niche, sat a woman.

As we came nearer I noticed that she was not old, as I had also expected, perhaps no more than thirty, with a smooth untroubled face which I find it hard to describe. The features were not in themselves beautiful, yet they were composed to form a serenity which created its own beauty; also there was an absoluteness about her, such as you may see in the ancient figures of goddesses which are turned up by the plough or dug out of some old burial place from time to time. She seemed to grow from the earth, from the rock and the living water; her eyes, raised towards us, told me that she was blind.

Before her, in the floor of the cave, was an irregularly shaped pool, stirred no doubt by passing currents from the river outside. The woman lowered her eyes to this pool, and the water caused strange tricks of light upon her face. I hugged my cloak about me, for it was dankly cold. Neither the woman nor Thomas appeared to find it so. He indicated the rocky edge of the pool, and we both found places where we might sit. It was oddly comfortable, worn smooth by the endless action of the river which had once, it was clear, swirled through the cave, hollowing it out century after century.

The woman spoke suddenly in the rough peasant French of those parts, yet the tone was measured and thus easy to understand, as smooth as the water-worn rock or as her own face, and its authority was, I use the word again, absolute: 'Drink, my lords.'

She scooped up a little water with her hands, and we did likewise. It was icy cold and sweet, not river water, so that I now knew that a spring must well up here. I looked around and descried ancient marks and carved symbols upon the walls, so that I wondered for how many years – perhaps thousands? – this cave and this spring had been sacred.

After a time the woman spoke again: 'There is no peace,' she said. 'I have looked many times for peace since you last came, but there is none.'

'None?' Thomas queried her easily, as if in conversation with me.

'I see none.' She frowned. 'Years, perhaps many years. Dimly. Man is not made for peace, more's the pity.'

'One may change conditions,' Thomas said, almost pleading. 'Times change, men change, tempers change.'

'Everything changes, but what will be is there. That does not change. It is.'

Something in this made me shudder. All our hopes, our arguments, our prayers and our wars, did they in truth come to this? 'What will be is there. It is.'

Thomas leaned forward. 'Will I . . . Will he and I . . . meet?'

I think that until this moment I had no inkling of the bond, no, let me say of the shackles which chained my lord to his King. There was such anguish in his voice, such love, that I felt myself to be an interloper and wished that I was in my hard bed at the abbey. Thomas must have sensed this in me, for he put out a hand and rested it upon my arm in reassurance. To me he said, 'One cannot speak obliquely here, one cannot wear a mask. It serves no purpose. She sees.'

'Yes, I see.' She looked up at me. 'Do not fear. There is nothing to fear here.' And in answer to Thomas's question: 'Yes, you will meet.' Thomas gave a light gasp, and again leaned forward. She said, 'He will come here.'

'Here!' In astonishment his hand tightened upon my arm, hurting me with its grip. 'To this place? To you?'

She nodded. 'He will come, and then, hearing what I say, he may think of peace. I do not see it yet, but then he has not heard me yet.'

The grip on my arm had relaxed, I'm thankful to say. 'How shall I bring him here?'

'He will come. Not soon, but in the god's time.'

'He knows nothing of this place, nothing of you. How can he come?'

She gave a slow, strange smile. It was evident to me that her thoughts, if one may call them that, occurred in a reverse order to those of ordinary people. She knew with certainty that King Henry II of England would come to this cave hidden in a wilderness; how and why he would come were therefore not important; where there was an effect there would naturally be a cause, but it was not her concern. After consideration, no doubt wishing to accommodate our little practical minds, she said with sly mockery, 'Indeed what brings so great a king to kneel before a humble woman like me?'

I think in his impatience Thomas had been about to tell her, but the question had been rhetorical: 'All that interests the great is their greatness. So tell him this: the days of his greatness are already numbered. Tell him that there lives in Paris a woman who carries in her womb a male child but two months conceived. Tell him that this child will destroy his greatness.'

'The King!' I think that Thomas gasped out the thought without even knowing that he had done so.

'After more than twenty-five years of waiting, his third wife is to give him a son.' She looked up from the water, her sightless eyes fixed upon Thomas. 'Do you think *that* will bring him here, my lord?'

'By God it will!'

'By the gods,' she said, nodding to herself. 'I hope he likes what I shall tell him.' Thomas seemed to know that the meeting was at an end; he stood up, and I did likewise. As we turned to go, she added: 'Tell him also, your great lord, that the rose is sweet but others may bear its thorns.'

We both stared, not understanding. She said, 'You do not need to understand; neither will he until a little time has passed. Remember it, for it too will serve to bring him here: the rose is sweet but others may bear its thorns.' She leaned back, turning her face to the rock as if exhausted; and I thought then that so much knowledge, if indeed she possessed it, must lie heavy upon the soul.

We followed the girl with the lantern, who led us back to our companions. We rode to Pontigny in silence. I cannot say what thoughts occupied Thomas's mind, but I was filled with that sense of dread which these people always arouse in me.

When at last we stood alone together in the hall of the abbey,

I said, 'What can be achieved by such a meeting between you and Henry?'

'What can be achieved without such a meeting? And none can answer either question save the priestess.'

'Priestess? Is it then a temple?'

He nodded. 'And has been since before man's memory. To bed with your doubts, William; as good Cistercians we shall be awakened all too soon.'

Again I say it: mankind should not seek to look into his future; what good can be gained by it? Her voice haunts me to this day: 'Everything changes, but what will be is there. That does not change. It is.'

Next day Thomas himself wrote to the King, telling him what the woman of the cave had said concerning the heir who was at last to be born to King Louis of France and who would become a scourge to the Plantagenet, eventually destroying his greatness. He urged Henry to visit him in friendship and to go with him to see the woman who possessed knowledge of the King's future which she would divulge to no one else. At the end he quoted her strange words: 'The rose is sweet, but others may bear its thorns.'

He sent this letter by a loyal messenger, with instructions to deliver it into the King's own hand and no other, and to wait for an answer.

Meanwhile Pope Alexander had been trying different and more orthodox methods of bringing about a reconciliation and then a meeting between King and Archbishop. Unfortunately at this time Alexander's own position was made doubly insecure by Henry creating a union between himself and the Emperor Barbarossa; he contracted his daughter, Matilda, in marriage to the Duke of Saxony and Bavaria. It was a typical Plantagenet manoeuvre, forcibly reminding Pope Alexander that he might not always receive from the King of England that vital support which he so badly needed; for the Emperor, as I have written, patronized the anti-Pope Pascal, a scheming nonentity.

For this and other reasons Alexander judged it advisable to leave France and move closer to his true city of Rome, even though, upon arrival there, he could expect little but antagonism and controversy, and even open warfare. He left Sens in the autumn of 1165, and though we wished him heartfelt Godspeed and success, we were faced by the hard fact that it must now take a good four weeks, rather than an hour, for our news to reach him, and, after he had considered his answer, another four weeks for his reply to come back to us. To his everlasting credit, he never lost interest in our fortunes, even when personally harassed on all sides, and never failed to support us when it was diplomatically possible for him to do so.

Thomas's messenger found the King preparing to lead an army into Wales to assert his royal dominion over the ever-troublesome lords of that country; he had paused at Worcester to watch his justices and sheriffs at their work – for whatever other troubles he might have, and however we in our exile might hate him, and with good cause, none can ever deny that he was a lion among kings, ever watchful of his laws and quick to act against anyone in power who might seek to evade or alter them. Thus, though he spent but little time in England, measured by days, his spirit was always there in the law. It was not our law, and for this we were in exile, but in my loyalty to Thomas and in my personal dislike of Henry, I must not forget the great good that this most intelligent of rulers wrought for England.

His reply to Thomas's letter was short and sour. Firstly he had no wish to meet his Archbishop, who was a renegade, a traitor, and, as Thomas would know better than any other, a hypocrite; this last of course referring to the fact that my lord was behaving like a Christian when he was not one, in order to further his own ends. He added, 'I think it unlikely, in spite of your latest discovery in soothsayers, that King Louis, at his ripe age and after so many years of trying, will ever produce an heir. If by some miracle he should do so, you will excuse me, as a man of thirty-three, if I do not tremble before the might of a babe-in-arms.' He ended by saying that the tag, 'The rose is sweet but others may bear its thorns,' was hardly worthy of 'a gipsy at a fair'.

I had not understood how much hope Thomas had placed upon his letter until I saw how cast down he was by the King's reply. As I have often said, my belief in such things is not his, but I felt bound in pity to remind him that although the woman had said that Henry would come, she had added that his coming would not be soon. My words were of little comfort, particularly when a few weeks later we heard that Henry had left his army in Wales and was journeying to Angers to spend the Easter court with Queen Eleanor.

It seemed to Thomas but a short ride, by the King's standards, from his ancestral city to Pontigny, but Henry did not take it, returning to his affairs in England after a short stay with the Queen. Eleanor was rumoured to be once again with child, a condition evidently achieved in spite of their mutual disagreements, about which the world at large was beginning to comment.

Three months later, in August of that year 1165, on the day known to Christians as the octave of the Assumption of the Virgin, my illustrious colleague, Giraldus Cambrensis, then studying in Paris, describes how of a sudden, near midnight, the city burst out into a clanging of bells and a leaping of flames as great bonfires were kindled in all the squares. He ran to his window and saw crowds pressing through the narrow streets towards the palace. He shouted to them, wanting to know what was the matter, and a woman, recognizing where he came from by his accent, as he relates – though I personally have never found his French that bad – shouted back, 'There is a king born tonight, by God's grace, and he shall be as a battle-axe to your King of England.' The long, long awaited heir had been vouchsafed to patient Louis: Prince Philippe Augustus, Gift of God.

Another colleague, Walter Map, was with King Henry when the news reached him. He writes, 'Whereas all about him were openly astounded, some joking that Louis grew younger with the years, some, more bawdy, wondering who had been visiting the French Queen at night, the King turned away as if in shock or anger and was deaf to all joking, presently withdrawing to his private rooms. None blamed him overmuch in view of what awaited him there.'

You will understand that I quote Map's words out of context, for I did not read them until several years had passed. As for the matter of what awaited King Henry in his private rooms, we at Pontigny might well have guessed that it would concern a member of the opposite sex, but we would never in a hundred years have guessed that we ourselves held a vital clue, not only to the lady's identity but also to her importance.

The 'shock or anger' which Map had noted in the King's reaction to this news of the French prince's birth must surely have been caused by his realization that the prophecies of Thomas's blind woman were already proving true; and had she not also foretold that Henry would fall from greatness?

The many questions which all these matters raised in our minds were answered by an unexpected invitation. Queen Eleanor, still acting as her husband's regent in Angers, sent word for Thomas to visit her at that city, where she was again within a few weeks of childbirth. She assured him that under her regency he could make the journey in extreme secrecy and without the King hearing a word of it; but Thomas had much business at Pontigny, for he was on the point of persuading Pope Alexander to appoint him as papal legate to the province of Canterbury, a move which, if successful, would certainly confound all his enemies in England. In any case it would not have been wise for him to venture into Angevin territory; he knew that he could trust Queen Eleanor, but who could be sure how far she could trust those surrounding her.

I do not need to describe my alarm and confusion when my lord commanded me to go in his stead; I felt as though I had been ordered to walk into the lion's den. However Thomas gave me good Brother Edward of Northampton as my personal guard, and, early in October when all the plans had been made, we set forth, both wearing Cistercian white, accompanied by a troop of the French King's men-at-arms.

The weather was mild, and the wide countryside of France was abundant with all the riches of autumn, but I fear that my nervous anxiety gave me little opportunity to appreciate any of it. Moreover our Frenchman left us between Orléans and Blois, wisely, for had we met patrolling Angevin soldiers their presence would have betrayed our whole secret. We were thus forced to journey some miles alone, which was not to my liking, but Brother Edward seemed unperturbed and I, not wishing to appear as the coward I am, put on as brave a face as I could contrive; but I was heartily relieved to see men of Queen Eleanor's household waiting, as she had promised, at a certain boatmen's tavern upon the banks of the Loire. They accompanied us the rest of the way, and thus I came back to Angers which in the days of my lord's Chancellorship I had known so well.

The Queen had by now been brought to bed with the child, her seventh; yet even under these conditions she retained her regality, and was evidently one of those strong women upon whom, as I have heard, pregnancy bestows a calm and full beauty, even at the age of forty-three.

She said, 'I apologize, William of Colchester, for receiving you thus. You may blame nature or the King or whom you will, but not me, for I grow weary of this royal whelping, and if I'm granted another son I'll have done with it.'

I had been summoned to the royal bedchamber immediately upon my arrival, so urgent was her desire to talk with me. Now, while I sat down to the refreshment she had ordered for me, curtains were drawn about the bed, and her ladies helped her robe, for she considered it healthy both for herself and the child she carried that she should exercise every day, be it only to and fro in her own chamber.

Pacing thus while I ate, her ladies being banished from the room, she said, 'The Archbishop has spies in England.' It was a statement, but I answered, 'Yes, my lady.'

'What then have you heard of this girl, Clifford?'

My surprise must have shown upon my face, for she repeated impatiently, 'Clifford. The King's new paramour?'

I said, 'My lady, since you have spoken of the matter yourself, I may be bold and say that the Archbishop's spies do not report on every wench the King takes to his bed.'

'This is not one of those wenches. She is the daughter of one Walter de Clifford, a Norman knight owing allegiance to the King and holding estates on the borders of Wales. My lord chanced to rest there during the recent fighting; he also chanced to contemplate the man's daughter, and has kept her by him ever since. Six months!' She came nearer to the table where I sat, and I saw that her green eyes were afire with rage. 'He takes her wherever he goes; he lies with her at our own palace of Woodstock, in my own bed I have no doubt!'

I was shocked and alarmed, not so much by the news which, knowing the King, did not even surprise me, but by the anger which it aroused in this woman. Once, long before, she had said to me, 'I wonder what slut he beds tonight. It doesn't matter, I can forgive, and it saves a world of torment to forgive what you must.'

She watched me at my thoughts, sharp-eyed. 'You've heard nothing? Clifford, Rosamund Clifford?' And, with deep scorn: 'Whom he calls his rose of all the world?' She saw my expression change, though I think it did so in the least degree. 'Ah, you *do* know something!'

I was bemused; what I 'knew' was so ephemeral and perhaps so meaningless; but, with a shrug, I told her that it was simply the word 'rose' which had touched my memory; I told her of the blind woman in her cave and of what she had said regarding Henry. When I had finished she nodded to herself, deep in thought: ' "The rose is sweet but others bear its thorns." *When* did the woman speak thus?'

'In February, your grace. About the middle of the month.'

She laughed. 'And he did not meet Clifford until the end of March!'

I admit that like a nervous horse I shied away from this proof of the blind woman's foresight; but the Queen had already accepted it, pacing in silence with the odd majestic grace given to women heavy with child. 'And she also prophesied the birth of an heir to King Louis?'

'Yes.'

'And what of this other thing concerning Henry: "The days of his greatness are numbered"?'

'Of course it's absurd, my lady, but she said that this child would ... destroy King Henry's greatness.'

'Why absurd? The King is thirty-three. By the time the French Prince Philippe is twenty, the King will be fifty-three. A ripe age for destroying, William, if he proceeds as he does now.'

There was something, to me, terrible in the green eyes; they saw too clearly, not as the blind woman 'saw', but in terms of allegiances and crowns and wars. Then she smiled. 'What did Henry say when Thomas wrote to him of this ... rose?'

'That the tag was hardly worthy of a gipsy at a fair.'

'It was some six weeks before he met her; we may wager that he thinks differently now.' She recommenced her pacing, both hands on her belly. 'Now he will be . . . not afraid, Henry is, I think, never afraid; he will be uneasy. Every time he holds his Rose in his arms, finding her wondrous sweet, he will wonder about those thorns. Oh yes, I know him well; finding her so smooth he will wonder who bears her thorns.'

She sat down suddenly, lost in thought, looking out across the fair city to the golden October countryside beyond. After a time she said softly, '*I* shall bear those thorns, William. He comes here before Easter, and by the blood of God he shall find a very thicket of thorns, I shall wield sweet Rosamund's thorns like a sword.' Her head dropped upon her hand. 'I am tired now; the child kicks like a boy, let us hope it is one. Please ring that bell for my ladies.'

As I did so, she added, 'We will talk again before you leave. I dare not write to Thomas, but you can carry my words in your head. There is profit in this for both of us.'

Thomas, for his part, knew very well what the Queen meant by 'profit'. Any move that King Henry might make which belittled him in other men's eyes was profit to his Queen, who planned to leave him, and to his Archbishop, who was appealing to the world to judge how unfairly the King had treated him. Moreover both Thomas and Eleanor knew that because the blind woman had been proved correct by the birth of an heir to France and by the tag 'hardly worthy of a gipsy at a fair', concerning Rosamund, Henry would not be able to resist visiting her in her cave; for the most powerful lure, that concerning his own greatness and its decline, still remained most potently in the future.

I think that the King, for his part, was wise and clever enough to understand that he sorely missed the guidance of these two people who had loved him; but I think he was also the kind of man in whom this sense of loss generated not desolation but renewed anger, and he grew determined to show them that he could well manage his affairs without them.

Giraldus Cambrensis, who attended the court in England at

this time, told me that Queen Eleanor was not alone in taking such exception to Henry's new paramour, the fair Rosamund; it seems that there were many near to the King who also looked askance upon the affair. Giraldus added that you might hear bawdy songs about her in any London ale-house, and that much play was made upon the Latin 'Rosa-mundi' meaning Rose of the World, and 'Rosa-immundi' meaning Rose of Unchastity. For this he could give no reason; the girl was indeed fair and quiet and never one to make use of her position; she gave offence to none, yet she called forth a kind of criticism which had never been accorded to any of the fly-by-night ladies of no virtue and less reputation who had shared the royal bed in the past.

There is a point at which the very success attending some men seems to turn against them. In some ways it may be said that in the year 1166 King Henry II stood upon the pinnacle of his power, and yet the words of the blind woman, that 'the days of his greatness' were already numbered, were also in their way true.

Ten days after my return to Pontigny, Queen Eleanor gave birth to her seventh child by King Henry: her ninth, if one includes the two daughters she had given to Louis of France. In spite of that strong kicking it proved to be a girl, and was christened Joanna.

Meanwhile we, at the abbey, were greatly taken up with Thomas's determination to be affirmed as papal legate to the province of Canterbury, but the Pope demurred and hesitated on the matter, for he knew that if such power was granted Thomas would let fly at those bishops, and others, whom he considered to have betrayed him at Clarendon and Northampton; this would anger King Henry, and Alexander could not afford to be instrumental in angering King Henry. So the quills scratched away, on both sides of the Alps, and the messengers rode out with their burden of words, and Herbert of Bosham enjoyed every moment of it, and nothing was achieved. Winter passed, not too severe, and the first little buds of spring were early on the lowest boughs.

In March of that year 1166 King Henry left England, ostensibly to hold the Easter court at Angers with his Queen; in fact she had reported increasing unrest and rumours of rebellion, a usual occurrence if the King stayed too long absent – for it must be remembered that apart from brief visits it was now a full three years since he had shown himself to his liege-men in the wide continental domains. Moreover the nobles of France, led by Henry's old enemies of Champagne and Blois, had taken strength from the birth of Prince Philippe, Dieu-donné, and had not forgotten the insults and broken allegiances of the Plantagenet.

As for the manner of Queen Eleanor's greeting her lord that Easter, you may read in other chronicles that on such and such a day 'the King and Queen held little conversation', or that 'the King rose early in a high temper and went hunting all day until late', or that 'the Queen was disposed to be merry that evening, with music and dance, but the King pleaded an ague and retired early'. We may detect a certain puzzlement in these entries, and no doubt the rumours flew about the great castle of Angers like so many startled bats.

Again, I was more fortunate than my colleagues in that I had been granted the good fortune to know what was in the Queen's mind. Certainly I would not for all the world have been in King Henry's boots when, all unknowing, he came roistering into Queen Eleanor's presence at the end of his journey to be at once encircled by that 'very thicket of thorns'.

Certainly he would have given as good as he got, demanding to know why, in God's name, she should object *now* to what she had always accepted so sensibly before? But it would have been at best a sorry argument, for what husband, be he cowman or king, can truly withstand the anger of a wronged wife? I am sure that the Queen 'wielded sweet Rosamund's thorns like a sword' with terrifying dexterity, and continued to do so until she had plunged her husband into the deepest and most devilish of Angevin rages.

No doubt he would have liked to shut her up then and there in some remote tower, but he well knew that Poitou and Aquitaine were restless and any move he might make at this moment against their lady would bring them rampaging into the field against him.

No wonder the Queen was 'disposed to be merry that evening, with music and dance'; no wonder the King 'pleaded an ague and retired early'. Small wonder, also, if his mind turned to the blind woman who had foretold all these things, and to Thomas, that good friend now lost, who would have smoothed over this Easter débâcle with his charm and wit; who would, more likely, have so advised him in the matter of Fair Rosamund that no word of the affair would ever have reached the Queen at all.

A week after the King's arrival at Angers, Thomas received a note: 'I come on the 22nd of the month, about dusk. All that passes between us must be private beyond all other privacy. I will visit your blind sorceress that same night, and ride from Pontigny before dawn.'

3

If, as Thomas has said, that midnight meeting in the barn in December of 1153 was the first turning-point in his relationship with King Henry, and if the confrontation on the last day at Northampton in 1164 was the second, then the third must certainly have been the King's visit to Pontigny on 22 March, 1166.

Since the King's clothes were always plain and without show, those who did not know him personally would, once the royal banner no longer flew at his side, see in him merely an ordinary knight riding a fine horse. Thus he came to the abbey, attended by ten of his men.

Only the Abbot knew the identity of this guest, who was at once ushered into the Archbishop's private quarters, and only I witnessed the meeting of the two men who had not spoken together alone for three years. Thomas was about to kneel, but Henry raised him quickly before he could do so, and peered into his face; his big red hands kneaded my lord's shoulders where he held him, and he said, 'Thomas, you grow thin, you grow sickly.'

My lord replied, 'As plants will when the sun is denied them.'

At this the King gave a grunt, I think of pain, and pulled his one-time friend against him, and they embraced closely. Their two faces seen together were more than ever a contrast, the one ruddy with fresh air and good health, the other pale and strained. All that they possessed in common was that both looked older than their years, Henry being thirty-three, Thomas forty-eight.

Turning, the King offered me his hand and, as I bowed over it, said, 'Greetings, Good-Right-Arm! And be gone!'

What then passed between them Thomas dictated to me immediately after, as was his wont, while the King slept; for, as usual, he had ridden hard without stopping and the blind woman would not see him until after midnight.

Henry was ever one to discard preliminaries, and he did this now by saying, 'Thomas, I need you by me; I need your wisdom. I am served by men who don't understand me, agree with all I say, and blow away like thistledown when I shout at them.'

Thomas replied, 'Yet, my lord, you do not like men who stand firm when you shout at them.'

The King gave a hard smile, accepting this. 'Even I can grant that a man may stand firm in defence of his own life; I've done it myself a hundred times.'

'You speak as a King.'

'Perhaps. Let us now speak man to man, as once we did.'

Thomas said, 'You tell me you need me by you, but what of Canterbury?'

'Yours. All the estates, all revenues. Eye and Berkhamsted too, if you wish.'

'My lord King,' Thomas said, 'what are you buying with this munificence?'

'The only man I ever trusted. The only man I regret having turned upon.'

Thomas told me that at this point he suddenly thought of the many legends concerning the devil's blood that is supposed to run in these Angevins; and he thought of the devil's voice that tempted the Son: 'All these things will I give unto you . . .'

He said, 'My lord, I desire more than anything in this world to have your friendship and to grow strong again in your sun; but I know that what you are asking me to sell is my God. If I couldn't do this in my days of plenty, how much less can I do so in my days of poverty?' And he raised a hand to stop Henry speaking, for he knew what the words would be. 'No, I am not a Christian, and I am not speaking as a Christian.'

'Then give me the Christian church, it means nothing to you, and only you can gain me its obedience.'

'Do you not have it already?'

'You know I do not. I have a body without a head.'

Thomas shrugged. 'You are right, that church means nothing to me.'

Henry threw up both hands and cried, 'Then do as I ask! Let us waste no more valuable time in enmity.'

Very gravely, Thomas replied, 'My lord, tell me how I may give you the Christian church without betraying God, and I will do it tonight.'

Henry stared at him; then said, 'There is something in you, Thomas, that was not there hitherto; I think I fear it a little.'

'It was ever there, but your grace would not allow yourself to see it.'

Henry nodded, still staring, but did not speak.

Thomas continued, 'I wish with all my heart for nothing more than to return to England, dedicate my life to your service, and be your friend again as once I was.' He went and stood directly before the King and said, 'I love you well, my lord, and your heart knows it.'

'But your "god" comes first.'

'Have I ever pretended otherwise?'

The King slapped his knee with his heavy gauntlets, and stood up abruptly. 'No! If you love me as you say, you would not fight me with this Christian balderdash.'

'I do not fight *you*, my lord.'

Henry turned sharply and gave him, as Thomas described it, 'a strange and wondering look', and he believed that in this moment the King had finally understood for the first time what lay between them. He said, in an uncertain voice, 'You . . . you fight my kingship, is that it? Everything I hold against the church?'

'Not for the sake of the church. For the sake of God, yes. For the sake of such Christians as are worthy of him.'

The King stared, and Thomas prayed. Later he said to me, 'Oh, Will, Will, it was all understood between us. Nothing divided us. Peace reached out for our two hands.'

Then Henry swung away, his voice growing hoarse with anger: 'By the blood of the Bull, Thomas, you could twist an oak-tree with your words!'

'But my lord . . . ?'

'If you loved me there would be no ifs and buts; you would do what I ask, you would be my man as you once swore you were, and I would return your love. But no, that cannot be upon my terms, only upon yours.' He turned back, red in face, dark eyes blazing. 'So I will fight you, Thomas, you leave me no alternative; I will fight you to Rome and back, to Hell and back, I know not where. And I shall win.'

'I think,' said my lord, 'that you will very likely "win", but I too will fight, with what little I have.'

'You shall have nothing, *nothing*; I shall take it all.'

They faced each other so, neither willing to give an inch. Then Thomas said, quietly, 'Henry, when you have taken all, I shall fight you with love, for that you cannot take.'

At this the King again fell silent, regarding him with that same wondering curiosity. Then he shook his head and gave a weary smile, opening his arms to embrace my lord as he had done upon their meeting. 'Thomas, Thomas,' he said, 'had things been otherwise, we could have captured and ruled this world, you and I. None could have stopped us.'

After King Henry had rested and supped – alone, for Thomas would not abandon the hours of his Cistercian hosts – we took horse a little before midnight. Thomas had to prevail upon the King to leave behind eight of his ten men: 'We go to a holy place, my lord, not upon a military patrol.'

The King obeyed unwillingly, and I must say that in this at least I understood him well and admired his courage; for was he not deep within France, the land of his enemies, about to be led he knew not where by a man whom he had wronged with cruel ferocity? Most probably he had left no word at Angers of his destination, it was far too secret a matter. How easily he might be taken, his men killed, himself betrayed!

On this night Thomas led the way by those half-hidden tracks and forest rides, until we came to the tangled banks of the river, turning south along that path under the whip-like willow branches; at length we reached the rocky hill, all grown about with trees now bursting into fresh leaf. An east wind blew, and it was bitterly cold.

We dismounted, and immediately that same wavering light moved among the tree-trunks and the same silent country girl came towards us with her lantern.

King Henry said, 'There are others here! I feel others all about us.'

Thomas replied, 'Many, my lord. Perhaps three or four living.'

This had been my own first reaction to the place, and I was not surprised that the King would not put aside his sword. The girl laid a hand upon the hilt and shook her head.

Henry said, 'I will not disarm.'

'Then,' said Thomas, 'you will not see the priestess. For more than two thousand years no honest man has entered this place bearing arms.'

Still the King hesitated. Thomas said, 'My lord, if there had been a trap, it would have been sprung long since, and not upon sacred ground. This is a temple of your own ancient religion; you know its rules better than I.'

After a moment, Henry nodded, disarmed, and handed his sword to one of his men. Again let me say that I admired his bravery; of all men in the world, I think that only Thomas could have led him into that cave, Thomas and devouring curiosity. 'All that interests the great is their greatness.' The blind woman knew too much; and I was glad to remain outside with the two soldiers, sharing their uneasiness and the bitter wind.

My day-book describes in detail what occurred within. On this cold night two heavy iron braziers had been set at either side of the pool.

They gave out not only warmth, but the heady scent of some herb or perfume, the smoke of which made the cave more than ever hazy and indistinct. Their dull red glare illuminated the face of the blind woman who sat as before in her rocky niche, but it did not touch the slow-moving water of the spring, which remained darkly green, shimmering with bubbles from time to time.

As before, she bade both men drink, adding, 'This is the water of earth's purity, before man befouled it with his evil. May it make us pure as the earth is pure, for otherwise the god will have no traffic with us.' Then she leaned forward, as if peering with her sightless eyes into the spring.

After a while she glanced up at Thomas and said, 'You have not found the peace you sought between yourself and this man.'

'In part perhaps.'

'Peace does not come in parts; it is entire or it is not peace. I told you before, I could not see it.' She plunged a hand into the spring, shattering its smooth clarity, and turned her blind eyes upon King Henry. 'And you, my lord? Are you strong for what I will say?'

'Men count me strong.'

'The strength of men is one thing; to draw the arrow-head from the wound is strong, but a greater strength is needed here.'

'Is what you see so terrible?'

'I see a thing which at first I would not believe; I tried again, and saw the same. Then I closed the entrance with elder branches and I cleansed the temple with fire and water, for I feared that others had been here in secret, profaning the god. After thirteen days I came again, and looked again, and saw the same thing. Therefore I ask if you are strong.'

'I am strong.'

She nodded and once more leaned over the spring; it seemed a long time before she spoke again : 'The rose droops upon its stalk and dies.' She cast the words aside as if they were of no importance, but Thomas saw how Henry's big hand clutched at his heavy cloak, and he guessed that Rosamund Clifford must indeed have grown close to the King's heart.

Then she said, 'Alas yes, it is the same. I see a great eagle wearing a crown; beset by four eaglets. Two tear at the outstretched pinions; the third plunges its talons into the breast and tears the flesh with bloody beak, while the fourth hovers on beating wings and pecks at the glaring eyes.'

My lord reported that Henry's face was like granite. After a few moments he said, 'I have but three sons.'

In her gentle voice she replied, 'I see four.' Thomas noted that she did not deny that the eaglets were Henry's sons.

'Continue!'

Again she plunged a hand into the water as if wishing to break whatever image her blind eyes 'saw' there. But as the ripples settled again she shook her head. 'You command me to continue?'

'I command it.'

'I see a sapphire ring, the stones set in a serpent of gold.'

Henry started in surprise; Thomas was no less astonished, for this ring was a part of the royal treasure of the first Henry and the King had recently worn it very seldom, since in his opinion few occasions called for jewels. They exchanged a glance.

'You have sent this ring to a young man who lies at the point of death. There are holy men present who would take the ring, but even though it is too big for the finger it will not be moved. I see it on the finger of your eldest son.'

At this, Henry could not contain himself; he gave a strangled cry and was upon his feet. 'He lives, he grows strong, his beauty and grace are the wonder of all.'

'He dies, and his death is the wonder of none.'

My lord reported that the King's face was working with violent emotion, whether terror or rage he could not, in that dim red glow, be sure.

Calmly the blind woman said, 'I warned you; and I cannot dissemble in what I see, for that would be sacrilege and the power would visit me no more. Better you should go.'

Henry fought with himself for a full minute; then swung back and sat down again. 'I did not come thus far for nothing,' he said. 'Neither is it my habit to turn tail and run.'

She nodded, and returned to her contemplation of the gently stirring water. 'Now of the four, three eaglets remain.'

'I have but three sons in all.' He repeated it doggedly, but she ignored him. 'The second is that which tears at the eagle's body, searching for the heart.'

Thomas, knowing that this could only refer to Richard, Queen Eleanor's favourite and heir, did not dare even to glance at the King.

'And does he have the heart?'

'Yes. Both these young birds take what they desire.'

'Will you talk in riddles?' Henry demanded, angry and impatient. 'You spoke of three, now you say "both".'

'The third also dies, I do not see this clearly. Horses' hooves and lances. In battle perhaps.' Thomas noticed that she dismissed

Geoffrey in an odd imitation of the manner in which Henry himself had always dismissed him. A haunting irony which was evidently not lost upon the King, who asked less roughly, 'And this . . . fourth, which I have not?'

'You shall love him well, my lord, as men love their last-born. He also wears a crown.'

'And in all this, what of France?' A trace of contempt had crept into his voice. 'I had heard that some babe in France crossed my destiny.'

'Why,' she said, 'they *are* France.'

Henry jerked forward, staring, his face all red in the glow of the braziers. 'What do you mean?'

She looked up directly at him and said quite evenly, 'One takes your heart, one takes your eyes, and all is treachery, for both love France better than they love you.'

There was a second of appalled silence before the King's pent-up passion broke loose; he leapt to his feet and turned on Thomas. 'You plotted this, all, all these lies, I should have known it!'

'*No!*' It was the first time that Thomas had ever known the blind woman to raise her voice, and he described it as a terrible cry like that of a wounded animal in the night. She stood now in her niche, seeming high above them in the wavering smoke, and she was pointing at King Henry. 'Do you think to profane this holy place *of your own religion?*'

'Lies, lies!' The King was beside himself.

'If you think yourself strong, my lord King, you needs must think again. As for this good man here . . .' Her finger moved to Thomas. 'At the time of which I speak he will be long dead, and not a day shall pass but that you mourn the loss of him.'

'Lying bitch!' He kicked out at the brazier which stood by him. It crashed over in a blaze of embers and a cloud of smoke which swirled across the cave.

Thomas admits that he does not know exactly what happened next; he says that he looked up to the blind woman and found that she had disappeared. Between gusts of smoke he glimpsed, standing in her place, the figure of a man, horned, with arms outstretched in supplication. Henry, seeing this too, let out a stricken cry and fell back, for however it had materialized, it was the god of his old religion, part bull, part man.

At the same moment a monstrous voice, which might have been that of the blind woman raised in her animal-like howl, screamed directly above them, 'The temple is profaned!', and on that instant there was a rushing and roaring of water; even before they felt it, icy about their legs, they saw by the light of the remaining brazier that it was pouring into the cave from all sides.

They stumbled to the steps. There, at the top, calm as ever, stood the country girl with her lantern. Thomas said that they were both shaking with cold or terror or both, as they climbed the flooded steps, no easy task, and reached her side. Moreover they had to pause there, gasping, while she stood by expressionless, until they had regained enough self-possession to rejoin the two soldiers and myself awaiting them. Nor, I must add, had we heard any sound or seen any sign of what had happened to them below; though I noticed at once their soaking boots and clothing. My lord gave me a look of flint, and I remained silent.

Thomas led the ride back to the abbey, and he rode hard so that none could have spoken even if he had wished to. He wanted, I understood later, to give Henry time to think, to look inwards and to calm himself after the ordeal which he had undergone.

At Pontigny, Henry paused only long enough to don dry clothing; then he turned to Thomas and looked long and searchingly into his face; then, to my utmost surprise, and I think Thomas's, he said, 'Give me the Kiss of Peace, my Brother, for God knows I have need of it.'

Thomas did so. Henry nodded curtly. 'Thus in private, with only Good-Right-Arm as witness. But in public, never!'

Thomas bowed. 'As God wills.'

'As the King wills.'

'As God wills.'

Henry swung away, hard-faced, and out into the courtyard. His men were already mounted, and the horses' hooves slid and stamped upon the cobbles; then they began to move.

Thomas stood motionless, listening intently, until the last sound of them had died away.

Before continuing my narrative I must add that Thomas and I often discussed, not only the words which the blind woman had spoken to Henry, but also the nature of what took place at the end of their meeting with her.

It seemed to us both that the niche, hewn from rock, in which the priestess sat, was not in reality solid, as it looked, but had access to it on one or both sides; thus, in the semi-darkness and smoke, she could have stepped out of sight while the figure of the horned man took her place, possibly upon a higher level.

Make no mistake, my lord never doubted for one moment that the blind woman possessed the true gift of prophecy, for she had proved it, but we all know that every temple of antiquity had its machinery of illusion, however simple. Of course many hundreds, even thousands, of years have passed since the most ignorant peasant has thought of the horned man as the god himself. He is only a representation, but nevertheless imbued with magic powers. As for the unearthly voice which cried, 'The temple is profaned,' this may well have been produced by means of a natural echo in the vault of the cavern, the height of which was always concealed in darkness. The flood of water presented the least of these problems, for the river had originally hollowed out the rock, as its smoothness bore witness, and the cave still lay below water-level. All that was required was the opening of a sluice-gate, and had not the blind woman herself said, 'I cleansed the temple with fire and water'?

To satisfy our curiosity we rode out one afternoon to visit the place by daylight. As we drew near, a countryman started up from among rocks and roughly asked us our business; but before we could reply he seemed to recognize my lord, thus implying that other eyes, perhaps many, watched over the blind woman while she was at her work; he said, 'The cave is flooded, there is nothing there.'

Thomas asked politely if we might proceed in any case, and the fellow let us pass with a shrug.

It was as he had said. A turbulent, thundering flood had repossessed the temple; the rough steps disappeared at once into a dark maelstrom; neither, search as we might, could we find any sign of a sluice-gate or other mechanism to control it. That too was a part of the mystery.

Withered branches of elder fixed at each side of the entrance told us that once again the temple was being 'cleansed', undoubtedly as a result of King Henry's profanity.

At Easter in that year 1166 Pope Alexander at last gave way to Thomas's pleading, and created him papal legate for the see of Canterbury. At once rumours and counter-rumours concerning excommunication filled the air, and there was near-panic in many an English bishopric.

As for Henry Plantagenet, he personally cared not a whit for all the anathema in the Christian church, for as we know he worshipped other gods and had scant reverence for them; only in one respect did he fear what Thomas might now do. Young Prince Henry was twelve years old, and he had not yet been crowned as future King of England; this was the King's own fault, and he had admitted it in his conversation with Thomas for had he not demanded the ritual death my lord would long since have performed the coronation. The situation was compounded by the birth of King Louis' heir, Philippe Augustus, Dieu-donné, by which Prince Henry's standing at the French court had been reduced to that of a mere son-in-law. The crux of the matter was that only the Archbishop of Canterbury was authorized to crown the heir to the throne of England, and since Thomas had openly said, in reply to Henry's threats, that he would fight back with what little power he possessed, it was more than ever certain that he would refuse to perform the vital ceremony. Excommunication was no 'little power' if applied in the right quarters.

There was more. Ten days after Henry's visit to Pontigny one of Queen Eleanor's men delivered a letter to Thomas; in it she wrote, 'What did your blind woman do to my lord? He left here in as foul a temper as I have ever witnessed, but he has returned a sick man; so sick that even my hardened heart goes out to him, and I nurse him with my own hands, having first assured him that I have no intention of poisoning him, a prerogative of queens since the beginning of time! He improves a little, but only a little, and has neither hunted nor hawked since his return. I think this to be a sickness of the soul rather than of the body.'

Had not Thomas heard directly from the Queen concerning her lord's health he might well have deduced, as did many others, that Henry was feigning sickness, for a sick king cannot be excommunicated. In any case, if he spoke of anathema it was only in the presence of certain Christians, knowing that it would please them; he had no intention of attacking Henry in this way because he knew that the blind woman's words were more awesome, in the King's estimation, than all the fulminations of the Christian church.

However, those who sensed that excommunication was in the air were not wrong. The Archbishop of Canterbury came forth from the celebrations of the Christian Easter, which we Cathars share in part, and proceeded to the great Cluniac church of Vézelay.

Thomas was ever one to rise to a great occasion, and Vézelay that spring was certainly a great occasion. Word had gone out that he would preach on the Christian Whitsunday, and there was a distinguished gathering of nobles and prelates from many parts of Europe, as well as a great crowd of pilgrims and onlookers, ever prepared to witness this struggle between the hated King of England and his wronged and exiled Archbishop. He told of the harsh injustice with which King Henry, that champion of justice, had acted towards him, and he threatened the dreadful possibility of excommunication if the King did not, upon arising from his sickbed, mend his ways. He spoke thereafter of the meaning of Pentecost, moving many to tears by his eloquence and humility.

Then, processing with all the clergy to the narthex by the Western door, a part of the church which Christians consider to be unconsecrated, he saw the seven candles lit: for John of Oxford, always so close to Gilbert Foliot, and Richard of Ilchester, both of whom had attended the Emperor Barbarossa and his anti-Pope: for John of Balliol and Richard de Luci, the King's lawyers who had been instrumental in drawing up the Constitutions at Clarendon: for Randulph de Broc and two others who had appropriated lands rightfully belonging to Canterbury.

The ringing words of anathema were proclaimed; bells were rung; and the candles, one by one, were extinguished and trampled underfoot; then the names of all those who had been excommunicated were posted at the doors of the church, so that all might know that they were henceforth cut off from their faith and forbidden ever to enter a holy place for any purpose whatsoever. It was, I must say, a most effective ritual, alarming even to a confirmed 'heretic' such as myself.

Meanwhile Henry lay sick at Angers, grappling as best he might with that vision of himself beset by all his sons, with the promise of the death of his beloved and beautiful Prince Henry, and of course Geoffrey also, and with the bestial prophecy that the remaining two would turn upon him and rend him – and, worst of all, do so hand in hand with France.

The descriptions which reached me, at the time and later, of the King's condition during his illness are so reminiscent of Northampton, that, if one may for a moment cast aside all legendary theories concerning devilish ancestors, one is left wondering whether King Henry II may not be afflicted by some recurrent disease of the brain. We know that Julius Caesar suffered from the falling sickness, more often than not being able to hide the attacks, and certainly proving that it in no way impaired his brilliance as a general or a ruler. It is a question to which others must seek an answer, for I have not the knowledge; yet I do know, and have seen with my own eyes, that the King can be intelligent, quick and forceful at one moment, and at the next a mere bullock of childish obstinacy and black unreason. Even his very aspect changes, at times almost beyond recognition, so that one can well understand the assumption of simple people that he is possessed.

It is impossible even to guess at the thoughts which haunted him as he lay in a fever at Angers, but to judge from his subsequent actions it would seem that he chose in some way to defy within his own mind the terrible words of the blind woman. Knowing that she had prophesied correctly in the past, he could obviously not bring himself to ignore her, and so it seems to me that with a typically Angevin, and indeed almost superhuman, determination he sought to change the situation around him, particularly by his later actions at Montmirail, so that the very world upon which she had based her prophecies would no longer be the same; perhaps in this way he thought to render the future invalid.

There is something both courageous and pathetic in this defiance, something thoroughly and warmly human which almost makes me love the man; particularly when I contrast his reasoning with that of the blind woman herself: 'What will be is there. That does not change. It is.'

How often have I come to the brink of liking King Henry only to draw back swiftly at what next I hear of him!

Some weeks after our return to Pontigny Thomas received a letter which might have seemed, to any but my lord and myself, to have come from one of his spies near to the King. It did not, however, bear the secret symbol, and at first we suspected some trap; but then the very first sentence proved to be a paraphrase of that short note which Queen Eleanor had written upon Henry's return to her in March: 'What did the blind woman do to the king?'; and later, words were used which she herself had spoken in secret conversation with Thomas at Canterbury in the summer of 1164. Doubtless she judged that these two identifications, known only to the three of us, were proof enough that the letter was indeed sent by her. I may say that such precautions were well advised, for the substance of it was subversive if not treasonable.

What did the blind woman do to the king?

You should know, my lord Archbishop, that following a violent attack brought about by your lordship's excommunications at Vézelay, he has long since risen from his sickbed and has not been idle. With one hand he has disbursed large sums of money to certain 'friends' within the Curia; with the other he has paid even larger sums to the Emperor Barbarossa to encourage his ambition of laying siege to Rome itself. Meanwhile he has dispatched the cleverest of your enemies to appeal to the Pope; part of this appeal will consist of veiled hints concerning King Henry's budding friendship with Barbarossa, a friendship which does not exist, and concerning his possible support of the German Popeling, whom he despises.

You will appreciate that he is thus catching and holding Pope Alexander in a vice, at the same time cutting away the ground from under your feet. The Pope will not be able to help you at this moment, so do not expect it.

Though I am not exactly privy to the King's thoughts regarding the future, I will go further and say that it is in his mind to defy papal authority altogether if that need should arise. His own religion, as we know, would present him with no personal feeling about this one way or the other. At all events, following his sickness he is in high good spirits and speaks openly of 'having Rome in his purse'.

As for the Queen, you will be surprised to hear that she is yet again with child. The King swears that he has absolute foreknowledge (from whom, you may be able to guess better than I) that it will be a son. The Queen swears that be it boy or girl it shall be the last. She has been brought to bed ten times in all, having, it may be remembered, given King Louis of France two healthy girls before she ever became Queen of England.

The wonder of the court is that she permitted the King to lie with her at all; relations between them are, to say the least, strained, and the Queen was lately heard to say to certain ladies that her husband had become 'a bore and a boor'. One can only assume that the King forced her, which, knowing the lady, I find unlikely, or that, since he does not lack for charm, as you know, one of their conjugal arguments ended classically between the sheets.

All in all, my good lord, have a care! Great forces are deployed against you. My advice is to stand firm, bide your time, and say as little as you may. God be with you.

Thomas was deeply touched by this letter, showing as it did the warmth of Queen Eleanor's feeling towards him. Her warnings were, as usual, well founded. King Henry had bound Pope Alexander hand and foot; when he had told Thomas that he would fight him 'to Rome and back, to Hell and back, I know not where', he had meant every word of it.

Referring to that conversation, Thomas now said, 'Well, there is the crux of it, Will. He said that if I truly loved him there would be no ifs and buts, I would be his sworn man, and then he would return my love. Then he said, "But no, that cannot be upon my terms, only upon yours." ' He sighed, took the Queen's letter to a taper and began to burn it. 'I see now the pattern of the future; it is to be a battle between his "terms" and mine. I do not believe he will ever give way, and I . . . I cannot give way without betraying myself and our faith.'

'Yet,' I said fearfully, 'there is no such thing in all nature as a deadlock.'

'No such thing.'

The letter fell as ashes into the fireplace, and the look which my lord turned on me was bleak indeed.

4

The months that followed were a nightmare. Life became an end-less penance of largely meaningless correspondence, punctuated by the coming and going of various ecclesiastical spokesmen, some in-telligent, others idiotic, and of papal legates who either fell out with my lord, or with the King, or with both.

As I have said before, if Alexander III had been firmly seated upon St Peter's throne at Rome, some order and sense might have arisen from all this confusion, but he, poor man, was almost as hard-pressed as were we ourselves. Under the relentless weight of King Henry upon one side and the Emperor Barbarossa upon the other, there was often little that he could do to help us. All was now being played upon the 'terms' of the King. Did Thomas sometimes wonder, as I confess I did, whether his chance would ever come? He said no word, not even on that terrible 14 September when King Henry, taking advantage of a general meeting of the Cistercian order, accused them of defying him by harbouring his enemies; if this continued, he said, he would instantly confiscate all their many possessions and lands in England.

Thomas arranged to move at once from Pontigny where we had lived for two years and where he was greatly revered and loved, for the last thing he wished was for the King's anger to fall upon those peaceful men who had helped him and his followers so generously. Hearing of this situation, King Louis came to our aid once again, bidding us make ourselves at home in any abbey in the whole of

France. Since we were well known at Sens, from the days of Pope Alexander's residence there, we asked to be admitted to St Columba of that city, and the good Abbot opened his doors to us with the same generosity which had greeted us at Pontigny.

Queen Eleanor had gone to England in October of that year 1166, taking up residence at Oxford, where she no doubt made it her business to learn much of what had passed between Henry and his Rose at nearby Woodstock. On the day after Christmas she gave birth to her last child, a boy as the blind woman had foretold. He was christened John.

Meanwhile Henry was spending Christmas in her own city of Poitiers, at the splendid new castle which he had built there and which she proposed, before long, to occupy herself. He had taken young Prince Henry with him in order to present the child to the Queen's liege-men, for although Richard, as Eleanor's heir, was to be their Duke, young Henry, as future monarch, would be his brother's overlord.

Here again I sense Henry Plantagenet's defiance of the prophecy which had driven him to profane the cave-temple beside the river. He would not allow himself to believe that his own beloved boy, his own heir to Anjou and Normandy and England, would never live to sit on the throne. Let the witches and soothsayers cry death and destruction, the Devil was in the Angevins and the Devil would protect his own!

Expert in flattery and deceit as they are in those southern parts, I am sure that the noble lords of Poitou and Aquitaine exhibited boundless courtesy and charm, but in their hearts they were impatient of this deference to 'foreign' rulers, first King Louis of France and now Henry of England.

Queen Eleanor knew this impatience well, knew how swiftly these glowing embers might be fanned into full flame; it was the cornerstone upon which her plans were built.

Henry may or may not have been convinced by the quality of the homage paid to himself and his eldest son by the Queen's lords, but he can have had no doubt that the southern realm was alive with conspiracy and rebellion. The Queen, I think, must have derived some amusement from the fact that her husband had to spend almost the whole of the year 1167 fighting for the rights and borders of her domains. I have even heard it said that she encouraged those fiery lords of the Auvergne and the Limousin to keep the King occupied while she completed the plans which, if all went well, would leave her as feudal ruler of the very lands which he was now struggling to subjugate.

Henry took up the sword to good purpose, as ever, methodically razing castle after castle and, as methodically, driving those whom he had dispossessed to seek refuge in France under the patronage of King Louis.

Could he not see, as Thomas very clearly saw, that already he was beginning to fulfil the destiny of which the blind woman had forewarned him? Every lord whom he drove from his own lands and into exile in France added one more to the many waiting in impatient rage to regain what had been taken from them. Could he not see that even if a father was killed in this fighting, there would be sons to cherish their family's revenge: sons, perhaps, of an age not very far removed from that of his own.

'And in all this,' he had demanded mockingly of the blind woman, 'what of France? I had heard that some babe in France crossed my destiny.' And she had replied, 'Why, they *are* France.' An answer which now began to assume a wider significance by including, as well as the French Prince Philippe, as well as his own babes, these dispossessed sons who would grow under the tutelage of France to share a common hatred of one man: Henry Plantagenet.

When at last he emerged victorious, Eleanor, with all her entourage, was waiting for him at Argentan. Here they held their Christmas court, and after it set off in state, King Henry escorting his Queen, Countess of Poitou, Duchess of Aquitaine, on a royal progress through her domains.

The world was led to understand that she was but moving the capital of her regency further south; the King's understanding was a little different, for he had no intention of leaving her alone among her own volatile people. Thus he placed her under the 'protection' of one of his most loyal barons, Patrick, Earl of Salisbury. However, as soon as he left her and turned northwards again, the Queen's procession was attacked by a desperate band of those very men whom the King had recently evicted from their lands: Lusignans, well-known as some of the most powerful and warlike of all the Queen's liege-men. It seems that they intended to capture the lady and hold her in ransom until their possessions were returned to them; but Queen Eleanor, even at forty-five, knew how to handle a horse, and it was the Earl of Salisbury, protecting her as she galloped away to take refuge in a nearby castle, who bore the brunt of the attack. The outcome was that my lord of Salisbury was killed, as were those of his men who did not run for their lives.

Once again there was a rumour that Queen Eleanor had not been totally ignorant of this attack, and that its purpose was not her capture for ransom, in which it signally failed, but a secret one which was signally successful: Eleanor of Poitou and Aquitaine was now a free woman in her own kingdom. The first part of her plan was achieved; now she turned to the second part of it, that which would render her heir Prince Richard the most formidable overlord on the European continent.

Already one of the eaglets had flown the nest and was circling overhead, testing the power of his wings, the strength of his talons, the sharpness of that beak which, if the blind woman had spoken true, would one day rend King Henry's heart.

It must not be thought that during all this royal manoeuvring the King forgot to pursue his bitter altercation with Thomas of Canterbury; there was indeed a lull, but during it Henry had once again used the threat of joining the Holy Roman Emperor and the anti-Pope. By this means he squeezed from Alexander papal authority for the Archbishop of York to crown young Prince Henry, though only under certain unusual circumstances; he also obtained a papal letter preventing Thomas from excommunicating either himself or any of his English nobles, lay or clerical.

Thomas held his anger in check concerning both these matters, for he knew that Alexander was not deceived by Henry's threats; indeed, upon examination he found that the English King's declarations of friendship for the Emperor and support for his

'Popeling', to use Queen Eleanor's word, were empty and unconvincing. He therefore dispatched a new delegation with orders that Henry must settle his dispute with Thomas by Ascension Day, at which time, if nothing had been achieved, the Archbishop would once again be granted full powers of excommunication.

This was the kind of ultimatum which King Henry II did not appreciate, and it moved him a little closer to the decision which Queen Eleanor had mentioned in her secret letter: that of 'defying papal authority altogether'.

In all these things – the continuing dissension between King and Archbishop, Henry's bloody campaigns upon the borders of Poitou and Aquitaine, his Queen's sudden and startling reappearance as a ruler in her own right, complete with heir apparent, the growing power of France, the Pope's continued salvoes despite the royal pressures brought to bear upon him – there were signs of integral changes, cracks and fissures, in the whole feudal structure of Europe; and it was this general feeling, as much as any direct command from King Louis or from the papal nuncios, that brought about the great conclave at Montmirail, a meeting, first, between King Louis and King Henry, and later between both sovereigns and the Archbishop of Canterbury.

Henry's actions at Montmirail mystified the Angevin chroniclers, who had mistakenly thought to understand him well, and astounded the world at large. We, who are in a position to see them against a background unknown to others, will find them easier to understand.

Montmirail lies between Chartres and Le Mans, a little nearer to the latter. The two Kings met at the castle there in full state on the Christian day of Epiphany, 6 January 1169.

It was immediately noticed that not only had King Henry brought his three eldest sons, but that each of these was accompanied by a proud escort of noblemen from the domains which their father had granted to them at birth. The Princes were too young as yet to understand the full meaning of power, but the lords attending them were very well aware of their distinct positions *vis-à-vis* King Henry and his liege-lord Louis of France. I have heard it said by many who were present that from the beginning there was a sense of tension, even of danger, which Louis by his watchful mildness did much to alleviate.

Firstly the King of England, as Duke of Normandy, paid homage to France, using in place of his accustomed terse delivery, graceful words, making much of the day of Epiphany, of the gifts which the three kings had brought to the newly born Son, and of his own gift of three fine sons as liege-men of France; and then occurred the ceremony which so amazed all present, and indeed, upon their hearing of it, the whole world.

Henry brought forward his namesake and favourite, and again confirmed the boy's inheritance of his own lands, Maine, Anjou and Normandy, and in this understanding young Henry paid homage to Louis. After him came Richard, Queen Eleanor's best-loved son: again Henry confirmed, before King Louis and all his court, the boy's entitlement to his mother's wide lands from the Loire to the Pyrenees; and there was not a man there, least of all the southern barons escorting the Prince, who did not realize that here stood the power-balance of Europe. He who had Richard for an ally would need no other.

There was, I am told, an audible gasp when the King of France proposed and the King of England accepted, his daughter Princess Alais, a child of nine, as future Countess of Poitou and Duchess of Aquitaine. It is even said that King Louis could not quite believe his ears upon hearing Henry's acceptance, and had to be prevented by his advisers from repeating the offer out of pure amazement; he even added to the girl's dower the county of Berry, which Henry had often considered appropriating by force since it strengthened the borders of both Anjou and Poitou beyond the River Creuse.

Prince Geoffrey, now aged nine, was confirmed in his over-lordship of Brittany which, as I have written before, was in reality the French King's property. However Louis, overjoyed one would say by the liaison of France and Aquitaine, blithely bestowed upon this youngest Prince the true heiress of the province, Constance of Brittany.

Now all this was solemnly sworn before a great company, the Princes on bended knee laying their two hands between those of King Louis, signifying the most sacred of homages, so that what all present were witnessing, in stupefaction, was the division, and thus the destruction, of that great Empire which King Henry Plantagenet had fought and negotiated and married and, some might say, cheated to build and to defend.

Many were the wild guesses made as to his motives, ranging from presentiments, or even knowledge, of his approaching death, to some devious and deep-laid plot by which the Plantagenet proposed to become a second Charlemagne, ruling all Europe. Let us remember that none present knew of his meeting with the blind priestess in the cave, and of her prophecies of division and disaster.

It is here, as I have said, that I believe Henry (who undoubtedly considered himself godly in some respects) sought to overthrow the world upon which she had based her knowledge; for I also believe that he thought her prophecy to be ruled as much by intelligent forethought, perhaps prompted by Thomas, as by her pure and undoubted gift of foresight. Of course it is obvious that on a more practical level he hoped to correct that balance of power which Queen Eleanor had overturned in favour of Richard; for, ignoring Geoffrey of Brittany who was in any case made vassal to Normandy, if Prince Henry was Count of Anjou and Maine, Duke of Normandy and King of England, he could well stand against his brother if the need arose, particularly as they were all to be wedded to daughters of France.

During this meeting of Kings I had been waiting with Thomas in another part of the castle. There was a particular stillness about my lord which I had grown to recognize as the prelude to bold and often enraged action, and I must say that the very sight of that pale, self-contained face made my heart beat a little faster in apprehension.

Many differing accounts may be read of the meeting which now took place between the King of England and his Archbishop, but since none knew that they had already met at Pontigny in secret, nor of what had passed between them there, all are based upon a primary error and proceed from there to further inaccuracy, when not marred by pure romantic invention.

I can assure you that Thomas did not prostrate himself weeping before the King. He knelt upon one knee and kissed Henry's hand. The King then raised him and they embraced, afterwards searching each other's faces for a few seconds. No doubt there were many present who were deeply touched by the seeming frailty of the Archbishop's appearance; King Henry had seen it before at Pontigny and I doubt if he underestimated the steel that lay beneath, even if the onlookers did. His pallor was caused by anger as much as by ill-health, and his words, as he pleaded for 'the cause of the Christian church' meant one thing to the ears of admiring bystanders and quite another to the King, who knew him well enough, I think, to understand where all this was leading.

As an experienced tactician in the field, he had obviously appreciated that at some point he would have to allow Thomas to attack upon his own 'terms'. I could tell from the expression on his face that he was expecting a sting in the tail of all this 'Christian' eloquence: 'Before the most mighty King of France, before the power of the Pope, as represented by his legates here present, before your noble and princely sons of England, I commit all disagreement between us to your royal justice . . .' a mere flicker of the eyelids '. . . saving my order and the honour of God.'

It was, of course, a scarlet cloth waved under the nose of the bull, and Henry charged at it: 'By God's blood,' he shouted, 'do you mean to drag us all back to *that* old bone of contention?'

As ever his anger had led him astray, for to many around him the order of priesthood, let alone the honour of God, far from being 'old bones of contention' were the very foundation upon which they ordered their lives.

Henry was quick to see that he had lost, and Thomas had thereby gained, the sympathy of the conclave. He turned hastily to Louis and made a conciliatory speech, concluding with the words, 'I only ask that the Archbishop concedes to me what the most saintly of his predecessors always conceded to my forebears,' which, to all but Thomas, sounded more than fair. There were cries of support and encouragement for the King.

Dangerously quiet and still, Thomas said, 'What my predecessors conceded to your forebears may be read word for word in a foolish document, already rejected by His Holiness the Pope, called the Constitutions of Clarendon.'

At this body-blow, Henry lost his temper completely. King Louis caught his arm and many lords and bishops besought him to be patient, while others surrounded Thomas, begging him not to cast away this chance of peace.

In a ringing voice, my lord cried out, 'What? Am I to consider my own "peace", or that of any other man, before the duty I owe to God? Are these the . . . *terms* I am expected to accept? Know you, my lord, I have *terms* of my own, which do not barter the church and God as if they were vegetables upon a market-stall?'

Of course from the very beginning Thomas had been determined not to give anything to Henry except this payment, in good measure, for months of insult and of enforced separation from his only ally, Pope Alexander.

It is said that as the two monarchs rode away from Montmirail, not even kind King Louis could find it in his heart to defend the Archbishop against Henry's rage. Certainly as *we* rode away I noticed that Thomas had lost a little of his pallor, and that his eyes, lack-lustre for many weeks, were afire again. He said, 'How many days until Ascension, Will?'

Only at that moment did I appreciate the full cunning of his plan, for it will be remembered that on Ascension Day, if peace were not made, the Pope had restored Thomas's full power of anathema. Thus on Palm Sunday, 13 April 1169, Thomas excommunicated Gilbert Foliot, Bishop of London, and Jocelin of Salisbury, as well as renewing his fulmination against Randulph de Broc and all those others who had seized the estates and revenues of Canterbury. He ordered this matter so that his agent delivered the letters of excommunication at St Paul's Cathedral in London during the celebration of Mass on Ascension Day itself. This agent told the priest that in the name of the Archbishop of Canterbury and of His Holiness the Pope the letters must be read out to the congregation before the Mass might continue.

Foliot at first refused to accept his fate, claiming in his usual tendentious manner that the see of London was not subject to Canterbury, but it seems he did not absolutely believe this claim himself, which caught him in a cleft stick, not knowing quite what to do. Naturally he wrote a cluster of appeals to the Pope, but then found that King Henry forbade him to send any of them, for reasons which will presently be apparent. I was told that Foliot suffered greatly in this matter, and I confess that I was heartily pleased to hear it.

The King was naturally enraged by the whole chain of events. Thomas, with few friends and, in comparison with Henry, no power at all, had outwitted him and dealt him a crushing blow which might well be the first of many. In fact it began to look as though, if he did not come to terms with his Archbishop, and the 'terms' in this case would again not be the King's, he might well find the whole of England placed under papal interdict, all churches locked, all priests forbidden to carry out any of their duties. What then of Prince Henry's long-awaited coronation?

For this reason in particular, though the King still had various plans regarding the coronation which he had not yet revealed, he now took the step which Queen Eleanor had mentioned as a possibility many months before; he promulgated a whole series of decrees to keep the power of the Pope out of England altogether. Any agent bringing letters of interdict into England was to be considered a traitor; and if despite this precaution interdict was imposed, all who heeded it, priests included, were to be exiled with all their kin and without possessions or money, while anyone showing the slightest sign of allegiance to Pope or Archbishop, and this included appealing to them, was to suffer virtually the same fate. Nobody was to leave the country, while all those entering it were to show a passport and be searched for letters. To top it all, everyone in England over fifteen years of age must officially swear to observe the decrees.

Here again I seem to detect the same unbalanced lack of reason which attacked the King on so many occasions, notably at Northampton and when he banished from England all Thomas's relatives, and when he took to his bed, sick with rage, at Angers. In none of these actions against papal power can we even recognize the great law-maker, great general, great ruler, whom at other times we must acknowledge him to be.

As before, having thus allowed the fury full release his whole character seemed to change, for he now turned all his attention upon that other aspect of the coronation which I have mentioned above.

He approached King Louis, stating a somewhat uncharacteristic desire to worship at the shrine of St Denis in Montmartre outside

Paris. He would bring with him his second son, Richard, who was about to receive the customary period of education at his future father-in-law's court and make closer acquaintance with the Princess Alais who was to be his bride. Now, if during all this religious and feudal parleying, Louis could persuade Thomas also to visit St Denis, why then there would be a meeting between King and Archbishop which, by its seeming casual nature, might achieve more than any heralded conclave before an audience of barons and bishops and useless papal nuncios.

King Louis who, particularly following Henry's recent anti-papal decrees in England, wished nothing better than to see King and Archbishop in amity again, arranged everything the English King had requested.

Queen Adèle and her son came out a little way from Paris to greet Henry. Having paid his respects to the mother, he squatted down upon his heels and drew the little Prince to him, studying the smooth childish face for a long time – as if searching in it for some visible sign of what the blind woman had told him; then he sighed, shaking his head, and gave the boy his blessing.

Meanwhile Thomas had gone to Montmartre; and let no one believe that he did this unwillingly, as many writers of history assert. Just as he had known, before Montmirail, that he, not Henry, held the cards, so now at Montmartre he was sure in his own mind of what was to come and was well-prepared for it. The King had taken great pains to arrange the meeting, and no doubt planned to conduct it upon his own terms; Thomas knew that by the very nature of things this could not be.

He had therefore armed himself with a formidable list of all goods and properties and revenues of which, in his own word, he had been 'robbed' since leaving Canterbury nearly six years before. It was a massive accounting and I do not think that Herbert or I or his clerks had missed out one farthing. It was also a weathercock, for if Thomas had judged King Henry aright, and his reason for desiring this meeting, the account would be accepted without demur.

Henry accepted it without demur.

I caught a glint in my lord's eye as the King took his arm, leading him away from the rest of us in private conversation, which my day-book notes word for word.

Thomas said, 'If I may make so bold, your grace, what has caused this change in your temper towards me, following your recent fortification of England against my assaulting of it?'

Henry laughed. 'It is as I said at Pontigny; if I have not your advice upon such things I go too far. We have no business to be in discord, Thomas, it is against nature.'

'And,' said my lord quietly, 'you want me back at Canterbury so that I may crown your son and heir.'

This came too swiftly for the King, catching him out; after a moment he smiled and said, 'It is my sincerest wish.'

'Yet you have papal permission for that master of treachery, Roger of York, to perform the ceremony?'

Clearly Henry had thought this to be a secret, for he was again taken aback. 'Come,' he said, 'we both know that Roger of York will not do. Would I have *my* heir crowned by a Christian? Only you, as Canterbury and as Archbishop, shall lay your hands upon him.'

'Your grace does me great honour. In view of our many years of disagreement.'

Henry dismissed this with a wave of his hand. 'Let us not speak of Clarendon, nor my royal customs, nor the dignity of your order; all will be settled in friendship at some later time. Say you will return!'

Thomas hesitated, eyeing him more with amazement than any other emotion; for at times, as he said to me in dictating this, 'the blinkered self-esteem of Henry Plantagenet comes near to madness. I truly think that if he desires a thing strongly enough he believes that it will be accomplished by the very strength of his will.'

Now he said again, more eagerly, 'You will come, Thomas, will you not?'

'If I understand you aright,' replied my lord, 'you, the King, are now asking me, your Archbishop, to crown your heir in the year 1170; ten times the sacred seven since William Rufus gave himself to the ritual sacrifice, and seven years since I myself last refused. Do you think I am unhinged by exile, my lord, or do you think I cannot count?'

This quiet savagery drove King Henry a step away, but before his anger could break out, Thomas swung back towards King Louis and the great men of church and state surrounding him, and cried out in a clear voice, 'My lord the King and I are agreed. All is well between us.'

This was naturally greeted by a burst of congratulation, praise, pure relief. Thomas continued quickly: 'I need no contract, no guarantee, no protection from the Pope. All I ask of my lord in token is that we exchange, here and now, the Kiss of Peace.'

His eyes were glittering as he turned back to King Henry with open arms. It was of course the last straw. The King exploded into rage, and strode away shouting, 'Never! I vowed never again to give the Pax to this man, nor do I ever break my oath!'

None present could understand King Henry's rage. A certain lord quipped that this must be the only oath that the King had never broken, while King Louis was naturally exasperated by all the trouble he had been put to, purely at Henry's request.

As for me, and for you who have read thus far, we know as did none other at Montmartre that Thomas only played with words when he used the word 'exchange' regarding the Kiss. Once again, he, the elder, the Archbishop, and the Perfect in our true Cathar faith, would have given the Kiss of Peace *to* King Henry, not the reverse; and thereafter, had there been any thoughts of the ritual death, it would have been Henry who must die and not my lord. Thomas had fought and won, all over again, but this time in a single sentence, the long battle of 1163.

It had always been my suspicion that the French King knew more of things than he pretended. Later he said to Thomas, 'My lord Archbishop, if I were you I would not return to England under these circumstances for my own weight in gold.' And he offered Thomas any among the high ecclesiastical positions in France. Yet the good-hearted King did not know that my lord was not a Christian: in this wilderness of doubts he had to find his own way, and it was a harder way than any saving himself might understand; for now he stood alone, as all men must upon the great crisis of their lives.

After Montmartre I sensed a change in him, a withdrawal, though he continued ably enough to act out his part in public. Often, as I covertly watched him, solitary with his thoughts, it would seem to me that the man before me did not differ greatly

167

from young Thomas of London; he was but the same man pared down to his essential structure, stripped of all excess, worn smooth by all that he had experienced as a stone is worn smooth by the endless action of the sea. I had watched him wrestle with worldly ambition, knowing it to be his enemy, which indeed it had proved to be, and emerge from that battle with a sure sense of his own conscience; with him, I had followed the tortuous path of that conscience to his inevitable defiance of the King; I had stood by his side at Northampton and seen him bowed to the very ground by the King's vindictive rage. Yet he had not fallen, neither then nor in the long humiliations of his exile. He had found an inner strength to go forward upon his lonely journey, never surrendering to King Henry, for as he had said, 'I cannot give way without betraying myself and our faith.'

Now, although I could not know that the final testing was but a few weeks distant, nor guess at the form it would take, it seemed to me that Thomas had at last cast off entirely the values of the world, which had once meant so much to him. He stood alone and he stood prepared.

5

Meanwhile, to the surprise of no man, Pope Alexander had finally fallen out of patience with King Henry. He demanded a conclusion; Henry must accept Thomas's return to Canterbury, restore all his properties and revenues, and pay him a large sum in recompense. Thomas, for his part, was to offer his services to the King unconditionally, with the single proviso, 'saving the freedom of the church'. If Henry refused, England was to be placed under the dreaded interdict, and if he agreed he was to be instructed, after a reasonably face-saving interval, to abandon the Constitutions of Clarendon altogether.

But before the papal envoys could even state these conditions, the news half-expected but still astounding, reached us that King Henry had finally dispensed with prudence and thrown wisdom to the wind; he intended to have his heir crowned in England by the Archbishop of York. He was clearly enraged by Thomas's bettering of him at Montmartre, and by the fact that though he had spent huge sums in bribery within the Curia and upon the strengthening of the Emperor's army against Rome, Pope Alexander refused to be silenced. As for Thomas, he had defied Henry twice, and twice he had won the day. His final demand for the Kiss of Peace at Montmartre had surely set the seal upon what the King was now about to do. He must then have known that he himself was ultimately responsible for the fact that he was not crowning the boy; and yet there was no mistaking the pain and anger he felt upon hearing the news.

Pacing about the room which the abbey of Sens had set aside as his study, he said, 'So! Roger of York will crown the prince in the sacred year 1170! By the Two Faces, I hope that my lord King has prevailed upon him also to die the ritual death!'

I pointed out that the Archbishop of York was a Christian.

'He is a mealy-mouthed turncoat who desecrates the name of God every time his mouth speaks it. I find it fit that he is to crown a King who will die before he ever sits upon the throne.'

I asked, 'Do you so firmly believe the blind woman?'

'Do you not, William?'

After a moment's thought, I confessed then, for the first time, that I was indeed beginning to accept her prophecies.

My lord laughed again. 'And have you forgotten a certain woman in Winchester who foretold *sixteen years ago* that the boy would be crowned but would never rule?'

I had not forgotten, and never would; too much misery had been quietly predicted in that small room of Winchester castle in 1154.

'You will see,' said Thomas savagely, 'that as soon as this crowning is done with, the King will be back, full of good cheer and begging me to return to Canterbury.'

'And you will go?'

'Will he exchange the Kiss?'

'No.'

'You have your answer.'

Needless to say, when the Pope heard of the proposed coronation he acted at once and with absolute authority. He wrote to York and to all the other bishops that there was to be no such ceremony unless it was performed by the Archbishop of Canterbury; to even begin to make this possible the King must at once annul the Constitutions of Clarendon and the oath against papal authority which all the English people under the age of fifteen were supposed to have sworn. These letters left Benevento where Alexander was then in residence, on 25 February 1170, and did not reach Thomas until 17 March.

Roger of Worcester was at this time in Normandy, and my lord summoned him to take the papal letter, with certain of his own, directly to York and to deliver them into the hands of the bishop himself.

My lord of Worcester left next day; but King Henry had crossed the Channel in great haste more than two weeks earlier, on 3 March; he had set forth, as was his habit when pressed, into the teeth of a terrible gale. On this occasion he had not been so lucky as before; one of his newest ships was destroyed with the loss of 400 lives. Many saw in this an omen presaging bad fortune to the mission on which he was bound. The King ignored such talk, and his first action upon landing was to strengthen all his earlier laws and precautions against those who might be carrying letters from the Pope or the Archbishop. I do not know whether so noble a man as the Bishop of Worcester, himself a cousin to King Henry, would have been stopped and searched; the occasion never arose since he was prevented by the King's agents in Normandy from taking ship at all.

He communicated this news to Thomas, who at once sent another and less prestigious messenger, Benedict; this man took the letters from the Bishop, and eventually found ship during the first week of April.

Now the coronation was planned for 14 June, so that even with the delays I have described, and even supposing Benedict had the utmost trouble in evading Henry's guards, he must have delivered the letters by the middle of April. Moreover, if circumstances had delayed him until the end of that month, which is unlikely, six weeks would still have remained for York and the others to answer or to take action.

It has been said that the letters were not received until the very eve of the coronation, a story which no one believes, and Roger of York even went so far as to claim that he never saw them at all, but this was a year later when he himself stood in danger of excommunication. The truth is certainly that all the recipients allowed themselves to be ruled by their fear of the King. So much for the conscience of a Christian bishop! In my experience one may find loyalty and good faith aplenty among the humbler sort of Christian, and precious little of it in their overlords who are for the most part barons disguised in vestments, more dangerous than their lay brothers because they tend to be better educated.

The pending coronation was not without other hazards. Chief among these was the young Prince Henry's maiden wife, Marguerite of France. Would King Louis be more insulted if she were temporarily left uncrowned, or if she were crowned by men whom he would certainly consider to be acting against the right of Canterbury and the decrees of the Pope himself? Though she was held ready in Normandy with her princely husband, for fear of interdict being imposed upon England, it was finally decided to keep her there; a second coronation would be held in due course.

Queen Eleanor had journeyed north from Poitou to take charge of these royal children, thus bringing her regency closer for a time to the drama being enacted in England. For the present she wished to co-operate in every way with the King, her husband; it suited her that they should remain on the best possible terms; but as ever with this woman there was a deeper and more dangerous reason for her desire to be in Normandy in the middle of this year 1170.

She chose to occupy the castle of Caen, not merely because of its proximity to the coast, but because part of it had recently been modernized and was therefore warmer and more comfortable than others in the vicinity.

While Henry had been busying himself with abortive meetings at Montmirail and Montmartre, and with safeguarding the coronation of his heir, the Queen had been much more positively employed in her southern domains. Using all her considerable knowledge of statecraft, not to mention her considerable charm as a woman, she had been proclaiming Prince Richard to all her vassals with such a show of grandeur and majesty as had not been seen in those parts for many years. She took advantage of each of these royal journeys to make peace between warring lords, and to restore, in the Prince's name, those estates which his father had seized. Thus, most of the exiled noblemen came home again with the sons of others whom Henry had killed; their love and loyalty towards Eleanor in no way softened their hatred of her husband. Everywhere she went, the strong young Prince at her side, she demonstrated in deeds no less than words that Poitou and Aquitaine constituted an ancient and honoured realm, and that they were now being restored to the power and prestige of which they had every right to be proud.

Prince Richard would be recognized as ruler-designate of all this richness and tradition in two years' time, when he was fifteen. It would be an occasion just as splendid as that which was about to see the crown of England placed upon his elder brother's head in Westminster Abbey, and it would suffer none of the absences and anomalies which attended the coronation of the 'Young King Henry' as he was now officially to be called.

Not that the ceremony of 14 June wanted for splendour. Henry Plantagenet was determined that it should gain in visual majesty what it lacked in traditional and legal sanction. Yet in spite of this, I have been told by many who were present that there was a strange feeling of unease. To begin with, though it was a common enough practice in France and Germany, this was the first time that an heir to the throne of England had ever been crowned while his predecessor was alive. King Stephen, it will be remembered, had wished it for his son, Eustace, but Henry's ambition, Thomas's legal skill, and a dish of eels, had intervened. Many now felt that it was in some indefinable way unfit to have a 'Young King' and therefore, by inference, an 'Old King' sharing the same throne; they recognized it as self-evident that nature would all too soon see to it that the Young King grew to full manhood, while his father, though still no doubt a power to be reckoned with, would by then be past his prime. Could there be anything in this but an open invitation to dissension and even rebellion? Others asked how this most holy and important moment of the young Prince's life could be properly consecrated without the presence of the Archbishop of Canterbury and against the wishes of the Pope.

The King hoped that such doubting and carping would be

silenced by the magnificent banquet which followed the ceremony; this was indeed, by every account, a most splendid feast, yet I cannot help feeling that William of Canterbury's story concerning the boar's head, which he has assured me is perfectly true, for he was there, must have summed up in many estimations the peculiar character of that whole day.

It seems that when this dish was brought to the royal table, the serving-man was seen to be none other than Henry Plantagenet himself, a kingly gesture to tell the world in what regard they should hold this 'Young King'.

Roger of York, servile and unctuous as ever, exclaimed, 'Ah, what Prince can claim to have been served at table by a King!'

Young Henry, at all times spoiled and at this time no doubt over-excited by his new grandeur, replied, 'My lord, do you think it a condescension for the son of a count to serve the son of a king?'

Was Henry (son of the Count of Anjou indeed) so proud of his wonderful boy that he laughed with those who dared to laugh at this merry quip? Or did his eyes narrow, as I have seen them narrow a hundred times, reading in this audacity a true sign of the boy's developing character which was to cause him so much future trouble?

While all this was going forward, a strange thing happened at Sens.

From time to time the good Abbot prevailed upon Thomas to conduct a Mass. As I have said, we Cathars may use the ritual, though our reading of it is somewhat different from the Christian one. Thomas would agree perhaps once a month, because he would do nothing to hurt the feelings of this man who had been so generous towards us. On the Sunday before the coronation Thomas was asked, and once more agreed, to officiate.

As ever when my lord appeared in the abbey, there was a great press of people, so that when it came to the consecration of the Host there was hardly a Christian man or woman (for many came who were not Christians) who did not wish to receive the bread and the wine which, to them, represent the body and blood of the Son.

I feared for Thomas's strength, for this was a long and tedious part of the ritual, but he declined assistance and continued alone.

Now even I, watching closely in anxiety for his health, did not notice the woman, nor my lord's reaction to her, nor indeed the fact that she did not properly receive the sacrament. Only as she rose from her knees to leave the church did I realize that a man led her by the arm and that she was blind; that she was, in fact, the blind woman of the cave. My astonishment was only matched by my uneasiness, for it must indeed have been a matter of great importance which had brought her nigh on thirty miles from Pontigny, and then into the abbey itself, a place for which she can have felt at the least no affinity and at the most a very real distaste.

As soon as the Mass was over and Thomas once more alone, I went to him immediately. He was sitting at his desk, his head supported in his hands. Looking up, understanding my expression, he said, 'You saw her then?'

'Yes.'

'She brought me . . . news.'

'What news?'

He stood up and came to me, putting an arm around my shoulder; I never doubted his affection for me, but any physical showing of it was so rare that I was taken aback. I saw that his face, as he looked up into the summer sky, for we stood by a window, was all skin and bone, and yet not haggard. At this time he possessed a strange physical beauty, as of a sculptor's marble, refined and refined and finished in ascetic perfection. But now I fall over my words; the truth is that he looked what he was, for had he not struggled these many years with temptations both of the spirit and of the flesh in order to become what, in our true Cathar faith, we call Perfect?'

'What news?' I asked again. 'What did she say?'

'I am to be called,' he said quietly, still staring up at the pale blue sky. 'Called to judge myself.'

I suppose, weak as I am, that I could not suppress a small shudder, and he felt it through the arm that rested lightly upon my shoulder; he looked at me and smiled. 'There is nothing to fear, Will. I have done the best I can; if it has not been good enough then I merely join the great majority of men, do I not?'

Reader, be patient with me! We come so close now to many

things of which I am forbidden to write. The great secrets of our faith may not be revealed because revelation can bring danger and even death to other Brethren. The Council of Tours, which my lord attended in May of 1163 was in itself a sure sign that the Christian church intends, eventually, to brook no rival religion. The days of freedom are dwindling fast, and it will not be long before we, like all minorities at all times, will have to face persecution. Then the Christians will proclaim that the great days of faith are born, when in reality they themselves will have killed faith, which is not one thing to all men, but all things to all men. The Christians will sacrifice God himself to the glory of their church; already they have confused the two in their own minds.

Of this calling to self-judgement, which is one of the corner-stones of the Cathar faith, let me simply say that it is in part like to the confessional of the Christians, and in part a court of law, more terrible than any other on earth because he who is called must judge himself from the depth of his own soul, yet aloud in the hearing of others; for we do not believe that one man has the right to judge his own brother, all being equal before God.

Thomas dropped his arm from my shoulder and turned away with a deep sigh. 'Let them call me soon, for then I think I will find rest.'

My lord's estimation of King Henry's actions following the coronation were exact. First of all he wrote from England to the papal legates, saying that he wished for nothing more than to obey Pope Alexander's instructions and to make his peace with Thomas. Then he took ship for Normandy, and hastened to meet the legates in person; he listened patiently to all that the Pope demanded of him, and agreed to all, with one exception which hardly needs to be mentioned to those of us who already know the true facts: he would not exchange the Kiss of Peace.

He said that he would consider this at a later date, and we may be sure that the date he had in mind was to be after 31 January 1170, when the sacred year, and the chance of Henry himself becoming the Divine Victim like his ancestor William Rufus, were safely passed.

He then moved on, all piety and goodwill, to seek audience of King Louis. Once again he begged the French King to arrange a meeting with Thomas at which all their differences would be solved. One may almost hear the sigh with which King Louis agreed, but agree he did.

I cannot, however I may try, imagine what the outcome of this meeting would have been. Who can say how long these two obstinate and proud men, each defending what was, to him, a perfect right, would have continued to fight and to obstruct each other? Until the end of their lives perhaps; and the good God alone knows what distress and misery this would have wreaked upon hundreds, even thousands, of innocent people, let alone upon Henry and Thomas themselves! But before King Louis could summon my lord to meet Henry Plantagenet yet again, the call came and all things were changed.

On the evening of 14 July I persuaded Thomas to leave the abbey and to take a little fresh air for the good of his health, and thus we rode together some miles out into the pleasant countryside surrounding Sens.

We both knew instantly what was to come when, circling a clump of poplars some four miles distant from the city walls, three horsemen wheeled from cover and reined in, waiting for us. As we drew near, one cried, 'Thomas of London?'

My lord, coughing a little for the dust swirled under our hooves, replied, 'I am he.'

The man said, 'I would be saved and I would save. Amen.'

Thomas replied, 'I would hear and I would be heard. Amen.'

The man then pointed along a track leading away from the city and we all spurred forward. Glancing at my lord's tranquil face, I was ashamed at the turmoil in my own mind, let alone that in my stomach.

After an hour's riding through woods and across fields loud with birdsong, sweet with the scent of newly mown hay, I saw upon the horizon a castle, and guessed that this was to be our destination.

It was not a large place, and its outward mien was grim, heavily fortified against troubled times. The courtyard within seemed to belong to another world, for here a spring surged up and splashed into a round basin, and vines shaded the south-facing walls, roses tangled amongst them, so that the calm air of evening was sweet. Doves fluttered about a stone cote, their pure whiteness grown pink in the light of the setting sun.

We were led into the castle, directly to the great hall which was empty. A big carven chair had been placed at its centre, facing the high table of whatever lord owned this pleasant place. Six chairs had been set there, and flanking each were candles in holders of heavy gold, seven in all. In the wide hearth burned a fire of huge logs, which seemed to me unnecessary on a warm evening of July; yet this, like all else, was planned.

Thomas sat down in the solitary chair, seeming small and frail within it, while I was conducted to a curtained archway, beyond which steps led upwards to the gallery, not prepared for the usual making of music, but, as I had guessed, for my making of notes: a table and a chair, fine quills and parchment.

Six men came in by a side door, ordinary men to look at, though of high rank, each wearing such clothes as his day had demanded of him, and took their seats facing Thomas. Three of these I recognized; one was head of a noble house near Poitou, and had travelled far for this duty; one was a man of some importance, often seen at the elbow of King Louis of France, who was, I am sure, unaware of the faith he followed; the third was an abbot who had often attended us at Pontigny, though at that time he had given no sign to me that he stood as high in the Cathar church as he did in the Christian one. The others were unknown to me, but I think that Thomas recognized them all.

A manservant lit the seven candles, which did not yet vie with the glow of sunset, and then withdrew, leaving the seven men to their business.

The noble Poitevin said, 'A mirror am I to thee that beholdest me. Amen.'

Thomas repeated this: 'A mirror am I to thee that beholdest me. Amen.' And added, 'I would hear and I would be heard. Amen. A door am I to thee that knockest at me. Amen.'

How can I describe the majesty of the scene below me, for it was of such simplicity. There is a majesty of the soul which defies description by word and is only appreciated in the heart. All I can say is that all the mighty panoply of our ride to Paris when Thomas was Chancellor, and all the rich magnificence of the conclaves at Westminster or Montmirail, were as nothing to this simplicity.

In the calling to question there is no man of higher position than any other, yet by the laws of chance or nature all men are not equal upon every occasion, and upon this particular occasion five of the questioners deferred to a sixth who was much older. I understood later that this man, long ago, had instructed my lord in much of our faith, and had conducted him through the ceremony of the Consolamentum, thus initiating him as a Perfect.

This man now said, 'Thomas of London, all here know you as Perfect, and your love for the true faith is not held to question.'

Thomas bowed his head.

'Tell us of your King, and of your love for him, and of your oaths to him.'

I think perhaps my lord was truly startled by this, for he raised his head sharply and stared at the six faces, intent in the candlelight. 'All?' he said. 'All that long story?'

The abbot said, 'You are well versed in speech and law; you will, I think, make it shorter than the nigh-on twenty years that you have known and served him.'

So Thomas told them, in the neat phrases for which I have always admired and envied him, of the many things he had done since our meeting with Queen Eleanor and Henry and his father in King Louis' palace on the Ile de France. They listened intently and in silence. The sun set; the doves fell silent in their stone cote outside the windows.

When my lord came to the midnight meeting with Henry in the barn on 3 December 1163, he said, 'And then the King asked me if I was his man, "his man unto death" were the words, as I recall; he asked me upon God's will and the two faces of Mary, upon the blood of the Bull and of the Son who died. And I . . .' He nodded to himself and cleared his throat. 'I replied, "I would be united and I would unite. Amen." '

'And have you stood by this oath?' It was the first question for perhaps half an hour to break the single sound of Thomas's voice, and it was the older man who asked it.

My lord answered swiftly, 'I was but a clerk at the time, and he Duke of Normandy.'

'Have you stood by this oath, Thomas?' It was the nobleman who stood so high at the court of King Louis who repeated the question.

There was a long silence. Then my lord sighed deeply and said, 'No.'

'You are Perfect, you have your reasons.'

'I did not consider, I do not consider, that he has the right to bid me die for him.'

'In the sacred year of his Old Religion, 1163?'

'Yes.'

'Yet you had sworn to be his man unto death, sworn upon our Book.'

'I never swore to die in a ritual sacrifice which is not a tenet of our faith.'

The Poitevin leaned forwards and said gently, 'It is a tenet of King Henry's faith, and you had sworn to be his man. Surely, Brother, you thus swore to die for him in terms no less certain than any half-educated knight who may kiss the King's hand and fall in battle the very next day with an arrow through his brain. Think, Brother. And continue.'

They waited long for my lord to continue; but at last, and I thought in a fainter voice, he told them of Henry's coming to the throne, and of the great things he accomplished for England, aided by his Queen and his great Chancellor. He told of the power which he had then wielded, of his princely standing.

Again the question, from a younger man unknown to me. 'In all this power and pomp we know that you prayed very often, sometimes all night, and subjected yourself to the lash, and gave richly to the poor. But what of your heart, Thomas? What of your spirit?'

Sitting alone in my dark gallery I thought of my lord's bedchamber in his palace at Westminster; I recalled the figure lying there upon the bed, back bloodstained from the penitential lash, and of the agonized voice which cried, 'I mock my boasted Perfection, do I not? I mock our whole faith and the truth I claim to bear. Answer, Conscience! Is my immortal soul in danger of damnation?'

I recalled also how, stricken, I had given the easy answer – that his very condition, his very self-questioning were all the answers his soul required – and how he had risen from the bed in rage, crying, 'Do not mince mindless words with me, William!' before falling unconscious in my arms. After another long silence he said, 'I loved power too much; I allowed ambition to rule me.' He did not tell them how desperately he had fought with that ambition, goaded in part by me, and I supposed that, in him, he knew that they would take this for granted.

'Continue.'

Does the reader understand now why I have called this procedure terrible? If not, let him look inward and judge, in all honesty, the actions of his own life.

It was dark now, owls calling far and near for there was an early moon. Thomas's voice rose in the candlelit gloom of the great hall, recounting the story of that vital struggle which had ended in his becoming Archbishop, defending himself against his own judgement of himself. 'It was a trick. The King is full of tricks. At Winchester I showed the Prince of my own free will, but I accepted Canterbury at sword-point.'

The six men were silent, knowing as well as Thomas did that no trick could vitiate an oath sworn upon the sacred Book, and that the trick itself arose directly from that ambition and lust for power which my lord had already admitted. Dear God, how simple it seemed, all that tangled past, in this quiet hall where seven intelligent men sat together in merciless trust and love.

I was remembering another room in a humble farmhouse where I had lain in a fever, having fallen from my horse during the return from Paris of the Chancellor's mighty procession. How cravenly I had cried, 'Great times and greater times are for such as you, Thomas. I fear too much greatness, too much power, too much show.' Yet now I sat above him, secure in my minstrels' gallery, while the great man I could never hope to emulate sat below me in self-judgement and self-inflicted agony.

I wished at that moment that I might leap to my feet and defend him, for if all were such as I and none such as he, the world would wither for lack of sustenance; yet, as I wished it, I knew that he was not suffering a judgement or an agony of the world, but of his own inmost spirit.

So, through the angry confrontations of Woodstock, Westminster, Clarendon and Northampton he led them to his flight from F~ ~land into final exile.

Again they were silent.

Thomas said, wearily, 'Yes, yes. I was his sworn man, and I loved him as I love him now; and I left him when he most needed me and my guidance.'

One said, 'Had you returned, he would have imprisoned you for life or had you killed.'

Thomas shook his head. 'I loved him and fled from him.'

Did he, I wondered, down there in his darkness, even realize that the roles had suddenly been reversed; one of the six had defended his action, and Thomas himself had condemned it?

The older man said, 'Brother, in exile you have suffered greatly. We only have to look at you . . .' My lord held up his hand, and the other fell silent. It was a silence which lasted for a longer time than before. The owls hooted at their hunting. Logs settled gently in the hearth. At last Thomas rose wearily to his feet and said, 'I would be saved and I would save. Amen.' And, after a pause: 'I swore upon our sacred Book to serve King Henry in all things, and, these last six years of exile, I have fought him in all things. I have even fought him with the Kiss of Peace, and forced him to have his heir crowned illegally.

'Before then, I practised the outward show of our blessed faith, but I knew in my spirit that ambition and the desire for ever greater power ruled me and had their will of me. I have betrayed my friend and King even though I loved him . . .' His voice broke, and the older man said, with great tenderness, 'Do not think that you have not suffered every provocation, every humiliation. The whole world knows it.'

Thomas replied, 'As ever, the "world" knows nothing.'

'Do you then judge yourself?'

'Yes, yes.' It was little more than an impatient whisper and it held the whole weight of his weariness. 'I have judged myself these seventeen years. Thomas of London is guilty of breaking an oath sworn upon the body of the blessed St John, the beloved of Christ; guilty of using that oath as best it suited his own will. He is guilty of worldly pride and ambition which made a mockery of his pretended Perfection in our true faith. Worst of all, he is guilty of betra,.ng love in its most profound meaning, as it existed between John and the Son.'

Silence. Then : 'And do you sentence yourself?'

'I do.'

They did not need to ask him what that sentence might be. Neither did I; but I know that I leaned my forehead upon my arms alone up there in my minstrels' gallery, and wept.

When I looked up the six men had gone. Thomas lay upon the stone-flagged floor of the hall, his arms outstretched as if upon the hated cross. The seven candles had been placed in a circle around him.

In sudden panic, I took my taper and tumbled down the twisting steps, but my fear was unfounded, he was only sleeping. His soul had found the rest he so deeply needed, and his body had followed it.

Understanding now the purpose of that fire upon a warm night of July, I piled it with more logs, for God knows the stone floor was chill enough; then I sat near to it, watching him. He never stirred. I dozed and awoke; dozed and awoke. His position remained the same, so that I knew that this was no ordinary sleep, but the sleep of ancient knowledge.

A little after I had heard the faint crowing of the first rooster, when all but two of the candles had guttered out, Thomas opened his eyes. The windows were grey with dawn. He remained lying thus for a little time; then stirred and stood up easily, as if from a feather-bed rather than one of stone; for the first time in many months I saw a trace of colour in his cheeks. He smiled at me and said, 'They will be worrying about us at the abbey. Let us make haste.'

We never spoke, then or later, of what had occurred in that hall. The final turning-point in the life of Thomas of London passed in silence.

Part four

Henry, when you have taken all, I shall fight you
with love, for that you cannot take.

Thomas of London, March 1166

I

There is no one who was present, neither lord nor bishop nor chronicler, who has not expressed amazement at the change in Thomas's attitude to King Henry when finally they met at Fréteval on 22 July 1170.

It was little over a month since the King, in the eyes of the world, had submitted his Archbishop to the final indignity by commanding Roger of York to crown his heir. All men there and then agreed that now there could be no possible reconciliation between the King and my lord.

The speed with which Henry, following the coronation, had hastened to Normandy to meet the Pope's envoys, a breed he was ever ready to avoid at all costs, showed how clearly he realized what the repercussions to his action might be. Certainly he must also have had grave doubts concerning this encounter with Thomas, and he must indeed have been surprised when, contrary to most of the official descriptions, it was his Archbishop who took the initiative, hurrying to the King and bending the knee to kiss his hand. Thereafter they embraced and immediately walked a little apart: it was noticed that Thomas spoke quickly and decisively and that the King listened, nodding; then both men returned to the Archbishop of Sens, who had led my lord to this meeting, and openly discussed before him and his advisers the disagreements which had divided them for so long. Henry, fully aware of how the world judged him regarding the coronation, seemed eager to please; he swore to banish all those men who, in Thomas's estimation, had counselled him injudiciously and selfishly, and to accept the historical claims of Canterbury as my lord envisaged them. Thomas, for his part, again knelt before the King, swearing obedience without mention of 'his order' or 'the rights of the church'; no reference was made to the Constitutions of Clarendon, and none to the Kiss of Peace.

To say that all who stood by were astounded falls far short of the truth; the chroniclers were faced with the additional task of trying to make sense upon parchment, and therefore in public, of what they had seen and heard. As for the Archbishop of Sens, he wasted no time in wonderment, but set his clerks to work at once upon a document of reconciliation; he was doubtless amazed to find that Henry had not even changed his mind next day, and signed it without question, only adding the words, 'saving the honour of my kingdom'. At once all heads turned towards Thomas, awaiting the expected objection; they waited in vain.

News of all this was immediately dispatched to King Louis in Paris; he can certainly be forgiven for saying, 'God be praised! But let us not praise men too hastily, for they are liable to change where God is not.' More than any other human being, that patient and quiet monarch had good reason to doubt the faith of the two protagonists.

Amid all this astonishment, doubt and disbelief, my reader again stands with me upon a different eminence from which we may gain a slightly different view of the proceedings. On the evening of the 22nd, while the clerks were hard at work drawing up their documents, there took place between Henry and Thomas the last of those secret conversations, each of which was a milestone in their relationship. Only in a full knowledge of what passed between them in private can there be any understanding of their public actions during the day that was ending, and during the five months to come. This is why, once again, all who chronicle those months do so as in a maze, struggling to find a way out of their confusion, disregarding facts which make no sense to them, and enlarging others which fit their own particular theory but which are of no importance at all. Thus the whole becomes at best distorted and at worst nonsensical contradiction.

In his private rooms at Fréteval, King Henry said to my lord, 'Now that all is decided in principle, when do you plan to go back to Canterbury?'

Thomas replied, 'There is much to be completed in France, debts to be paid, documents to be destroyed or correctly preserved; and in all I must stand upon the orders of my overlord, the Pope.'

He told me later that he could see Henry watching him carefully as he spoke, almost with held breath. This made him smile, and he said, 'Know this, my King and my friend, I will go there before the end of this sacred year 1170, and I go there to die.'

He says that the ruddy good health which was always evident upon Henry's face actually paled. He released his breath in a gasp, made as if to stand up, and then, as if unable to find the strength, lay back slowly in his chair, staring.

Thomas then told him quickly how he had been called to the question, and how, in that quiet hall before his Brothers and friends, he had come to certain irrevocable conclusions about himself, his motives and his actions. During this, Henry looked away out of the window, where the late dusk of July was falling upon the forests and meadows of Fréteval. When Thomas had finished he was silent for a long time; then he said, 'Do you recall how at Pontigny, when I swore to fight you until you had nothing left, you replied, "Henry, when you have taken all, I shall fight you with love, for that you cannot take"?'

'I remember very well.'

'It seems,' said the King, 'that you win the battle after all.'

'The world will say, with truth, that *you* win.'

'It is of little comfort to "win" upon the death of a friend . . .'

'Yet only by dying do I prove my love of you.'

'. . . the death of my only friend.' He stood up and looked into my lord's face, reading there the marks of privation and the soul's torture. 'For mark this well, Thomas, you were, and ever have been, my only friend. Is it not odd that I who have so often wished you dead for this or that reason, now wish you not to die.'

'It is beyond your willing. Beyond mine also.'

The King but stands upon the edge of our faith, yet others of his family have been true believers since the beginning; he knows very well the meaning of the call. 'Why did you judge yourself so harshly?'

'Is it not clear? In breaking my sworn oath to you, I broke at the same time every single tenet of the faith. I was not worthy even to be called a believer, yet I still called myself Perfect. I cannot even claim honest self-delusion, for I knew it all in my heart. You gave power to my over-ruling ambition and I thought of nothing else. Only when you called me to Canterbury did I begin to face the truth.'

'Then it is I who have destroyed you.'

'I have even tried to believe that lie. What I did, *I* did; and for that I have judged and sentenced myself. Though I think the world will blame you directly for my death.'

Henry shrugged his disdain for the world's opinion.

'You will have to undergo the ritual spilling of your own blood, which the Christians have absorbed into their own faith under the guise of penitence.'

'You warn me as my great Chancellor was used to do.'

'For half an hour I must be that Chancellor again, if your grace wills.'

'I desire nothing better. But our world has changed, Thomas, the world we made in our youth. Sometimes I fear the words of your blind woman.' He stood lost in thought for a moment; then said, 'Proceed, Chancellor!'

'We have harmed England greatly by our antagonism; all that you strove to make strong we have weakened.'

'I know this.'

'However we may think of it personally, the Christian church is one cornerstone of that strength. The church must be strong with the King. Therefore your grace must call the bishops to council and make peace with them; it will be easy without my interference.'

Henry smiled at this, suddenly boy-like again, so that my lord found himself smiling also, as of old at some private joke. Then, more seriously: 'I shall return to Canterbury, and the people will flock to me because they will know that I am come to die for them. Now in this it may suit you well to read signs of rebellion which, from the King's point of view, could make good excuse for my death. Your barons will applaud you, for they dislike me heartily, and thus they will join the church at your side.'

'The Pope, I think, will be less pleased.'

'Alexander will fulminate as the situation demands; but he is too clever a man not to capitalize upon what it offers, using it for his own ends, as your grace himself will do.'

Henry nodded, once more staring as if in wonder. 'You speak of your own death as I've heard you speak of . . . procuring a tax for the rebuilding of the keep at Angers. Are you not afraid, Thomas?'

'I have been, and will be, but am not now when I act as your

Chancellor, for it is another man, not the Chancellor, who is to die.'

'I was a fool ever to have lost you by forcing Canterbury upon you.'

Thomas remained silent.

'Was I not? Chancellor?'

'Yes, my lord; but things work out as they will, and now we must make do with what we have, and that, used correctly, contains power; for I think that what I desire most greatly from my dying is England strong at your back once more.'

King Henry shook his head, again in that kind of wonder, and said, 'Thomas of London, are you so little Norman at heart that you care so much for England's future?'

Thomas told me that he had not thought overmuch on this, but that when the King spoke thus he realized for the first time that he was indeed more English than Norman. He replied, 'Thomas of London I am; others aplenty will care for Normandy.'

'My son and heir, the Duke,' said Henry, with an edge to his voice, 'cares little; except for show and his own grandeur.'

Thomas said nothing. The King turned sharply away in the nearly dark room. 'I was wrong to divide my lands as I did at Montmirail, was I not?'

'My lord it is done,' said Thomas gently.

'Would you, as Chancellor, have advised that division?'

'No, your grace.'

'I was wrong. The eaglets try their wings, but I am still strong, and they do well to recognize the fact.'

'Your grace is but thirty-seven years old.'

'I bear many scars.'

'Scars, once healed, do but toughen the skin.'

The King turned back to him then, smiling. He lit a candle and brought it near, once more examining his friend's face. 'So, my good Chancellor, you advise that we emerge from Fréteval as we have emerged from other such conclaves, uncertain of each other's temper.'

'I think,' said Thomas, 'we must have seemed to find conciliation, lest others lose all patience. Edgy conciliation. It must be judged delicately; too many close to you wish so ardently for my death that any real show of amity between us now may lose you their support.

Before I go to England I will give you . . .' My lord admitted to me that here his courage did indeed forsake him, but only momentarily: 'I will give you the date. As for the Kiss of Peace, which has plagued us enough, it is obvious now that you must continue your refusals; we must never exchange it in public in this year 1170, yet I must seem to seek it as before. All who surround you are not fools, and if I do not, one or another may guess the truth which must not be guessed.'

'But,' said Henry, 'I would receive it from you now, in secret, as I did at Pontigny.'

Then Thomas gave him the Pax, and the King went down upon both knees before him. My lord blessed him in the name of the Bull and of the Son who died, making the ritual signs upon his forehead. Then he said, 'I, Thomas of London, being your anointed high-priest and thus a part of your royal body, do swear upon the word of the blessed St John, the beloved of Christ, and upon the gods of the Old Faith, that I am now become the Divine Victim in place of my King, and that until my last breath is drawn I, not you, wear the body of the god who must die. Amen.'

The King said, 'Amen', but did not rise from his knees. After a time he spoke again: 'I will ever thank you, Thomas my friend, for teaching me the meaning of the word "love". I shall not live by it as you have striven to live by it, for I am not strong as you are strong. But through you I have at least understood its meaning, and even that is denied the great majority of men.' His voice broke a little as he added, 'The gods go with you.'

Thomas said, 'God go with you, my lord.'

Henry rose to his feet, and they studied each other's countenances as if, my lord said, they both wished to rediscover, if only for a moment, the great trust and friendship which had for so long bound them one to the other. Then the King said, 'Lest there is no other opportunity for it later: farewell, Thomas, my only friend.'

'Farewell, Henry, my King and friend. We are truly as one now, all else may be forgotten.'

So they embraced for the last time in private, and so they parted.

Now it may be understood, by those who have never understood before, why, when the Pope once more imposed a censure upon all Thomas's enemies, which he did a few days later, Thomas pleaded with him to spare such unworthy men as Gilbert Foliot and many others who had betrayed him. Of course this action makes no sense if it is not seen against the background of what passed between King Henry and my lord, in secret, regarding England.

Only one, Roger, Archbishop of York, did Thomas abandon to papal justice, for he had been at the centre of opposition, and had crowned Prince Henry with his own hands against the Pope's personal command. Much has been made of Thomas's saintly nobility in this matter, but of course the truth as we know it is that he wished all those lords of the church to support the King and if they were excommunicated their power in this would have no meaning.

All noticed, of course, that the relationship between King and Archbishop had cooled somewhat since Fréteval, for that was exactly the impression both men wished to give; there were also several occasions when the Kiss of Peace might have been exchanged in public, and none failed to comment on the fact that it was not. In fact a whole flock of little legends grew up around this single subject; all of them noted that in this way and that Henry would avoid all chance of the Pax, even, in one crowning feat of some busybody's imagination, going so far as to call for a Requiem Mass on a certain occasion at Tours, lest Thomas might officiate and exchange the Kiss as part of the ritual. It is not, I should add for those unacquainted with the quirks of Christian behaviour, included in a Requiem.

Further fuel was added to this make-believe fire when Henry, without apparently consulting his Archbishop, summoned the Bishops of London and Salisbury to Normandy to advise him upon the settling of church matters in England. All looked towards Thomas for an indignant reaction, which he willingly gave, even though Henry had summoned the bishops upon his own urgent advice.

All, as you will understand, was now double, for in a sense, the Christian sense, Thomas no longer regarded himself as Archbishop of Canterbury; his mind was already fixed upon other matters, and he was steeling his spirit to meet and accept gracefully the crisis that awaited him, terrible to us, but to him merely an inevitable self-sentence of death, a final reckoning in that lifelong struggle with his own spirit and, at the last, a greatly desired victory.

John of Salisbury, who had been sent ahead to find out how things fared at Canterbury, returned in great distress; it seemed that the King had made none of the reparations so blithely promised at Fréteval, and that the de Broc family, among others, still held the church lands which they had been given upon my lord's flight into exile. Thomas had to soothe John's anger while at the same time hiding from this very Christian Christian that he cared not a whit who held what of Canterbury, that he had long since rescued his own people there from any deprivation, and that he was now simply a Perfect of the Cathar faith; Canterbury must wait for a Christian successor to fight its battles and put its affairs in order. Again, he had other matters to occupy mind and soul.

I have said that Henry and Thomas were never alone together after their meeting on the evening of 22 July, but there was, at Tours, another secret conclave between them, four other men attending.

William de Tracy held estates in Devon, Somerset and Gloucester where he was a knight of substance and standing, as was Richard le Breton, another knight of the West Country; Reginald FitzUrse was the son of one Sybilla, a grand-niece of the first Henry, and Hugh de Moreville was a great landowner in the north of England. All were held in high regard at the King's court and had served both Henry and England with good faith and loyalty; so let no man pretend, as many have, that those who would come to Canterbury with drawn swords to exact the ritual sacrifice were adventurers or mere assassins. They were courtly men of solid wealth and position, well known to my lord.

To each, in that privacy, he gave the Kiss of Peace and said, 'What you will do, do with an unburdened soul, for God demands it of you, and I shall willingly accept it.' He warned them, however, that none could tell what situations might arise upon their arrival at Canterbury on the given day, for there would be many who wished to protect him, many who would not perceive, or would not dare to perceive, the reality of what they were witnessing. 'These,' he said, 'are not important, my lords, and we shall circumvent them. Our sole concern is that what occurs between *us* be cleanly and well done, so that those with eyes to see shall know its meaning and be joyful.'

The four knights, for their part, commended his courage and prayed that their own might be equal when it came to the testing. It was William de Tracy, holding estates in the westernmost parts of England where the old faiths are stronger than in the south, who said, 'I understand why the true motive for what we must do is to be hidden from those who have not eyes to see, yet upon arriving at Canterbury we must be heard to speak out in anger against the Archbishop, or none will believe our presence there.'

Hugh de Moreville, who had been a witness at Clarendon and was a Justice, perhaps understood more of politics than his colleagues; he said, 'As King's men we can once more object to the courts of the church, demanding in your grace's name that Thomas dismiss them forthwith.'

The King shook his head, not deeming this a strong enough excuse, and Thomas said, 'Let excommunication be the bone of contention.'

'But,' argued FitzUrse, 'your lordship has just pleaded with the Pope to lift all censure save upon Roger of York.'

The King smiled. 'What the Archbishop has done in charity he may swiftly repent of; it will not be the first time.'

So it was decided that presently my lord would change his temper regarding certain bishops and also certain laymen who opposed him, such as Ridel, the Archdeacon, and Randulph de Broc; and it would be these excommunications which would be the knights' excuse for violent words and finally for violent action when at last they came to Canterbury.

So it was done.

Let me add that at least one of the legends is true: when Thomas mounted his horse upon leaving Tours, King Henry did indeed hold his stirrup for him, and it was indeed a mark of signal deference. All who witnessed it have expressed their hundred explanations of its meaning; we of the Brethren who were present might, had we been so minded, have paraphrased the words of the Young

King Henry to wretched Roger of York at the coronation feast:
'My lord, do you think it condescension for a king to hold the
stirrup of a god?'

All our business at Sens was completed by 3 November. Thus,
as we rode forth on that sunny winter's day towards the port of
Wissant, it was exactly six years since Thomas had set foot upon
the coast of Flanders as an exile.

To mark that he returned in triumph, King Louis, for one
reason, and King Henry, for a reason very different, saw to it that
my lord was attended by a noble escort of a hundred horsemen.

As I have said, all was now double, and if the French people
who cheered his passing read in that pale, grave face the true mien
of a Christian archbishop restored at last to his real might and
power, I could recognize in it a complete absence from us; his
mind was far away, engaged in some final subjugation of the rebel
spirit or of the unwilling flesh, for he knew that these were in
one sense his last hours of peace, and that his arrival in England
would be all tumult – of this he had already been assured.

Our way to Wissant led us to the east of Paris and of Beauvais.
Between this last city and Compiègne there is a small nunnery
upon a hill, dedicated to St Anne. As we drew near, a man on horseback rode towards us; we could tell from his black habit that he
was an Augustinian and a lay brother, and it was clear that he
recognized Thomas, for he came straight to him and reined in,
saluting him. He said that the Mother Superior of the little convent lay upon the point of death and, hearing who passed that way,
had begged that the Archbishop attend her for a few minutes.

The captain of the guard, knowing as well as the rest of us that
Thomas was surrounded by enemies, sensed a trick in this, and
insisted on accompanying us with two of his men, others standing
ready at a little distance, in case the brother was indeed setting a
trap. Thomas nodded to me, and I also accompanied him.

Arrived at the convent, we were all admitted to the courtyard, and
it was immediately obvious from the attitude of the nuns going
about their work, as well as from the atmosphere of the whole
place, that no harm was about to come to my lord. The captain

and his two men remained in the court, while Thomas and I were led into the simple buildings which accommodated the sisters. The nun leading us opened a heavy door and gestured us to enter the sunlit room beyond.

Eleanor of Aquitaine was the sole occupant of this room, though to judge by the dress she had thought it advisable to wear, she might indeed have belonged to some Order of the Christian church.

'You did not think,' she said, 'that I could let you go upon this journey without saying farewell.' By a very slight accent upon the word 'this' she informed us that she already knew, by what means only she could say, that Thomas was to die at Canterbury.

Thomas said, 'Your grace honours me; the more so since you cannot approve of what I am doing.'

She shook her head. 'What you do, you do upon your own good judgement and of your own free will; who am I to approve or disapprove? Had you acted thus in 1163 under the intolerable pressure brought upon you by the King, I would not have held you in the great respect I now do. Neither would we have become friends.' Suddenly and swiftly she knelt before him and kissed his hand. As Thomas raised her up, I saw that there were tears in her eyes, and that she turned away across the bare room to hide them; and turned again to face him. 'Now,' she said, 'you know me. Whatever the cause I would have travelled this far in secrecy, and further, to bid you farewell; but in thinking and planning on it, other ideas entered my wily head.' She spread her hands, still expressive and beautiful though she was now in her forty-eighth year. 'These days it seems that my every thought slips into the form of a plot.'

Thomas smiled. 'I would hazard a guess that your grace is not alone here.'

The Queen also smiled. 'Thank God,' she said, 'that the King, addled though he may be, at last realizes that losing you as Chancellor was the fatal mistake of his life. What is your guess, my lord?'

'That somewhere in this . . . convenient place there waits a boy thirteen years old.'

She came back to him, remarkable green eyes afire. 'You did not crown Henry, therefore the Young King is no king at all. Will you, my lord, honour my son, Richard, by laying your hands upon him?'

'Most willingly.'

I have mentioned earlier that her visit to Caen upon the King's business regarding the coronation was not quite all it seemed. She had once again used her great knowledge of statecraft to read signs which few others could even see, and, when her reading of them began to prove itself correct, she must have sent for her beloved son and heir immediately.

Extraordinary woman! How glad I am that in our last encounter with her she did not fall short of her own extraordinary standards.

As we moved down a dim corridor, led by one of the nuns, she took my arm and whispered, 'Good William, take what care of him you may.'

'I shall try, my lady.'

'Of course, for you are his good friend; I wish that I had been granted such a one.' She flashed me a glance which was still, I swear, that of a young girl. Then doors were opened before us and we were entering the little chapel of the convent; a choir broke into sweet song.

I saw that fifteen or twenty men waited there, and even had I not recognized more than one from our journeys to Poitou and Aquitaine, I would have known them by their complexion and bearing as lords of her own southern domains. That they came so easily into France was no longer surprising, for the links between them and King Louis grew stronger yearly, in direct proportion to their weakening with King Henry of England. And was not the comely young Prince, who was now led forward, himself affianced to one of the French King's many daughters?

He too knelt as Thomas approached him, and made a sign which indicated to all with eyes to see that already he had been initiated into our faith. At this my lord hesitated, looking about him at the open faces of the good nuns; he then spoke in words which would be meaningful to the Queen, to her son and to their lords, but which might still be translated into Christian terms, affronting none: 'In the name of God and of the Son and of the blessed St John, and in the power of our true faith and its Perfection, which shall be shown to all by what I will do at Canterbury, I bless you,

Richard Plantagenet, Count of Poitou, Duke of Aquitaine, and bid you ever follow the true faith upon whatsoever terms God may grant you the strength to do so. God be with you and all those over whom you will one day rule. Amen.'

When all had echoed 'Amen', Thomas looked around at each of them and said, 'I beg you, remember me in your prayers.'

Only the Queen left the chapel with us. She held out her hand in that straightforward man's gesture which I had seen before, not for courtly kissing but for grasping. Thomas took it between both his.

She said, 'God grant you courage, my lord.'

He said, 'God grant you peace, my lady.'

So they parted. I am not sure which was to desire more heartily the blessing of the other, but I am sure that I have ever been thankful that I was granted to know this great woman whose gift it was to make of life something more vital, more worth the living, than any other mortal I ever met.

Thus we rejoined our three guards and rode back to the men of the escort who were watering their horses at a nearby stream.

When we reached Wissant the blustering sea air was full of rumours and challenges, so that Thomas found it advisable to remain there for some time before crossing to England.

My lord had long since taken the first steps in the plan he had formulated with Henry and with the four knights who would come to Canterbury; he had sent ahead a messenger, one Osbern, with the first letters of excommunication which were to become the 'bone of contention' between the King's men and the Archbishop upon their meeting. These letters were, I am uncharitably happy to say, addressed to Roger of York, Foliot of London and Jocelin of Salisbury, all of whom had officiated at the Young King's coronation; neither could the matter have fallen out more neatly, for the messenger found the three men at Dover, waiting for a ship which would carry them to further consultation with the King – he handed them their letters of excommunication without more ado, and the three bishops, had they been mummers well versed in their parts, could not have acted more perfectly in accordance with what had been planned.

Reverberations of their rage were now recrossing the Channel, and my lord did not need the assurances of others to convince him that were he to sail for Dover his life would be in immediate danger. Though he was prepared for death, it was to be no random blood-letting upon a quay. Thus we changed our plans and set forth towards our own port of Sandwich.

Thomas's enemies might indeed have attacked him here, had not the huge crowds of people upon the shore made it very clear to them that they, in their turn, would not have escaped alive, but would have been torn limb from limb; for it seemed that all Kent had left hearth and home to welcome my lord's homecoming. I have never witnessed such scenes of joy, bordering upon a kind of madness; many hundreds of men and women even ran into the freezing November waves to protect his ship, to haul it in, to be the first to receive his blessing.

It was a slow but triumphant progress from Sandwich to Canterbury, since there was barely a yard of the way which was not lined with shouting, jostling, praying people. Reeds and evergreens and even much-needed cloaks were flung upon the road before him, and my lord must have stopped more than a hundred times to dismount and to lay his hands upon the beseeching masses, many of whom had brought their children, even the tiniest babes in arms, to be touched upon this day of days. Whether they considered him a returning Archbishop or a returning god come to die for them, or a hazy mixture of both, was a secret held in their own minds.

The writers of history point out, with some truth, that the laws of King Henry II and the reforms he had made for the ruling of England in his absence by sheriffs and justices, great though they were and are as exercises in kingship, were harsh indeed upon the ordinary folk; thus they might have seen in Thomas, a man who had opposed the King for so long, a returning hero, a triumphant patriot: but I beg to say, as an eyewitness, and one with a certain knowledge to understand what I saw, that the great majority simply knew that this was the Divine Victim returning in the year 1170 upon the second day of December, a good three weeks before the sacred 25th, birth-day of the god Mithra, birth-day of the invincible Sun who would assuredly return to bless their crops and cows and ewes, to bless their lives.

King Henry had received the Kiss of Peace from this very man in 1163, as all knew, but he had failed them, failed to act as 'god' or 'devil', the words being interchangeable. Now the arch-priest was come, and none doubted the meaning of his presence; he had come as king and as god, and this was the sole explanation of the extraordinary, almost violent popular joy and enthusiasm which carried him, as upon a huge wave, to Canterbury and to the gates of the monastery.

Within, the quality of the welcome was entirely different of course, but no less enthusiastic; the Archbishop had returned in triumph three weeks before Christmas; the six long years of leaderless insecurity were at an end. Canterbury was Canterbury once more. The bells rang; the hymns were sung with abundant fervour. 'Blessed is he who comes in the name of the Lord.'

Thomas was exhausted, but somehow, by delving into those deep spiritual resources which seldom betrayed him, he found the strength to greet each of his old friends individually, and to join them at table. Then I helped him to bed, for he was barely able to stand from fatigue. Just before he fell asleep, he smiled at me and said, 'It is done, Will. I shall rest now.'

His tone suggested that everything was over, all accomplished; and I wondered greatly at it, knowing what lay before him.

2

On the very next day representatives of the Bishops of York, London and Salisbury were at the gates before sunrise, demanding immediate absolution; they were presently joined by royal officials representing the absent King, who argued that Thomas's actions in this matter were illegal.

We heard, from other sources, that Gilbert Foliot and Jocelin of Salisbury would have been content to abide by the censure, but that Roger of York, ever the troublemaker, had convinced them that he was rich enough, in his own words, 'to settle both Pope and King': a singularly unfortunate statement, coming from this singularly tactless man, which presently reached King Henry's ears, with what results you may well imagine!

As for Thomas, he truthfully replied to these envoys that the excommunications were the Pope's command and that therefore only the Pope could remove them. In fact, and for obvious reasons, he was not interested in placating any of these men, and his abstracted attitude only served to irritate them the more; which also suited his intentions.

Naturally he was assailed on all sides with a hundred complaints from his own people of Canterbury and from all those who had suffered under the de Broc family and others of the same ilk. Thomas disassociated himself from them as gently as he might, promising that presently he would direct the power of the church against the miscreants, and this he was indeed to do upon Christmas Day.

As for all the general matters concerning Canterbury, it only needed his presence to set the clerks at work once more, so that almost immediately the centuries-old machinery of the see began to operate of its own accord. I myself took the small precaution of reading all documents before my lord should sign them, for I believe he would have signed whatever was set before him.

Of all the matters demanding his attention, only one truly touched his heart, and it did not concern the Christian church. He felt a deep pity for the Young King Henry, who was now held a virtual prisoner at Winchester by his father's lords; Thomas had heard, even from Henry himself, that the boy was growing up arrogant and self-willed, and he knew that this was in great part because, however his father might adore him, he was invariably absent, and because his mother cared only for his brother, Richard. Therefore the Prince had never known any security or continuing love since he had been torn away from my lord's own household seven years before.

Thomas believed implicitly that Young Henry, now seventeen, would die before his father as the blind woman had predicted, and the uselessness of that wasted young life touched him deeply. He would like to have visited his erstwhile ward, and I think the boy himself would have been delighted, for he had always loved Thomas; but, to no one's surprise, his guardians forbade it and

Thomas must needs content himself – and he hoped the boy – by sending a gift of three proud war-horses, richly caparisoned.

Another duty, which he was less eager to perform though pressed on all sides to do so, was to visit London, showing himself to the people and clergy of that city in solemn proof that he had indeed returned to them. An anxious company of Christian prelates came three miles from the gates to meet him with a great procession of clerks and scholars singing the *Te Deum* and *Benedictus*, escorting him in triumph to Southwark cathedral where Mass was celebrated; but I know that it was the vast crowds of ordinary people which moved him the more deeply, surging around him to touch and to be touched, many with tears pouring down their cheeks.

He had long realized that his coming death would mean different things to these two estates of the people; it was inevitable, if ridiculous, that the Christians would claim him as a Christian saint, but this was a matter upon which he wasted neither time nor thought. His deepest feelings on the subject had already been spoken at Tours to the King and to the knights: 'Our sole concern is that what occurs between *us* be cleanly and well done, so that those with eyes to see shall know its meaning and be joyful.'

The day which he had finally named to Henry was Tuesday 29 December. The time, sunset.

On Christmas Day, falling on the preceding Friday, further great crowds filled the cathedral to hear him preach or simply to see him; many who had travelled half the night could not find a place within, but my lord went out to them later and blessed them.

For the first time in public he spoke of his imminent death, and at this moment, had it been possible to see every face, one might have recognized at a glance those of that great crowd who were Christian and those who were not. The Christians alone expressed horror or disbelief; the others had known for a long time that one would come to die for them: had it not always been thus since time before memory?

At this ceremony Thomas also continued the preconceived plan of excommunication, censuring all those who held the lands and churches of Canterbury without his permission.

It has been wrongly asserted that next day he sent close friends and servants, including Herbert of Bosham, to the court of King Louis in France because he feared that they too might suffer violence at the hands of the King's men. This, as we know, is absurd nonsense, for the chosen knights were honourable and proud, and had no business with any but Thomas himself. My lord's motives were more devious; he wished Louis to be informed, from a purely Christian point of view, how matters stood at Canterbury; and he did *not* wish Herbert to describe, from a purely Christian point of view and therefore inaccurately, what was to happen in three days' time.

Meanwhile the King had spent a stormy Christmas at Bures, less a castle than a fortified manor, near Bayeux. He had for company enraged bishops and infuriated noblemen, the one group complaining bitterly of unlawful excommunication, the other claiming that if the people continued to rise in clamorous support of the Archbishop as they were now doing, there would soon be widespread rebellion throughout the whole of southern England.

Henry, knowing much that they would never know, appeared to be making plans to contain the Archbishop's popularity; from long practice, much of it under the tutelage of his Chancellor, he was adept at giving an impression of intense activity whilst in reality setting nothing in motion. This must have been particularly easy during that Christmas at Bures; amid so much violent talk and so much coming and going, all were so occupied with personal complaint that none even noticed the departure of de Moreville, Fitz-Urse, le Breton and de Tracy who left separately and separately took ship from Normandy, having agreed to meet at Saltwood Castle, illegally held by Randulph de Broc.

It is true that Roger of York told Henry that he would never have peace in England so long as Thomas lived, but the King's much-quoted remark, 'What idle cowards surround me, that they allow me to be mocked by a low-born clerk,' is an invention. Since the knights were already on their way, and the King of course knew it, such words would have been very far from his mind.

The sea was calm, strangely for that time of year, and the four men arrived at Saltwood within a few hours of each other on Innocents' Day by the Christian calendar. They rested – uneasily de Moreville has said, for though they were experienced soldiers and men of honour, and knew very well the true meaning of what they must do on the morrow, it seemed to them a cold-blooded affair, far removed from the instant demands and heat of battle.

I think them brave men, as dedicated in their way as Thomas in his. I could not, under threat of torture, have done what they had to do, any more than I could have taken the place of my lord.

Thus, grey and unmerciful, dawned the appointed twenty-ninth day of December, and in the bitter cold of midwinter all things stood frozen, waiting.

3

There were many witnesses of what was to occur at Canterbury on that day; four of them have written accounts which have long since been accepted, no reader seeming to care that each differs in the detail, sometimes in every detail, of what took place. Of course the Christians have taken great pains to obscure the true facts, since it is indeed hardly suitable that a brand-new, and extremely profitable, Christian saint should be known by all to have died a 'pagan' death in an 'heretical' cause.

However that may be, the four other 'eyewitnesses' cannot evade all blame, supplying as they have the source material, or lack of it, upon which all other historians have had to base their own accounts.

On 29 December 1170, there were two other Williams present in the monastery, myself apart: William of Canterbury and William FitzStephen; Edward Grim had but recently joined us from Cambridge, wishing to pay homage to Thomas; he is an eager and straightforward man, but knows too little of the past upon which the present stands. As for John of Salisbury, who knew Thomas better than any saving myself, and had been with him for many years on and off, one would think from his account that he had been abed or had pulled his cowl over his face. He was present when the knights arrived in the Archbishop's presence, yet he does not write one word of what took place; and, upon their return to carry out the appointed sacrifice, he contents himself with saying that 'pity' forbids him to give any detailed account. For the word 'pity', I fear that we must substitute the word 'caution', for he was ever cautious. Make no mistake, he knew very well the true meaning of all he saw and heard. Alas that a man so honest and outspoken must be held guilty of prevarication and a wish to mislead those who have turned to him as the most notable witness of that day! For his own reasons, possibly good ones from a Christian point of view, he chose to omit what he could not falsify.

When I attended Thomas in his chamber early that morning, I found him in prayer, but I think he may have slept a little during the night. As ever in times of crisis, he was calm and withdrawn, and I think it possible that he may have used certain ancient knowledge to put himself in a state somewhat akin to that of trance, the better to face, not the final ordeal but rather the countless trivial ordeals of his duty as Archbishop.

When he was dressed, he turned and gave me all his attention. 'Well, my good William,' he said, 'I doubt if we can again rely on being alone together.'

I nodded, for I did not trust myself to speak. Thomas, understanding me as always, said, 'It is not a day for tears, Will. God knows we have passed many such, and have never shed a drop.' He took me by the shoulders, forcing my eyes to meet his. 'All is well with me. Wherever you are this day – and I bid you keep near me – I shall need to know that you understand this. I regret nothing and I have no fears, for what I must do is just and blessed. Think as I do, William, that this is but the Endura of our true faith.'

I break no vow if I say that the Endura is our last sacrament and testing of the soul, and that it invariably ends in death. We hold death to be better than doddering and helpless old age, when the senile mind is lost to reason and God knows what sickly thing may take its place. I must make it quite clear, for no other has, that Thomas was not only dying as a 'pagan' sacrifice in King Henry's place, and not only because he had judged and sentenced himself when called to the question. Queen Eleanor had, as usual, spoken the truth when she had said, 'A certain familiarity with death, even a desire for it, lies at the heart of your Cathar faith.'

Touching obliquely on this, I then said, 'My lord, it is strange; you know I have no spiritual power, yet when I fell from my horse as your great procession was returning from Paris, when I lay in that simple house, you took my hand and asked me what it was I feared or perhaps foresaw . . .'

'And you replied, "I foresee nothing. I fear too much greatness, too much power." It has long since struck me that you did indeed foresee something, but found no words to speak of it; you foresaw this day, and that also was your fear.'

I stared in astonishment, for he had spoken my very thoughts.

'Do not say you have no spiritual power, Will: all men possess it and may learn its use. That was your moment of vision, I never doubted it. Yet, however we may see the future, we may not change it.'

Bitterly, for I had always hated her words, I quoted the blind woman of the cave: ' "Everything changes, but what will be is there. That does not change. It is." '

'I fear she is right.'

There was a sudden chattering of voices outside the door, one raised in unmistakable panic. It brought us back to the present.

Thomas took my hands and said, 'Farewell, William, stalwart friend and companion. We have seen much together, and in all things you have been like a staff for me to lean on.'

I replied, upon a sudden inspiration, 'My lord, at least I can say that life in your service has never lacked interest, or contrast.'

'Northampton!' I had wondered whether he would recall and because he did I was absurdly pleased; the memory seemed to please him too for he smiled, and we embraced for the last time, both smiling. I think that of all men only Thomas could have parted from an old friend thus, upon the brink of death, with a moment of humour. I bless him for it constantly, for in one sense it is how I have always remembered him.

He gave me the Kiss of Peace; then said, 'Guard well your day-books, my friend; they may bear witness for all time, long after our bones are dust.' I swore to do this, and he added, 'Write simply and clearly of what you see and hear today, for I doubt if any other will do so.' He looked towards the door and sighed. 'Now let us see what proceeds at Canterbury.'

Outside the door of his chamber there was a feeling as chill and as grey as the day itself. The monks were prone to cluster together in small groups, talking fearfully in whispers, so that I lost patience with them and for once asserted my authority, scattering them as I came upon them, sending them flapping away to their several duties like so many broody hens. Presently their Archbishop's presence, as he went calmly and dutifully about the business of his day, put them to shame, and they too became more calm. But all watched and waited, and started up at any sound a little louder than was usual.

My lord went his customary round of the cathedral, and was seen and touched by many simple folk who had been drawn there either by knowledge or intuition; then, wishing everything to be in order regarding the church upon this final day, he made a confession to one William of Maidstone, though he considered the habit absurd, as do all we Brethren. If a man cannot confess to his God in his own soul, what can be achieved by the agency of a priest in a box, who may or may not be worthy?

Thomas then took dinner with his household as was customary, and afterwards went to his inner chamber with five of us, John of Salisbury included, to consider certain letters which had arrived from France that morning. But soon our words grew desultory and inept, and even Thomas fell silent, lost in thought, for now the time drew near and all knew it.

As for myself, I must say that as we sat in my lord's hall all things within me seemed to come gradually to a stop, and all my faculties took up abode in my stomach as if it were a place of refuge. I felt sick and lost, and though I knew very well its meaning and Thomas's willingness to accept death, I witnessed what I had to witness with both horror and disgust. That being said, to my detriment in the face of my lord's dignity and courage, I shall write no more of my unimportant personal feelings upon this long dark afternoon, but simply report what I heard and saw as Thomas had bade me do.

At 3 o'clock there was a commotion outside; the four knights had entered the courtyard of the monastery.

They had been much put out by the arrival of other King's men who wished to support them in their enterprise, but these they had persuaded to remain outside the locked gates for the ostensible purpose of keeping the townspeople in order and of preventing the

Archbishop's escape, though they knew that there would be no trouble from the people of Canterbury, the great majority of whom were fully aware that the knights were expected and accepted by Thomas, and that escape would be the last thing to occupy the Archbishop's mind.

In this way they cleverly managed to impose the necessary degree of secrecy concerning what was to occur within. They were accompanied only by their trusted squires and by a certain Hugh Mauclerc, who was, more than any other present, versed in ancient ritual. I may say no more.

They were met by the Archbishop's steward, FitzNeal, whom my lord had carefully instructed in his duties; he took the four knights to the great hall, Mauclerc remaining outside, and asked them if they would eat; upon their refusing, he conducted them directly to the Archbishop.

My lord bade them enter his private chamber and be seated. Much has been read into the silence with which they greeted Thomas and he them, but it should be remembered that what they might have wished to say to each other privily could not be spoken in front of such as John of Salisbury, (though, as we now know, he would doubtless have remained dumb enough concerning it!) and others who were present. They were therefore forced to proceed with the business so long prepared and rehearsed.

Reginald FitzUrse said, 'We have a message to you from the King, my lord; will you hear it in public or in private?' I think he spoke this last to give Thomas an excuse for clearing the room of all save myself, but Thomas, after a moment's thought, rejected privacy and bade them proceed.

So then FitzUrse brought up the matter of the carefully arranged excommunications, and demanded absolution for all concerned, to which Thomas gave his old reply: 'The sentences were not mine, but the Pope's; let them go to him for absolution.'

At this all four men broke out in assumed anger, accusing Thomas of acting against the King and against England, etcetera, etcetera, while my lord defended himself, citing Fréteval and Henry's promises of peaceful discussion in the near future.

De Moreville cried, 'That was before this madness of excommunication seized upon you and the Pope, your master.'

Thomas leapt to his feet, shouting, 'I will strike any man who violates the name of His Holiness or the right of the church.'

Le Breton shouted back, 'You speak in peril of your life!'

'If you have come here to kill me,' said Thomas, casting his voice as he had done at Northampton, so that the many who listened outside might hear, 'I commit my cause and my soul to the Judge of all men. I fled once from my duty, rather than face your swords; this time I stay. You will find me here.' He did not forget to add, 'And do not forget in whatever you may plan that you are my liegemen one and all,' thus giving the four an opportunity to exonerate themselves in public as they had already done in private. De Tracy shouted, 'We renounce all fealty to you, in the name of God and the King.'

By now they were pushing out of the chamber, and I am sure that none watching in ignorance doubted their rage. FitzUrse commanded us all to keep watch on Thomas, for if he escaped they would hold us all responsible; and Thomas again cried, 'Have I not said it? You will find me here.'

De Moreville shouted, 'To arms, to arms,' and they returned noisily to the courtyard where they had left their swords, pushing terrified monks and clerks out of the way and shouting, 'King's men, King's men!'

This was heard by their supporters outside, and many would have entered to join them but could not for the gates were still locked; lest the gatekeeper should lose his head and open, de Moreville set one of their own men in his place.

Within, all was confusion except in Thomas's mind. John of Salisbury was angry with him for not forcing the knights to talk calmly of Fréteval and of the King's promises: 'You're the same as ever you were,' he said. 'You speak too hastily, too irrationally, never asking advice.'

Poor, good, reasonable John! He was beginning to understand what was happening before his eyes. 'Don't you see, these men only want a good excuse for killing you?'

Thomas nodded. 'We must all die, John. And I think I am more ready to suffer death than they are to inflict it.' I truly believe I caught the ghost of an old mocking smile about my lord's lips as he added, 'God's will be done, my friend.'

Meanwhile the knights had armed themselves under the mulberry tree in the courtyard, and the monks had bolted all doors to the monastery and the cathedral. Thomas had foreseen that this would be their natural reaction, and he had instructed a faithful clerk to lead the four men, now accompanied by Mauclerc, round the wall of the kitchen and into the small orchard on the south side of the Archbishop's hall. Here was an outside staircase which workmen were at that time repairing. There is a story that the knights broke in using the workmen's tools, but this is not true, for Thomas had sent me to the door with orders to open it as soon as they appeared and to lock it behind them.

FitzUrse nodded to me as they passed through and muttered grimly, 'By the two faces, Brother, pray for us now!'

There is also a story that other armed men were at this time forcing a group of townspeople to leave the cathedral, but this also is untrue, for there was only a handful huddled there in the darkness, and any shouts and cries which may have been heard emanated from members of my lord's household in fear of their own miserable and unthreatened lives; though to give them their due, they did not know that none threatened them.

A more loyal and courageous group had, all this time, been trying to make Thomas leave the chamber where he still sat, and seek sanctuary in the cathedral. My lord refused. Some have stated that he had made up his mind to die, which is true enough, but feared that if he stood upon consecrated ground the knights would draw back, which is not true for the obvious reason that their business was in no way concerned with Christian observances.

In his own good time Thomas allowed these monks to over-power him, so that when I returned from admitting the knights, I found that they were half-pushing and half-carrying him towards the monk's cloister. The heavy door leading to it had been closed for many years, and none expected it to open; in this they were ingenuous, for that very morning it had been oiled by certain of the Brethren within the community. Thus Thomas was 'forced' around the cloister and into the north transept of the cathedral, which was where he had from the first intended to take his stand. Neither could he be moved from there, though some urged him to go to the altar while others tried to make him hide in the crypt or the roof.

Their entreaties were interrupted by a great clattering in the cloister, and the knights, following in Thomas's footsteps, now burst into the north transept. All fled, excepting Grim, who certainly did not lack for courage, and naturally myself. I seem to have been confused by some writers of history with a certain Henry of Auxerre who was carrying the primatial cross in the absence of Alexander the Welshman (he having gone with Herbert of Bosham to the French court); this is perhaps because it was my duty at this point to take the cross from the said Henry, who abandoned it willingly and fled.

All that was now happening, and about to happen, was accompanied by a great commotion and echoing shouts from the cathedral which was still in almost total darkness. Monks and the few townspeople who had ventured forth for Vespers, or, more likely, to witness my lord's sacrifice, were milling about in the nave. As planned, the north transept was empty except for those of us who knew the secrets and Edward Grim, who did not.

The north, you should know, is holy in all the old religions, so that any stories of Thomas standing before the altar are pure invention, as are any accounts of further argument between Thomas and the knights; they spoke only the last few ritual words. The death which now followed has been swiftly and thoroughly Christianized, so you will find in the records little true mention of what occurred.

First, de Moreville shouted, 'Where is Thomas Becket?' and my lord replied, 'I am here, the Priest of God.'

As they moved towards him, I stood forward with the heavy cross, and de Moreville struck at the hated symbol, severing the ornate shaft with, I'm glad to say, expert precision, though the wind of his great sword's passing was cold on my cheek. The cross fell and was shattered, which made poor Grim cry out.

Thomas now carefully mounted four steps (not seven; four is the sacred number in all the old religions, and the Christians know it), standing with his back to the great central column of the transept and facing the four men, Mauclerc still being in darkness. He pointed to Reginald FitzUrse and said, 'You, Reginald, you are my man,' meaning that he chose FitzUrse to deliver the first blow. This knight raised a hand and struck off my lord's woollen cap (he was certainly not wearing the mitre); he then lifted his sword.

Thomas said, 'I commend my soul to God, to the two faces of Mary, to blessed Dionysius and to St John, the beloved of Christ.'

FitzUrse struck, his sword cutting my lord's scalp and slipping to injure his shoulder. Grim, brave according to his ignorance, tried to ward off this blow, thus extending my lord's agony rather than helping him; his arm was deeply cut and broken, and I'm glad to say that he fell back to the floor.

Now de Tracy struck at the same point. Thomas dropped to his knees; de Tracy struck again, and Thomas fell to the floor, but I saw that he fell according to the ritual, his head to the north.

It was Richard le Breton who delivered the fourth blow, splitting the skull and ending the life of Thomas of London.

Throughout all, de Moreville had been turned the other way in order to repulse any who threatened to come forward from the nave, interrupting the ritual.

Mauclerc had now moved out of darkness. Every kind of vituperation has been heaped upon the head of this man, for the Christians realize, without understanding, that he was a dominating figure and that what he now did was at the centre of the sacrifice. He placed his sword upon the split skull and twisted the blade, scattering blood and brains.

At this there was a crying and wailing from the darkness of the cathedral – the voices of those who recognized the true significance of Mauclerc's action, bearing witness that what had passed between Thomas and the knights had indeed, as my lord had instructed at Tours, been 'cleanly and well done' so that those with eyes to see should 'know its meaning and be joyful'. The blood of the Victim had touched the ground, and the earth was now blessed by it, reborn by virtue of the Divine Sacrifice.

FitzUrse turned and spoke into the darkness: 'Mark well! He himself wished to be King here, and wished to be more than King.'

He was answered by a murmur of voices, some saying, 'So be it', some, 'The gods bless him', some, 'Amen'; and the voices of many monks were heard raised in protest, either because they did not know, or knew all too well, the meaning of what they were now witnessing.

The knights turned and left the cathedral with Mauclerc. At once there was a movement towards Thomas's body, reverent and quiet; and more than one bent to touch some rag or the hem of a cloak or a skirt against the freely flowing blood.

News of my lord's dying was known all over Europe, and as far away as Jerusalem, within the hour, but this will only surprise those who know nothing of our mysteries.

So at last Thomas of London, Perfect of the Cathar faith, my beloved lord and friend, had completed his life in a final gesture well befitting his own inner greatness, his love of King Henry, and his search for the reality of God.

I would be united and I would unite. Amen.
I would be wounded and I would wound. Amen.
I would mourn. Lament ye all. Amen.

Epilogue

Man is not made for peace, more's the pity.

The blind woman of the cave,

February 1165

Thus, almost abruptly, ends the chronicle of William of Colchester, except for an afternote of four short pages, which I have placed at the beginning of the Prologue.

It seems unlike him not to have added his final comments summing up all that had gone before, particularly as he had promised, following King Henry's meeting with the blind woman, that he would tell the outcome of her prophecies in their proper place.

Did he lack the time to go further, or did the death of Thomas seem so final that he lacked the heart? Was he killed as he feared, by King's men or Pope's men; or did he complete his story, arrange its hiding-place, destroy his day-books, and lose himself in anonymity, perhaps joining some Christian monastery under another name? In any case, some word of conclusion seems necessary, and if William himself does not supply it, I must.

The canonization of Thomas was declared by the Pope on 1 February 1173 – though miracles and signs were said to have begun on the very night of his death. If William outlasted Louis VII he would have seen Canterbury become the foremost place of pilgrimage in all Christian Europe; we must regret not having his, undoubtedly acid, reaction.

Thomas, no less than his chronicler, would surely have been amused by the fact that many modern religious authorities doubt his right to be a saint at all, some declaring that he was not even a martyr in the strict Christian sense. Yes, I think they would both have enjoyed that irony!

Contrary to various Christian legends, which invent violent deaths for the four knights, all of them continued to live respected lives and all died quite naturally in the fulness of time.

As for the prophecies of the blind woman, she was correct in all she foretold.

It is interesting that when Henry had the palace of Westminster refurbished, possibly in 1172 for the second coronation of the Young King and, this time, of his wife, Marguerite of France, he commanded that a large space on one wall be left blank for a design of his own making. When the fresco was finally unveiled it was seen to depict a great eagle with spread wings being attacked by four eaglets, in the exact manner the blind woman had described.

In 1172, at Avranches, the King agreed to restore all lands and goods taken from Canterbury and to make amends to those whom he had dispossessed during Thomas's lifetime; he may also have accepted the penitential lash at this date. In June 1174 he certainly went to Canterbury, crossing the channel in the usual storm. He spent a night in vigil at the saint's tomb, after which he was scourged by all the monks so that his blood did indeed drip upon the earth, thus fulfilling the promise he had made to Thomas and no doubt delighting 'those with eyes to see'.

But his sons were growing fast, not only in years but in duplicity, attacking him however they could. The great King did not abandon his greatness without a fight; more than once he counter-attacked swiftly, with all his old cunning, and more than once brought them to heel. He also caught Queen Eleanor, mastermind of this sedition, escaping into France dressed as a man, and, as she had guessed he would many years before, he locked her up in a succession of towers, among them Salisbury and Winchester, where she stayed until his death.

Amid all the confusion and discord the rose did indeed 'droop upon its stalk'. Fair Rosamund Clifford died as gently as she had lived in 1177, having born Henry two sons.

Meanwhile the prophecies of the blind woman continued inexorably to be fulfilled. Henry, the Young King, fell victim to a fever in June of 1183 while in open rebellion against his father. The King wanted to go to this favourite son, but was warned that the young man's illness might be a trick aimed at his own assassination. Thus far had their relationship disintegrated! He therefore sent physicians and 'a gift of gold', which reached the heir before he died.

Now this latter was indeed the ring, once the property of Henry I, which the blind woman had 'seen' upon the finger of the dying boy. Had Henry, forgetting her in his anguish, reached for the first gold that caught his eye? Or had he at last accepted her powers, and did he send the ring out of some grim desire to complete the circle? 'Everything changes, but what will be is there.'

His third son, Geoffrey of Brittany, charming and unreliable, also died young. Historians seem unsure of the date and of the cause but seem to think that he too may have been stricken by a fever, or may have been killed in a tourney. Since the blind woman mentioned 'horses' hooves and lances' it was probably the latter.

This left the Queen's favourite, Richard – Coeur de Lion, as we have come to know him – and young John who, after the death of beloved Henry, became recipient of all the King's affection, and repaid it by rebelling in the company of brother Richard and Philippe of France. Both Princes turned upon their father, as the blind woman had predicted, and both were to wear the crown of England.

King Henry II did not relinquish that crown easily, and his own death was, as one would expect, full of fury and broken grandeur: sick in body, betrayed by his sons now firmly allied to the old enemy, France, the empire falling to ruin around him, and no one to blame but himself and his own actions at Montmirail. He died at Angers in a typical rage, which was followed just in time by a less typical, perhaps apocryphal, desire for absolution. He was taken to the abbey of Fontevrault where he still lies.

Eleanor of Aquitaine outlived them all but one. Her darling Richard died in 1199 – at war, his invariable pastime. Though married he had no children, so that his brother John found himself holding the crown of England, to make of it what he might.

Eleanor died in 1204 at the age of eighty-two, and was laid beside Henry at Fontevrault; but long ago she had seen the Plantagenet sun setting, as it seemed, with the sun of King Henry II himself, and the mighty empire which they had built together, in the company of his great Chancellor, Thomas of London, was no more.